WITCHES *of* HONEYSUCKLE HOUSE

Also available by Liz Parker

The Other March Sisters
In the Shadow Garden

WITCHES *of* HONEYSUCKLE HOUSE

a novel

LIZ PARKER

alcove press

Books should be disposed of and recycled according to local requirements. All paper materials used are FSC compliant.

This is a work of fiction. All of the names, characters, organizations, places and events portrayed in this novel are either products of the author's imagination or are used fictitiously. Any resemblance to real or actual events, locales, or persons, living or dead, is entirely coincidental.

Copyright © 2025 by Elizabeth Mary Parker

All rights reserved.

Published in the United States by Alcove Press, an imprint of The Quick Brown Fox & Company LLC.

Alcove Press and its logo are trademarks of The Quick Brown Fox & Company LLC.

Library of Congress Catalog-in-Publication data available upon request.

ISBN (hardcover): 979-8-89242-2-901
ISBN (paperback): 979-8-89242-1-997
ISBN (ebook): 979-8-89242-2-000

Cover design by Lucy Rose

Printed in the United States.

www.alcovepress.com

Alcove Press
34 West 27th St., 10th Floor
New York, NY 10001

First Edition: October 2025

The authorized representative in the EU for product safety and compliance is eucomply OÜPärnu mnt 139b-14, 11317 Tallinn, Estonia, hello@eucompliancepartner.com, +33757690241

10 9 8 7 6 5 4 3 2 1

For everyone who can never go home.

Table of Contents

TABLE OF CONTENTS

TABLE OF CONTENTS

A History of Deaths at Honeysuckle House

1947: Helen and Christopher Caldwell
1960: Tillie Grey
1973: Violet Caldwell
1986: Regina Caldwell
1999: Robert Thomas-Caldwell
2012: Linda Caldwell

Part 1
The Hermit

A call for isolation and solitude.

Chapter One

Florence, Now

A witch's house is a living, breathing thing. When magic is as much a part of a person as air or water or blood, it refuses to stay in narrow, well-drawn lines. It infuses board and beam. It winks in windows and mirrors. It seeps out with every candle burned and every card turned, until, given enough time, it takes on a life of its own.

For Florence Caldwell, that place was Ink & Pages, a cozy, unassuming bookstore beneath her apartment in the heart of Burdock Creek. Florence had used her inheritance to buy it when it was on the brink of going out of business, setting up shop with her best friend. The first time she walked through the doors after that, the building had come to life.

The brick storefront beckoned customers, calling them off the street and through its thick wooden doors. One look at the window display and they'd find the exact novel they'd mentioned to their friend the day before, or the cookbook their brother had wanted for his birthday, or the memoir they'd seen online that afternoon. All it took was one step inside to feel like the shop went on forever. A work of clever architecture and proper shelf placement, or so Florence claimed to anyone who asked. The locals, of course, knew better. Florence was a Caldwell witch, and the Caldwells had a reputation in their little east Tennessee town.

The southern humidity had finally released its hold on Burdock Creek, and when Florence stepped out on the apartment landing above the store, her breath fogged in the morning air, steaming up the lenses of her thick, wide-rimmed glasses. A little thrill ran through her as the wind whipped her hair with the threat of rain. As much as she loved the sounds of summer, here the cicadas' songs lasted well into September and the thick heat right along with them. It wasn't until days after the old maple outside her window traded in its green for a full coat of yellow that the temperature made up its mind to match.

Florence wore a button-up blouse beneath a soft brown sweater, both of which she tucked into a long floral skirt. She'd traded her sandals for pointed green boots and calf-length socks that showed a flash of fair skin with each swish of fabric. As the apartment door closed behind her of its own volition, she pulled her sweater over her hands and started down the steps.

The town was already bustling, Burdock Creek's fall tourism season in full swing despite the dark clouds. Even now guests spilled out of the coffee shop across the street, owned by her best friend Angela Rider's parents. The fall chill called for pumpkin spice, but with the line as it was, Florence would have to wait for a midmorning break. October was the town's busiest time of year thanks to the festival Florence's younger sister Evie hosted at their childhood-home-turned-bed-and-breakfast, a point of contention between the sisters. For years, Florence had avoided the whole affair, but holding it this fall was more than tasteless.

It was dangerous.

This wasn't any normal October. This was a thirteenth year.

For the Caldwells, thirteen wasn't just an unlucky number. It was a curse. Thirteen years ago, Florence's mother died. Thirteen years before that, her father. Thirteen years before him, her grandmother. And back and back all the way to her great-grandparents. Every one of them on October thirteenth and every one of them in the Queen Anne Victorian at the edge of town. The place Florence's sister called home: Honeysuckle House.

If history had any say in the matter, in four short days, someone dear to the Caldwell witches would die on its grounds.

As Florence reached the sidewalk, her fingers itched to dip and burn a protection candle, but Florence hadn't used her magic since her mother's death. No longer did she set flame to wick and pull her desires into the world like the threads of tangible things. If her tarot reading thirteen years ago was to be believed, giving up her magic was the only way for Florence to stop the deaths that had plagued her family for almost a century. Not that her younger sister understood that.

Florence caught sight of Angela making her way across the road, two lattes in hand. Fresh twists fell down Angela's back, and her dark brown skin glowed in the morning sun. Her jeans were belted high, with an oversized sweater tucked in at the waist. Though her lace-up boots gave her a couple of extra inches, they still left her well below Florence's five-foot-ten.

"It's finally fall in Burdock Creek!" Angela said as she skipped the last few steps and held out one of the cups to Florence. At Florence's answering frown, Angela said, "I know it's a curse year, but we have to at least celebrate the change in the weather."

That, Florence couldn't argue with. She shoved her keys into her pocket, accepted the drink—the hot paper sleeve a welcome feeling against her chilled hands—and took a long, satisfied sip, awash in the smell of leaves and fog and fireplaces.

"Owen was at the coffee shop," Angela said with a grin as she held up a bag of pastries.

Florence rolled her eyes and reached for them, but Angela pulled them back.

"He's coming in for his tarot lesson this morning," Angela said. While Florence might not practice anymore, tarot wasn't something that belonged only to the Caldwells. Angela had been reading the cards all her life, and Florence saw no need to ask her to stop on Florence's account. Angela wasn't a Caldwell, so there was no danger in it.

"He asked about you," Angela said.

Florence's stomach fluttered. She pressed a hand to it, willing the sensation away. The last thing Florence could do right now was fall for someone. She'd kept the number of people she cared about to a minimum—her sister, her niece, and Angela—for their protection as much as her own. "Was he looking for a book recommendation?"

"Or a bookseller." Angela's laughter came out bright and loud and so much bigger than anyone would've expected by looking at her.

"Not an option," Florence said.

"And if we all make it past October thirteenth unscathed?" A touch of hope tinged Angela's words.

Florence hadn't thought that far. For the last thirteen years, every moment of anxiety, every nightmare, every fear ended four days from now, on her thirty-ninth birthday. She shrugged and held out a hand for the pastries.

"That's not a no," Angela said.

"Owen will be gone after the thirteenth, so it doesn't matter what it is."

Unlike her sister, the town, at least, had the sense to recognize the threat of a curse year. While the local businesses would still take part in their own way, those who lived in Burdock Creek had refused to staff the events at Honeysuckle House. The curse might only claim those close to the Caldwells, but the town still feared becoming collateral damage. That left Florence's sister to hire outside help, including Owen Grey, whom Evie had brought on to manage the honey harvest. He'd been in town for a few weeks already, staying at Honeysuckle House and getting to know Evie's bees. Florence wondered how much work he was actually doing, as he'd been in the shop almost daily taking tarot lessons.

Angela leaned her head against Florence's arm. "I just want you to be happy."

"Then give me that bag," Florence said.

With a laugh, Angela handed it over. Florence peered inside as Angela unlocked the door. "Sticky buns!"

"You really think I would've teased you about . . ." Angela dropped her voice to a whisper as she glanced down the sidewalk ". . . the curse, if I didn't have sticky buns?"

"All is forgiven." Florence took a giant bite and washed it down with a sip of her latte as they stepped inside.

Though Florence had left the Caldwell ways behind, she still tucked sliced lemons in hidden corners and blew cinnamon through the front door at each new moon. Houseplants and crystals kept company among the books. Just inside, a collection of spider plants and several raw chunks of black tourmaline prevented negative energy from coming through the doors. In the self-help section, a calathea and blue lapis lazuli offered clarity and strengthened intuition. Two monsteras framed the romance section, with several raw pieces of rose quartz scattered among the shelves, fostering self-love. Finally, a fiddle-leaf fig sat right near the register surrounded by bright orange citrine points for abundance and happiness.

These were the things Florence had taught herself in an effort to fight back against the candles her mother had once lit to control her—one that blinded her for a day when she'd mistakenly dipped a wick orange instead of red, another that muffled her ears for a week after she'd eavesdropped on her father accusing her mother of using her magic on him, a third that stole her voice for a month when she tried to tell a neighbor how her mother had locked her in her room without food for three days (the house had kept her fed, but it was the principle of the thing).

Was it magic? Only insomuch as the sun rising every morning and setting every night was magic. What mattered was that it wasn't the Caldwell family magic, which Florence was convinced had brought about the curse.

At least, that's what she told herself on that early October morning. In four short days, Florence would finally know if all of her efforts had been enough to stop the curse, or if her sister's decision to build a life around the very magic Florence abandoned would outweigh those efforts, leaving Florence with the most heartbreaking sort of "I told you so."

After the curse had claimed their mother and almost taken Florence along with her, the sisters had been determined to never let it happen again. Florence had wanted to leave Honeysuckle House behind, convinced the curse was tied to their childhood home. Every death had happened there. If they avoided Honeysuckle House, she reasoned, then maybe the curse wouldn't claim them. But to Evie, it was the witches who were cursed, not the house.

They turned to tarot, as Caldwell witches are known to do. But they'd been unable to agree on what the cards had shown them: The hierophant reversed, temperance reversed, the hermit.

The meaning had been clear for Florence. She had to be her own guide—she couldn't trust anyone else to lead her—and her plan to stay away from the house was the right path. Their power had gone out of balance, putting a curse on their family. The only way to undo it was to give that power up altogether. To become the hermits the cards told them they must be.

Evie hadn't seen it that way, and the sisters hadn't agreed on anything since.

Chapter Two

Evie, Now

The Caldwell family home stood at the edge of Burdock Creek. Honeysuckle wove around the handrails, up the thin columns, and all along the porch. Red-orange blossoms flowered on the vine, the wind whipping them this way and that. Storm clouds muted the soft yellow clapboard, a match for the maple leaves that littered the grass. In the far corner of the house, a turret rose up from the third story.

Evie Caldwell stood just inside one of the turret's black-framed windows, a candle on the antique bureau in front of her. Her wavy blonde hair hung loose about her shoulders, and her hazel eyes looked almost brown in the shadows cast by the oncoming storm.

She stared out at the grounds of Honeysuckle House. Wildflowers grew rampant along the creek bank, glistening with the first drops of rain. Her daughter Clara stomped her way through the grass in bright yellow rain boots, a spot of light in the fall gloom. Before Clara was born seven years ago, Honeysuckle House and the candles Evie dipped for the town had been her whole world. She'd been so desperate to prove to herself and her sister that she was right about how to end the curse that Evie hadn't let herself think of anything else.

She still remembered the diary the house had presented her with after her mother's death. The words inside that led her to this life.

She'd found it face down on her mother's bed, open midway through. She'd flipped it over to find her mother's handwriting scrawled across the paper. It had been so long since she'd read anything the woman had written. She'd trailed her finger over the words, which had taken her back to her childhood. To the years after her father's death when Linda left notes each morning because she dipped and burned candles late into the night and couldn't be bothered to rise with her daughters and get them ready for school.

Things like:

There's eggs in the fridge. Don't use them all.

The dishes in the sink won't do themselves.

Evie, stop leaving your bike out on the front lawn or I'll take it away.

She'd held her place with a finger and flipped to the front of the journal. The inside of the cover read, *Property of Linda Caldwell. 1986.* It was the year Evie's grandmother had died; the year Florence was born.

The window had opened, and a soft breeze blew through the room, flipping the pages back to the way Evie had found them. From what she could tell, they were notes her mother had written to try to understand the curse. In the center of the page, someone had circled a few paragraphs.

Can magic be good or bad?

I've never used my magic to hurt anyone. Yes, it made it easier to fall in love, to ease Robert's anxiety over the curse, but that's good magic, isn't it? And what of Mother? Her spells have helped us meet our needs. The town fears us because of the curse, so we've gotten by as best we could, and we have the magic to thank for that.

But is magic that's only meant for yourself—that doesn't help other people—inherently bad?

All my life, Mother has kept that magic here, locked behind these walls, unable to escape. Perhaps that is what has caused this curse. Too much power hoarded in one place. If we were to use our magic for the good of the town, could that bring balance?

Those words, Evie believed, had been what the tarot cards pointed to when she and Florence had consulted them for answers, no matter what Florence had said. The hierophant could represent tradition. Reversed, it was a breaking of tradition. By sharing their magic, that's exactly what Evie would be doing.

She had lost the journal soon after, as if it had never been there at all, but the lesson had stayed with her. The only path to restoring the balance of the Caldwells' power was to turn their backs on the way their mother and their grandmother had hidden it away.

Evie had done exactly that, sharing her magic with the town. Every month Angela joined Evie in delivering her candles to the various businesses along Main Street (much to Florence's disappointment), and, slowly, their dying town came back to life. Even business at the bookstore boomed despite Florence's refusal to burn Evie's candles. Over time, Evie had grown lonely. She'd invited a handful of guests into her bed, hoping for someone who might want to stay, but nothing ever came of it. Until her daughter, Clara.

Evie gripped the curtain gently and smiled. The fabric brushed against her hand, then her cheek, a reminder of all the love she'd fostered behind these walls.

She turned back to the bureau she'd set up in the attic above her room, once a place her mother wouldn't allow her, now claimed for her own spellwork. Yes, her mother may have died in the room, but it had the best view in the house, and Evie was done with letting her mother have a hold on her. Before her lay a deck of tarot cards and a black taper candle. For a Caldwell witch, the power of their magic was twofold—the creation of the candle with the intentions they poured into each dipping of string in wax, then the release of those intentions once they set the wick to flame.

This one she'd infused with love and protection, dusted it with basil and rosemary between the layers, and the all-too-familiar words: *May my magic be good, my loved ones be safe, and my work be a blessing.*

She pushed the sleeves of her burnt-orange sweater up to her elbows as she whispered the words again, then poured a circle of salt around the candlestick holder. Then she struck a match and lit the wick. For the third and final time she said, "May my magic be good, my loved ones be safe, and my work be a blessing."

She lifted a slip of paper on which she'd written the names of four people—Evie, Clara, Florence, and Angela—and held it to the fire. As the flame burned through the names, a scream echoed through the house. Evie stilled, the paper turning to ash and the fire licking against her fingers. She pulled them back before they could burn.

Then, she ran for the sound.

Down the spiral steps to her bedroom, across the hall of the third floor to the main staircase, to the landing on the second floor where the guest rooms were.

"Where did it come from?" she asked.

The floorboards shifted beneath her feet, pushing her to the right. She hurried down the hall, past cobwebs that hung in corners and photos of the Caldwell witches who'd come before her—both a reminder of who she didn't want to become and a part of the story she sold her guests of a haunted house in a small Tennessee town—until a sconce flickered beside one of the rooms.

Evie stopped abruptly in front of it and rapped on the door. The sound of shuffling feet came from the other side. When no one answered, she pulled her keys from her pocket and started through the ring looking for the right one. Before she found it, the door creaked open on its own. Evie dropped the keys as she reached for the handle.

"Hello?" she asked.

The door opened further, and Evie found a woman with light brown skin, dark brown hair, and a bright red lip standing on the other side. Evie racked her brain for her name.

"Harper," she said as it came to her. "I heard a scream. Are you alright?"

"Just a little scare," Harper said.

Her wife—Quinn, Evie remembered—sat on a small couch eyeing the four-poster bed warily. Her curly red hair was disheveled, and she held a fair, freckled hand over her pregnant belly.

"The mattress threw me out of the bed," Quinn said.

"Threw is a bit of an exaggeration," Harper said.

Evie's brow furrowed. The house played tricks on the guests as much as it did on Evie and Clara. Turning doorknobs, fluttering curtains, flickering lights. But it wasn't supposed to touch them.

"You're not hurt, are you?" Evie asked. "Do you need me to call someone?"

Quinn waved a hand. "I'm fine. It surprised me is all."

"I'm terribly sorry," Evie said. "This visit is on me."

"That's really not necessary," Harper said. "We knew the house was haunted, but none of the reviews mentioned falling out of bed. We might've waited to come another time."

"I insist," Evie said.

The two women shared a glance. When the pregnant one nodded, the other one said, "That's very generous of you. We've had so much fun. We'll definitely be back."

"If you need a little extra time before you check out, please let me know," Evie said.

"We were just heading down for breakfast, then plan to hit the road," Harper said.

"And you're sure you're alright?" Evie asked Quinn.

The younger woman nodded. "Sorry to make such a fuss."

"Not at all." Evie backed out of the room. "Come find me when you're ready to leave, and I'll give you a hand with your bags."

Once Harper closed the door, Evie tapped her fingers against the wall, a twisting feeling in her stomach. October thirteenth was right around the corner. She'd been so certain her use of magic would be enough to break her family's curse, but if a guest had been pushed out of bed . . .

She shook her head. This had nothing to do with the curse. It couldn't.

"No touching the guests," she whispered.

But if the house heard her, it didn't respond.

Chapter Three

Florence, Now

As Angela turned on the lights inside Ink & Pages, Florence switched off the alarm. They faced the room, eyes sweeping over the shelves and floors for any tricks the shop may have played in their absence. A few rows down, several books had been tipped off one of the seasonal end caps and scattered in the walkway. They were all stories about magical sisters. The shop had a way of knowing what worried Florence.

Angela started to reach for the books when Florence waved a hand. "I'll get them." If she let Angela take the message meant for her, the shop would simply drop them on the ground again, and as much as Florence had come to enjoy her back-and-forth with the shelves, she didn't want the merchandise damaged. As she put the books back in their places, a loud crack of thunder shook the walls of the store, and the sky opened up outside. She made her way back to the front and paused when the window came into view. Already, water dripped down the glass. The cloud cover cast the street in shadow, and though Florence worried about her sister's bees, she hoped the rain would stay through the week and force Evie to cancel the festival.

It was only when Angela cleared her throat that Florence noticed Owen had arrived. He and Angela sat in the front corner reading nook, a tarot guidebook on Owen's lap and their lattes on the small table between them. A lamp cast a soft yellow glow despite the darkness on the other side of the window.

Even seated, Owen towered over Angela. Florence would've put him at six-foot-three if she had to guess. He had just a hint of brown in his complexion; from what Florence had learned in eavesdropping on his sessions with Angela, his grandmother was Indian. He looked up, brushing dark hair from his face, and when his brown eyes met hers, her chest warmed clear down to her fingertips. He raised a hand in greeting.

"Good morning," she said brightly, trying her hardest not to think about what Angela had said about him earlier. She hurried over to the register and busied herself by looking over the list of preorders coming in that week, but she couldn't help listening in on the tarot lesson.

"I finished the guidebook." Owen's baritone was soft against the pounding rain. "I've been doing a daily pull like you suggested."

"And?" Angela asked.

"I almost can't believe how spot-on they've been." He ran a hand over his well-trimmed beard.

"You didn't think they would be?" Angela asked.

He shrugged. "I was mostly looking for a way to pass the time. My grandfather used to read tarot—something he learned from his sister . . ." He trailed off, shook his head. "I never really understood it, but I think I'm starting to."

Angela answered him with a grin. "Think you're ready to do a reading for someone else?"

Across the room, Florence tucked a receipt into one of the books and slid it onto the shelf behind the register.

"You want me to read your cards?" Owen asked.

Angela glanced in Florence's direction. "Not exactly. What do you say, Florence?"

Florence did, in fact, want a reading. With her upcoming birthday and the Caldwell curse and her sister's refusal to give up her magic and cancel the festival, she wanted the guidance only the cards could bring, but she would never risk pulling them herself.

"Maybe," she said.

Owen's eyes brightened. He opened his bag and started digging around. "They're not here," he said. "I know I brought them."

"We have plenty of decks in the shop." Angela waved a hand. "Go find one that calls to you."

He jumped up and started for the mystical section. Florence watched him until he disappeared behind the shelves.

"You're staring," Angela said, loud enough for only Florence to hear.

Florence ignored the comment. "Are we sure this is a good idea?"

"You've been watching us every lesson," Angela said. "Maybe a card pull will help put your mind at ease. Besides, you're not the one reading them, so there's no Caldwell magic involved."

Florence considered this. Before she could decide either way, Owen appeared once more, a box in hand. "This one was already open," he said as he sat down and started shuffling. He glanced up at Florence with a tentative smile. "What do you say? Want a reading?"

With a heavy sigh, Florence closed the register and came over to join them, perching on the armrest of Angela's chair. As Owen held the deck and bit his lip, it took everything in Florence to look away from his mouth and remind herself of the curse. Though Florence hoped her sacrifice would be enough to stop it, she wouldn't know for certain until October thirteenth, and she wouldn't risk anyone else getting hurt because of her sister's unwillingness to give up her magic, too.

Owen reached across the space between them until his face was close enough to hers to feel intimate, to feel a swirling right in the middle of her chest, but far enough that he was still somehow respecting her personal space. She dared a glance at his eyes, and when hers met his, he grinned, at once soft and roguish, and it was a good thing Florence had sworn off love or she'd probably have kissed him right then and there. She tugged at the leather cord around her neck, pulling a small piece of tourmaline from under her sweater. She clutched the crystal tightly in her hand.

Owen fanned the cards out in front of her, and her chest went cold.

She hadn't seen those dark green card backs since the day she'd given up her magic. They shouldn't have been there. Before she could say as much, Owen flipped one of the cards toward her. Four candles were painted in each corner, and in the center sat Honeysuckle House.

Florence stared at the card, her heart racing. Beside her, Angela gasped.

"The four of wands," Owen said.

A peel of thunder echoed around them, loud enough to shake the front window. Florence made a sound in the back of her throat. Maybe if she asked him to turn the card back over, she could pretend this had never happened.

He glanced up at her. "Is something wrong?"

She didn't know where to start.

"Is that—?" Angela didn't finish the sentence.

Florence nodded.

Owen looked between them, confusion clear on his face.

"That deck belonged to my great-aunt." The words came out before Florence could think about them, and as soon as she spoke them, Owen glanced from her to the card the way one might take in the varying veins of green and purple in a piece of fluorite, all beautiful on their own but ultimately part of a whole. She pulled off her glasses and started cleaning them with the sleeve of her blouse.

Owen opened his mouth as if he was about to speak, then closed it just as quickly as he took out a second book on tarot. The shop had developed a habit of dropping guidebooks at his feet, and he had developed a habit of buying them. He flipped a few pages and said tentatively, "The wands are the fire suit. The four is a homecoming card."

"It is," Florence agreed.

He lifted the card gently and ran his thumb along the painted surface in a way Florence had longed to do for thirteen years.

"Is this Honeysuckle House?" He nodded at the front of the card.

"It is," Florence said again.

Owen worried at his lip. "It also says the card is a good omen—a cause for celebration. Is your birthday coming up?"

"The thirteenth," Florence mumbled.

"You don't sound too happy about that," he said. "Do you want me to pull a clarifying card or . . . ?"

She did, and she didn't.

"I think that's good for now," Angela interrupted. "Why don't we pull a card for you?"

He glanced between the women then nodded. He held his hand over the cards, landing on one on the opposite end of the card he'd pulled for Florence. He picked it up, tilted his head to the side, then showed it to her.

Painted on its front were two cups held aloft by two hands. Honeysuckle vines twined around the fingers and up the stems of the glasses, binding them together.

Florence swallowed hard, ignored the very pointed look Angela was giving her, then once again started furiously cleaning her glasses.

"This is a much more fun card," Angela said. "Go ahead, what do you think it means?"

"Cups represent emotions, and twos represent unions," Owen said.

"Good," Angela said. "Which means . . ."

"A union of emotions?" Owen suggested.

Angela laughed. "Exactly!"

Owen's eyes flicked toward Florence, and when his met hers, his cheeks flushed. He tucked a fallen piece of hair behind his ear. Florence looked away.

"More precisely, it suggests a deep emotional bond between two people," Angela said. "It's a romance card."

"Not always," Florence said a little too quickly.

Angela quirked an eyebrow.

"It's a soulmate card," Florence clarified. "Angela and I are soulmates, and we're just friends." They'd tried dating once after they took over the shop—Angela suggesting that since she was the one person Florence had let in, they might as well give it a go—but they'd quickly realized neither of them had romantic feelings for each other.

"But it *can* represent romantic love," Angela pressed.

"Except that it's reversed, which indicates a lack of trust in a new *or* an existing relationship," Florence said.

Angela cut Florence a look, glanced at the cards. "It's facing the same direction as your card."

"Right, but Owen pulled this one for himself, not me."

Angela leaned forward. Her brow furrowed for a moment then smoothed just as quickly as she leaned back and clapped her hands.

"A reversal can *also* indicate an amplification of the regular meaning," Angela said.

Owen glanced between them, following their back-and-forth with a small smile playing on his lips.

"Maybe you should draw another card," Florence suggested. "Get a little more insight."

"Careful," Angela said. "Sounds like you're giving tarot advice."

"It's not like I'm reading the cards," Florence said.

"You don't read tarot?" Owen asked.

"Not for a long time," Florence replied.

"Well, I like the idea of a little clarification." He flipped another card.

Honeysuckle House sat before them once more. Only this time, it was on fire.

Florence stared at the card.

Angela stared at the card.

Owen stared at the card.

None of them spoke for a few moments.

"Oh. Well. Hmm," Angela said, breaking the silence. "I did not expect you to pull the tower."

Owen let out a choked sound.

"It's okay," Florence said, as much for herself as for him. "The tower doesn't have to mean impending disaster."

Angela blinked a few times, then nodded. "Right! Of course! The tower can be a sign of sudden change. Like . . . like . . ."

"Like taking a temporary job as a beekeeper in a small town?" Owen suggested.

"Exactly!" Florence said.

"It doesn't have to mean things literally burning to the ground." Angela laughed uncomfortably as she picked up the card and held it up for them to see. "The illustration is a metaphor."

As the words left her mouth, the lights in the shop flickered. There was a rustling of pages, and all at once, there was a loud crack, crack, crack. Florence turned in her seat, eyes landing on the black crystals surrounding the front door.

Each piece of tourmaline had split right down the middle.

Chapter Four

Evie, Now

Evie sat in one of the rockers on the front porch of Honeysuckle House with her arms crossed and her foot tapping lightly against the wood. The storm had eased its deluge, leaving behind only a gentle rainfall. Evie would've found it peaceful, were it not for the worry creasing her brow. On her way downstairs she learned another person had fallen from their bed, two people had been locked out of their rooms, and the cinnamon had been swapped for cayenne at the oatmeal bar. The guests had taken it in stride, excited to get the full Honeysuckle House experience. But these were not the usual tricks, and they unsettled Evie. Her mind strayed to the black candle burning in her attic, and she wondered, for the first time ever, if she shouldn't have left an open flame unattended.

She shook her head. She would not let her sister's paranoia get to her. She'd done everything the cards had shown her to break her family's curse. If it hadn't worked, the house would know, and it would tell her. Honeysuckle House loved her and Clara as much as they loved it. It wouldn't put them in danger.

So lost was Evie in her thoughts, she didn't hear the footsteps on the porch until Angela stood right in front of her. Evie pushed up from the rocking chair and grabbed Angela in a hug, holding a little tighter than usual. Angela took a step back, hands on Evie's forearms, and looked her over, eyes at once gentle and searching.

"Something's wrong," Angela said.

Angela might've been Florence's best friend, but she and Evie had a special bond all their own. Florence wouldn't set foot in the house, but where Florence couldn't be there for Evie, Angela had. It had been Angela who stood by Evie's side when the first guest booked a stay. Angela who had driven Evie to the hospital when Clara was born, who had helped celebrate Clara's first birthday and her second birthday and all the way to her seventh.

Evie glanced down at Angela's hands on her, and though she wanted Angela to keep them there far longer, she knew better than to get mixed up with her sister's best friend in that way. There was enough tension between herself and Florence as it was. She wouldn't give Florence something else to hold over her.

Not that it stopped Evie from gripping Angela's hand—lingering on the feel of her skin beneath Evie's fingertips, the ridges of her knuckles, her short-cut nails—and pulling her around the side of the porch, where the once-bright clapboard was now chipped and stained. The house had never been worn down when Evie was younger, but since her mother's death it had done its part to look haunted for Evie's guests.

"There's nothing wrong," Evie said, more for herself than for Angela. "The house is being a little more mischievous than usual."

Angela arched an eyebrow. "Not just the bookshop it seems." As she reached into her bag, Clara came running from the yard, followed by a stream of honeybees. She shot up the steps and barreled right into Angela, leaving a trail of muddy footprints in her wake. She wrapped her arms around Angela's waist, already quite tall for her age.

"Angela!" she shouted then buried her head into Angela's side.

Angela grabbed her in a hug. "Good morning to you, too."

Where Evie had her late father's blonde hair, Clara took after Evie's mother, making her look more Florence's daughter than Evie's, with an angled face and long brown waves that had managed to fall almost completely out of their braids. Evie was constantly trying to talk Clara into cutting it, but Clara wanted it long like Aunty Flo's. Evie didn't mind too much, as long as Clara was happy. The one feature all three shared: the hazel Caldwell eyes. Though, much to Evie's surprise, Clara had been born without a birthmark above her right cheekbone. Evie and Florence both had a freckle at the corner of their eye. It was one of the few physical features they shared, not only with each other but with their mother, and, if she was to be believed, with every Caldwell witch who'd come before them. Evie's hadn't become apparent until she was around Clara's age, so it was possible Clara's would arrive with time.

In one fist Clara held a handful of rain-damp honeysuckle flowers, which the bees were still attempting to drink from, in the other the taper candle she'd dipped the night before with Evie. Clara had been eager to learn magic the first time she saw Evie light a candle, and while Evie didn't let her daughter cast spells on a whim (at least, not without guidance), she did let her dip her own candles, as long as she promised only to use her magic for good.

"What've you got there?" Angela asked when Clara finally let go.

"Candle," Clara said, holding it up.

"Pink!" Angela said. "Aren't you a little young for a love spell?"

Clara laughed brightly. "Pink can do other things."

"If not love, then what?" Angela asked with a quick look at Evie.

Evie smiled and mouthed, *Thank you*. Angela didn't only indulge Clara, she listened to her. Treated her like a person. There was a reason her daughter loved Angela like she was a part of the family.

Clara pursed her lips in thought. "Friendship." she said. "Besides, it's not all pink." She gave the candle to Angela, and where Clara's hand had covered the base, the pink wax bled to blue. Evie used blue for healing, forgiveness, truth, or clarity—sometimes all four. It was the first time Clara had used the color, and the first time she'd combined it with another.

The choice had surprised Evie. She preferred working with multiple candles for a spell if she needed the properties of different colors, but she wanted to foster her daughter's intuition. Clara felt drawn to put two colors together in a single candle, so Evie helped her make it happen.

"What's the blue for?" Angela asked.

"All of us," Clara said. "But the house especially." She looked up at the windows, her brow furrowed. Then, she took the candle and sat on one of the porch rockers, absorbed in her own thoughts.

Evie stared at her daughter.

"Seems you're not the only one who's noticed something off with the house," Angela whispered. "What happened?"

But Evie shook her head. "The usual antics."

Angela narrowed her eyes, and Evie sighed.

"It locked a few guests out of their rooms, tumbled a couple out of their beds." She paused. "One of them was pregnant." Then, quickly, "Don't tell Florence."

"Florence is why I'm here." Angela reached into her bag and pulled out a tarot deck.

"Don't tell me you talked her into a reading," Evie said.

"It wasn't me," Angela said. "The bookshop managed to pull these cards out of the house during my lesson with Owen." She handed them over.

Evie had wanted to shuffle her sister's cards more than once these past thirteen years, but she left them untouched on a high shelf in the upstairs library, where Clara couldn't get to them.

"Did she pull any?" Evie asked.

"Owen did," Angela said. "Before she recognized the deck. The four of wands."

Evie arched her eyebrows. "Yet she sent you to our childhood home, instead of doing what the cards told her. Let me guess, she interpreted it as a sign she *shouldn't* come home."

"It's not only that," Angela flipped the top card, and Evie frowned at the sight of Honeysuckle House burning. "He also pulled the tower. It was for his own reading, but . . ."

"But?" Evie asked.

"Our tourmaline cracked," Angela said. "All of it."

Evie's eyes widened a fraction. "While that's concerning, it was in the shop, not here at my house."

"The house where Owen happens to be working," Angela said.

Evie opened her mouth to reply, but Angela cut her off.

"I know you and Florence see things differently, but you can't ignore this." Angela reached for Evie, then hesitated, eyes searching. "What if she's right?"

"I thought you were on my side," Evie said.

"So did I," Angela said. "But with the cards and now the house, I'm worried about the festival."

"We've spent the last thirteen years bringing this town back to life," Evie said. "The festival is at the heart of that. We can't cancel it."

The whole point of the festival was reclaiming what had happened to her family—she and Angela had come up with the idea together. When Evie told the house her plans for the bed and breakfast after she'd inherited it thirteen years ago, she'd asked for its help in renovating, and photos of the witches who came before her had appeared on the walls. These were the ghosts who haunted her home, or so she told the tourists. But the festival put hope at the end of all that darkness. After a raucous tour of the house, they sent each guest home with a candle and the promise there would be no more deaths at Honeysuckle House.

"What if you move it to the twelfth?" Angela suggested.

"It's too late," Evie said. "The rooms are booked."

"If this rain keeps up, we might not have a choice," Angela said.

But they both knew the house would help them find a workaround.

All at once Clara was beside them. She reached for the deck in Evie's hands, and to Evie's surprise, she let her daughter take it. Clara shuffled the cards. When she was finished, she lifted the top one, revealing the same thing Florence had seen—the four of wands. She looked up at her mother. "The house wants her to come back."

"We all want her to come back." Evie bent down and pulled the rest of Clara's hair free from her braids then started replaiting them. "She gets lonely in that shop."

"She's lonely?" Clara asked. "What about us?"

"She loves us, honeybee, but unless we go to her, most days she only has the books and Angela to keep her company."

"I make great company," Angela said.

"That was never in question," Evie said with a little heat in her cheeks. "I meant . . ."

Angela laughed and waved a hand. "I know what you meant. You're not the only one who thinks Florence needs more than just the three of us in her life."

Evie tilted her chin down, narrowed her eyes.

Angela wiggled her eyebrows.

With a quick glance at her daughter, Evie said, "Clara, why don't you go get your things together? I need to drop off candles around town—you can play at the bookstore while I do."

Clara looked from Evie to Angela. Evie's daughter loved to help with the deliveries. The two of them had spent the day before dipping green tapers to help promote prosperity.

"Can't I come with you, *then* go to the bookstore?" Clara asked.

"Don't you want to keep Aunt Florence company?" Evie knew the sorts of conversations she was in for today, and she'd rather not expose Clara to them if she didn't have to.

"She does get weird when you're around." Clara pressed her lips together then nodded. "Okay. But can I keep these cards?"

Evie considered the question. The shop had pulled the deck from the house, and Florence had never explicitly said she couldn't use it. Who was she to get in the way of that sort of magic?

"Don't tell your aunt."

"I'll go get my things!" With a bounce, Clara bounded across the porch and through the front door.

"Now," Evie said when she was sure Clara was out of earshot, "tell me what happened with Owen."

* * *

Evie couldn't take her mind off the thought of her sister finally having a love life—having anything at all other than her judgment of and worry over Evie—as she made the drive into town. Clara might not have dipped her pink candle with love in mind, but Evie found herself hoping the color would still do its work. Maybe after Evie's theories were proved to be correct, her sister would finally open her heart again, and they could be the family they hadn't been these past thirteen years.

She pulled her car into one of the few open spots on Main Street. There were still four days until the festival, but the town was already bustling despite the morning's storm. The pumpkin patch had opened for the season last weekend, and with most of the schools in the state on fall break, families looking for a little autumn fun flocked to Burdock Creek.

Evie stepped out of the car, basket of candles in hand, and squared her shoulders before she started for the antique store at the end of the strip of shops. It had been on its last legs thirteen years ago, but after Evie offered the owners a green candle, things had suddenly turned around. The launch of the festival a year later had brought even more customers through their doors, and ever since, business had never been better. Every shop on Main Street had a similar story. While Evie's goodwill had burned away some of the wariness her family's history had instilled in the town, echoes of fear lingered. She heard them now in the way the shop's owner, Stephanie Cooke greeted her.

"Welcome to—" Stephanie cut herself short as her eyes landed on Evie. The brightness in her voice dimmed. "Oh, Evie. What brings you in today? Any news about the festival?"

Evie forced herself to smile and keep a certain sweetness in her words as she said, "Do you mean have I canceled the ghost tour, the honey harvest, and the candle dipping?"

Stephanie avoided meeting Evie's eyes as she laughed, her discomfort clear, and turned her focus instead to the display of teacups she'd been rearranging when Evie had walked through the door. "With the curse, it might be safer for everyone."

Evie had already had a version of this conversation with almost every business owner in town after they'd decided to host this year's events in the park instead of at Honeysuckle House. The craft fair, the pumpkin carving contest, the face painting. Angela chaired the festival committee, but that hadn't stopped them from going around her with their own plans. While no one had explicitly asked Evie to avoid the downtown festivities this year, they also hadn't invited her to relocate her own.

"I don't think we'll have to worry about that this year," Evie said. It was the line she'd used every time, and while she didn't go into her reasons, she still felt the need to say it. "But, no, that's not why I'm here today." She grabbed a candle from the basket and held it up for Stephanie to see. "I figured we could all use a little extra luck this week."

"You're too good to us," Stephanie said as she accepted the candle. "Please be careful. You and Clara are such lights in this town, especially after your mother . . ." She trailed off, then shook her head. "I don't want to see either of you get hurt."

"Don't worry," Evie said with a forced levity. "I'll be burning plenty of candles to make sure that doesn't happen."

Chapter Five

Clara, Now

Clara Caldwell loved three things most in the world: Honeysuckle House, her magic, and her family. But every time she stepped inside Ink & Pages, that list grew.

She loved the smell of her aunt's fresh-cut lemons soaking up negative energy and the way the books sat on (and sometimes fell off) the shelves and the energy of the crystals and the magic in the plants and all the tarot decks, and she especially loved hiding in the reading nook the shop created just for her whenever she came to visit.

All of that, of course, came back to her aunt.

And Clara very much loved her aunt.

That was why even though she also very much loved helping her mom deliver candles, she agreed to spend the day in the shop. Because maybe—just maybe—she could help her aunt with whatever it was that was making her so lonely.

Clara burst through the door of Ink & Pages with a backpack full of supplies. She had the candle she dipped fresh the night before all pink and blue and set with intentions to help her aunt and help the house because while she didn't exactly speak the same language as the house, she knew whatever was happening—whatever her mom was doing her best to ignore—was tied to her aunt coming home.

So, she had her candle, as has already been mentioned, but Clara felt it was always best to start lists at the top. She also had matches and her favorite crystals—obsidian for protection (her mom and her aunt preferred tourmaline, but she liked how smooth obsidian was, and she especially liked her obsidian crystal because it was carved in the shape of a cat), pink quartz for love, and moonstone because another thing Clara very much loved was the moon.

"Aunt Flo!" Clara called as Angela came in behind her and carefully closed the door that Clara had thrown open.

Florence stepped out from one of the rows of shelves and in a singsong voice said, "Is that my favorite helper come to brighten up my bookshop on this gloomy day?"

"It is!" Clara cried, running straight for Florence and wrapping her arms around her. Clara came up to Angela's hip, but her aunt was tall, tall, tall, and Clara only just reached her thighs. One day, though, she knew she'd be as tall as her aunt because she had her aunt's hair and her aunt's smile, and she might not have her aunt's (or her mom's) witch's mark, but maybe she'd grow into that, too.

Florence bent down and kissed her lightly on the forehead before her focus landed on the door. Clara turned around, following her gaze.

"Your mom's not coming in today?" Florence asked.

"Nope," Clara said. "She sent me with Angela after you sent over those tarot cards."

Florence ruffled her hair and said, more to herself than to Clara, "Maybe she's sitting with my warning."

Clara answered her anyway. "She doesn't think it's a warning. She thinks it's a sign, like you do, but a sign you need to come home and stop hiding in the shop and being so lonely."

With a surprised laugh, Florence arched an eyebrow, her attention now on Angela. "You told her about Owen."

Angela pressed her lips together and gave a little shrug. "I might have mentioned him."

"She's never going to let this go," Florence said.

"Well, she is actively avoiding you," Angela replied.

"If I still worked the flame, I'd light my own candle to get her to come to her senses."

"What color would you use?" Clara asked. "I could light one for you."

Florence dropped down in front of Clara and gave her another kiss on the forehead. "Thank you, but that would only further prove your mother's point."

"That you don't like magic," Clara said.

Florence opened her mouth, then closed it. Clara knew her aunt didn't think she or her mother should be dipping candles, much less lighting them, but she never said it to Clara directly. Well, she had. Once. And the way her mom got after? Clara had never seen her so mad and never wanted to see it again, and that was apparently enough for her aunt not to bring it up anymore, at least not when Clara was around.

"It's okay," Clara said. "You don't have to say it." She walked back to the front door where the tourmaline still sat broken. She planted her hands on her hips and leaned toward it. "At least you know it's doing its job."

Her aunt's smile slipped as she looked at the cracked stones.

"And maybe you'll have even more protection now," Clara said. "More pieces means more crystals to keep you safe!"

Florence laughed. "That's certainly one way to look at it. Why don't we find you a book to read? Or do you want to help me stock some of the shelves?"

Clara didn't want to do either. She wanted the shop to open the path to her special little corner, then close it off from her aunt so she could light her candle without anyone knowing. But Clara also didn't like lying, so she decided she could read a page or two before she got started on her spell.

"Let's find a book." As the words left Clara's mouth, there was a shuffling of pages from the children's section and the familiar sound of a book hitting the floor.

Her aunt's lips quirked. "It seems the shop has something in mind."

Clara gripped her backpack tight as she ran down the space between the shelves until she reached the children's books. Here, every bit of exposed wall had been painted with characters from all of Clara's favorite stories (which were, coincidentally, her aunt and Angela's favorites, too). A very hungry caterpillar stood poised to devour an entire shelf. Winnie the Pooh and Paddington sat down to tea with Alice, while unicorns and penguins and a mouse eating a cookie ran along the wall. Right in the middle lay a book, face up. The cover showed a little bee perched atop a coneflower.

Her aunt came up beside her and whispered, "Thank you."

"Yes, shop," Clara said, much more loudly. "Thank you! This is exactly what I need to impress Owen with my knowledge of the bees!" She scooped up the book, turned back to her aunt, and said, "I'll go find somewhere to read, then."

Florence tilted her head to the side and said, "Sounds like a plan. Let me know if you need any help."

Clara flipped open the first page of the book and looked over the words. "I think I can handle this one all on my own."

Then she was off, weaving between the books until she reached the very back of the shop. She glanced over her shoulder, and when she was sure no one was watching, she knocked on one of the shelves. It swung open, revealing a small corner with a beanbag chair, a reading lamp, and a little table just for her. On its opposite side sat every single one of Clara's favorite books. After reading the first two pages of the new story the shop had given her and getting caught up in it and then reading three more pages, Clara finally set it down and got to work. She dug through her backpack—rocks she'd gathered from the creek, brown candles she used to get home in time for dinner, and everything she'd brought for today's spell.

First, she pulled out her candlestick holder. Then, she created a circle around it with her crystals, arranging her obsidian cat front and center. Finally, she put the candle in place. She struck a match and held it up to the wick. Once it caught flame, she shook out the match dramatically, stared into the fire, and said, "Bring my Aunt Florence a friend. And show me how I can help the house." She paused, gasped as she remembered what her mother had taught her, and said, "Oh and may my magic be safe, my loved ones be good, and my work . . ." She paused, furrowed her brow, then smiled with satisfaction. "And may my work be a blessing."

The fire glowed brighter with her words, and as it did, the candle began to melt. Rather than the slow burn she'd expected, slow enough to let her read the book and wait for her mom to come and get her, the wax melted quickly. It spilled out over the top of the candle, dripped down the edge, and pooled on the little table so fast that one moment the candle was burning and the next it had put itself out, the spell complete.

Her mom had always told her intention was at the heart of their magic, if she wanted something badly enough, she could bring it into the world. And right then she could feel her intention at the center of her chest, like she'd had a hot cup of cocoa and swallowed it down much too fast. It seemed the candle had felt it too, which was well and good because that meant she could get back to reading sooner rather than later.

The wall behind her began to shake, and she let out a small yelp as the bookcase opened to reveal her aunt.

"Is that smoke?" Florence asked, gaze shifting from Clara to the now-empty candlestick holder. She dropped to her knees in front of Clara's spell circle, a hand over her mouth and her eyes wide in a way Clara had never seen them.

"Sorry," Clara said. "I know you don't like magic in the shop, but it was for you. Mom said this was going to be a hard month for you, so I had to make the candle. Then when she said you were lonely, I didn't want you to be lonely because I love you and I thought I could help you find a friend and also the house needed it and . . ."

Clara could feel the tears starting to well up, and all at once her aunt's face shifted from fear to concern.

"Please don't stop wanting to see me the way you don't want to see the house."

Florence wrapped her arms around Clara. "I'll never want to stop seeing you." She held her tight, right up against her chest and rested her chin on the top of Clara's head. "I'm sorry if I ever said anything that made you afraid I would."

"It's just, you never come see me," Clara said.

Florence pulled back. "That has nothing to do with you, but your mom made me promise not to talk to you about it, and I have to respect that. If things were different, I'd be there every day to give you a hug and walk with you by the creek and sip nectar from the honeysuckles. Who knows, after my birthday I might be able to."

"You really think so?" Clara asked as she wriggled out of her aunt's arms to look up at her and better assess her answer.

Florence's face clouded. "I certainly hope so. But until then, you know I don't allow candles in the shop. And I thought your mom had a rule about casting spells for another person without their knowledge."

Clara's mom did, in fact, have that rule. But before she could say as much, a soft mewling sound came from behind her aunt. The shelf-turned-door opened wider of its own accord, and a small, long-haired black kitten stepped into the alcove. It blinked at them with eyes yellow as the moon. With a twitch of its tail, it approached Clara and rubbed its head against her leg. She scratched between its ears. Then, it crouched low, shook its back legs, and jumped in the direction of Clara's favorite books. It almost reached the shelf that was eye level with Florence, but fell just short. Florence caught it before it could tumble to the floor, though Clara knew it would land on all four feet. That's simply what cats did.

"Who let you in here?" Florence asked, holding it up to her nose.

No one let the cat into the shop. Clara's magic had called for a friend for her aunt, and the cat had answered. It was that simple. She couldn't wait to tell her mom.

"No collar," Florence said with concern. "And I haven't seen any pregnant strays around."

The kitten meowed again before wriggling out of Florence's grip, clinging to her sweater, and crawling up her shoulder, where it started purring furiously. Her aunt smiled so wide, Clara wondered if she'd ever really seen her smile before that moment.

"Are you gonna keep it?" Clara asked. "You have to keep it."

The smile slipped and, with a sigh, Florence said, "We should put up signs." She nodded at the kitten. "I'm sure someone is missing you." It burrowed in deeper against Florence's collarbone.

"Maybe it's here for you!" Clara said.

Florence glanced at Clara's setup—the spent candle, the crystals. Her eyes widened. "You . . . summoned a cat?"

Clara shrugged. "Not on purpose. Well, yes on purpose, but I didn't know it was going to be a cat. Mom and Angela said you were lonely and I love you and don't want you to be lonely. Can we call him Ink? I think that would be just perfect."

"Him?" Florence asked, holding up the kitten. She tilted her head, as if unsure how Clara could tell the cat was a boy.

"Feels right," Clara said.

"If someone comes looking for this kitten, you know I have to give him back, don't you?"

"Sure," Clara said. But she knew no one was going to come looking. "Until then, he's here with you in the shop." It wasn't a question.

Florence laughed softly as the kitten rose on unsteady legs and balanced on her shoulder before he leapt off and landed on the shelf he had missed earlier. He rubbed his back against the spines, then turned his eyes on Florence once more.

"He loves books!" Clara said.

"Ink it is," Florence replied. Then she scooped him up and said, "Come on, let's see if we can find him a saucer of milk."

Chapter Six

Florence, Now

Florence was not lonely. At least, that's what she told herself. That her sister *and* Angela had said it loud enough for her niece to hear, that her niece felt compelled to cast a spell in response, was at once deeply mortifying and unexpectedly heartwarming.

But it didn't change the fact that Clara had done magic inside Ink & Pages.

The moment Florence smelled the smoke, she knew. Seeing the spent candle had only made matters worse. She'd given up so much to keep her shop safe, afraid her family's curse would somehow extend inside its walls if any of them practiced magic there. Though she hoped one candle lit by a child wouldn't be enough to undo her sacrifices, the spell itself had been beyond anything Florence had ever done. She couldn't quite fathom her niece's ability to conjure a living being to her shop. Neither Florence nor her sister had ever had that strength with their magic.

Well, that wasn't fully true. When they were children, before their father died, her sister had managed to summon a hummingbird who took up residence in the tree outside her window. Their mother had been against pets, because she thought her daughters and the house got up to enough mischief on their own. The last thing she wanted was some strong-minded creature knocking over her candles.

Later, when they were older and realized they could hide a pet from their mother with the house's help, Evie had tried to do the same with a cat, but to no avail.

The kitten freed himself from Florence's hold and climbed up her sweater once more until he nestled his feather-soft head against her neck and purred loudly, right into her ear. Florence knew the magic was a danger, but she hoped desperately no one came looking for the kitten.

"Ink," she tried out the name. He purred louder, and beside Florence, her niece beamed.

Florence scratched the kitten's ears and gently lifted him from her shoulder. "We're going to have to do something about this digging your claws into my favorite sweater business," she said. "Do you want to hold him?"

Clara stared longingly at the kitten. She started to reach out, then she shook her head. "The universe sent him for you."

"Right, of course," Florence said. "But I need to see if I can give him oat milk, and I would hate for him to get lost in the stacks. Maybe you can watch him for a minute?"

"We definitely don't want him to get lost." Clara held out her arms and Florence gently deposited the kitten into them. Though he rubbed his head against her niece's hand, his yellow eyes never left Florence.

She started a search on her phone as they made their way to the break room, and she discovered she could give Ink a small amount of oat milk, which was good because that was all she had.

"Want to do the honors?" Florence asked.

Clara set the saucer on the ground and poured just enough that it only splashed over the edge once. After he'd had his fill, Ink shot through the break room door and into the shop.

"Wait!" Clara called as she chased after him.

Florence followed quickly behind her, but it seemed the kitten had already disappeared. She felt a pang in her chest at the thought that he might be gone for good.

Clara turned in a circle then planted her hands on her hips. "He'll be back. When he gets hungry. You're going to have to buy some cat food."

Florence laughed. "Am I now?"

"You're going to take care of him, aren't you?" Clara took Florence's hand as they made their way back to the front of the shop so they could keep an eye on the door should Ink try to escape.

"Of course," Florence said. "It's not every day your niece summons you a kitten. Even if she knows you have a very strict 'no magic in the shop' rule."

Clara pointed at the rose quartz and monsteras decorating the romance section.

"Crystals and plants don't count," Florence said.

"Then I think you should change the rule," Clara said. "No *spells* in the shop."

"And definitely no candles," Florence added.

When they reached the front, they found Angela at the register with Ink on the counter in front of her. He sat, licking one paw. She stood, staring at him.

"You found him!" Clara ran to the kitten. She gave him a quick pat on the head, then turned back to Florence. "He wanted to introduce himself to Angela."

"You got us a shop cat?" Angela asked.

Florence shook her head and pointed to Clara. "It wasn't my doing."

"His name's Ink," Clara said.

"Appropriate," Angela said. "And where did you find him? I know he wasn't here when I brought you in."

The kitten did a long stretch at the mention of his name, then wriggled his back legs as he prepared to pounce in Florence's direction. Before he could, she picked him up under the soft spot of his belly and set him on her shoulder. She was rewarded with more purring.

"I never took you for a cat person," Angela said.

Florence would've shrugged, but she didn't want to send Ink tumbling, so instead she said, "I guess we learn new things about ourselves every day."

She turned her head and pressed her nose to Ink's. As she breathed in his soft kitten smell, the bell above the door rang. She glanced over the top of Ink's head to find Owen on the other side with a rather large piece of tourmaline in his hands. Ink turned on her shoulder to face him, tiny claws clinging to Florence's sweater.

"Twice in one day?" Florence said. "Do you have another lesson?"

Owen held up the crystal with two hands. "My reading broke yours."

Angela stepped out from behind the register. "Where did you get such a big piece so fast?"

He ducked his head with a little laugh and said, "I bought it online a week ago after the crystal encyclopedia fell off the shelf in front of me." His eyes flitted toward Florence.

"The shop knew," Clara said, sagely.

"That I'd pull the tower card and crack all your aunt's tourmaline?" Owen asked.

"That she'd need more protection," Clara said. "And that she's lone—"

Before Clara could finish the sentence, Florence interrupted her by lifting Ink and holding him out toward Owen. "Clara got me a kitten."

Owen set the tourmaline on the counter and smiled so broadly that Florence had to force herself to look away.

"His name's Ink!" Clara said.

Owen accepted the kitten, cradling him in his arms. Ink bristled a little at first, arching his back and narrowing his eyes. When he started to sink his teeth into the pad of Owen's hand, Owen rubbed gently between his ears. Ink looked up at him and gave a soft, surprised meow.

"Nice to meet you, too," Owen said. Then to Clara, "Where did you find him?"

Clara looked up at Florence, the question clear in her eyes. Magic wasn't a secret in Burdock Creek—especially not with the way her sister used the history of the curse as a part of her branding—but to tourists, that's where it ended. A cursed family, a haunted house, and a candle for prosperity. The extent of the Caldwells' magic wasn't something they shared with outsiders.

"That's a little complicated," Florence said.

"Like books falling at my feet whenever I browse the shelves is complicated?" he asked with a gleam in his eye.

Florence laughed. "Something like that."

"Maybe I can buy you coffee and you can tell me about it."

A small smile spread across Florence's face, and for the first time in a long time, she found herself thinking about life outside of Ink & Pages. Owen didn't live in Burdock Creek, she reasoned, so how much could she come to care about him in a few days' time?

"Thank you for the tourmaline," she said, dodging the invite all the same. "You didn't have to do that."

"I know you don't like tarot," he said. "Now I know why. Does something dangerous happen every time you look at the cards?"

"Let's put this in the same category of complicated as the cat and the books," Florence said.

"Another topic for discussion over coffee, then."

"Perhaps," Florence said.

This conversation would be much easier if Owen wasn't staying at Honeysuckle House.

Ink wriggled against Owen's hold then leapt from his arms, landing neatly on all four feet before he started for the front corner, where Florence had tucked a lemon after that morning's incident. When he reached it, he looked up at her, sat back on his haunches, and licked his paw in a way that seemed to say, "Come and see."

Florence crouched down beside him to find the entire lemon covered in mold like it had been sitting out for weeks. The fruit was meant to absorb negative energy, yes, but she'd never seen it happen so quickly.

"That doesn't look good," Owen said. She glanced up to find both he and Clara had followed her.

"The lemon?" Angela called from the register, where she'd just finished ringing up a customer.

Florence nodded as she stood. "I'm going to need another, but we're fresh out."

"I was heading to the store after this to grab a few things," Owen said. "I can get you a bag."

Florence stared at him for a moment, afraid to let him in too much, too soon, especially after what had happened that morning and the cards he'd pulled.

"That would be great!" Angela said. "We'll be here."

But Owen's eyes were on Florence. She forced a smile and said, "One should do it."

"Grab at least two," Angela said.

Florence rolled her eyes but smiled, this time for real, and said, "Thanks again for the tourmaline."

Ink abandoned the lemon and started winding his way between Owen's legs.

"Do you need any food for this little guy?" Owen asked.

"Oh!" Florence said. "Yes, please. If you don't mind."

"Not at all." Owen bent down to scratch Ink between the ears. When he straightened, he caught Florence watching him. She flushed as he rubbed at the back of his neck. "See you in a bit."

Florence waved, lost for words.

As he stepped out onto the street, Evie's voice came through the open door.

"Owen!" she said. "I didn't expect to run into you here."

"Just dropping off something for Florence," he replied.

Florence could almost feel the satisfied look on her sister's face, and when Evie walked through the door, she proved Florence right. Her eyes found Florence right away, and she wiggled her brows before she set a small basket at the front checkout counter, empty save one green candle.

"Mommy!" Clara ran for Evie. "You'll never guess what happened!"

Ink gave up on the lemon and trotted across the shop toward Evie in greeting. He rammed his head against her legs, then looked back at Florence. She followed after him.

"You got a kitten?" Evie bent down to pick up Ink. She pressed him right up against her face. He squirmed in her arms and gave a small hiss. Affronted, she put him down, narrowed her eyes, and said, "I'm surprised you'd risk bringing someone new into your life so close to your birthday. Finally changing your mind about the curse?"

Florence's heart skipped over itself. She'd been so surprised by her niece's magic—and worried about its broader consequences—that she hadn't thought about the impact it could have on the cat himself. The last thing she wanted was for something so small and innocent to fall victim to the Caldwell curse.

"I didn't think . . ." Florence trailed off.

"Mom!" Clara said, arms crossed. "That's not very nice."

Evie glanced at her daughter and with a short nod said, "You're right. Sorry, Florence. I think it's great you got a cat. Unless it's not yours?" She glanced at Angela.

"He's mine," Florence said, and the smile Clara rewarded her with almost made Clara casting a spell in her shop worth it. Ink trotted over to her and meowed to be picked up. Florence obliged. "But I didn't adopt him. We have Clara to thank for little Ink here."

"Where did you find a kitten?" Evie asked.

Clara glanced up at Florence. "I broke Aunt Florence's rule and used a candle in the shop."

Evie's mouth fell open slightly. "You summoned a cat? With your magic?"

"Apparently she heard the two of you talking about how lonely I am," Florence said.

"It's true," Evie said.

"I might've let more people in over the past thirteen years if you'd listened to me."

"Instead, you gave up your magic without knowing if it would even make a difference," Evie shot back.

Neither of them knew for certain if their efforts to break the curse would work until the thirteenth came, but as far as Florence saw things, one less practicing Caldwell witch might just be enough to tip the balance the tarot cards had pointed to, undoing the damage wrought by the magic of the witches who had come before her.

"That's better than doing nothing!" Florence said.

"Helping this town isn't nothing," Evie replied.

"So, you're going to sit in that house and hope the curse doesn't come for you?" Florence asked.

They'd had the argument so many times that Florence knew what Evie would say next, so when Evie opened her mouth to respond, Florence cut her short. "You have *people* in the house. You have Clara!"

Evie took a step forward, pointing directly at Florence. "Don't bring my daughter into this."

"How can I not? You're putting her at risk."

"Keeping her magic from her is an even greater risk," Evie said. "Look at the beautiful things she can do. If I'd raised her the way you would've had me do it, there'd be no wonder in her world."

Behind Evie, Clara had taken Angela's hand as her eyes tracked back and forth between Florence and Evie, her lip trembling.

"I think maybe that's enough for now," Angela said.

Evie whirled around. "Oh Clara, honeybee, I'm so sorry." She looked back over her shoulder at Florence. "I raise my voice a lot less when you're not around, you know."

"Funny, so do I," Florence said.

"Come to the house. We can talk through this there," Evie said. "Your tarot card—"

"Was a warning," Florence said.

"Your own shop wants you to come home."

The lights flickered overhead. Evie arched her eyebrows.

"I'm not going to that house," Florence said. "Not until after the thirteenth."

"If my efforts haven't been enough to break the curse—which is a big *if,* since the tarot cards made it clear that using our magic is how we fix this—the danger isn't *until* the thirteenth," Evie said. "So come before then."

"I thought you said the house turned a few of your guests out of their beds this morning," Angela said.

Evie winced. Florence crossed her arms.

"It's October," Evie said. "The house was having fun. The festival is coming up."

"One of those guests was pregnant," Angela said.

Evie sighed. "You weren't supposed to say anything."

"I couldn't keep it to myself," Angela said. "Not with everything else that's happened today."

"Fine. It's a little worrying, but not *someone is going to die in our house* worrying." Evie shrugged.

"That is exactly the sort of worrying it is," Florence said.

"The guest laughed it off," Evie said. "No one was hurt."

"They could've been. And what about what happened here?" Florence threw out her hand toward the cracked tourmaline.

"Not every bit of bad energy has to be the result of a curse," Evie said.

"It's too much of a coincidence not to be."

"Then *do* something about it," Evie said. "The tarot told you to come home."

Florence shook her head. "I'm not going to the house unless you agree to shut down the bed and breakfast until this is all over."

"October is our busiest month of the year," Evie said. "People have already booked their rooms."

Florence shrugged. "Those are my terms."

Evie sighed and said, "Come on, Clara." She took the last green taper from her basket and held it out toward Florence. "I dipped one for you."

But Florence shook her head. "No candles."

Evie set it on the countertop by the register anyway, then she took Clara's hand and headed for the door.

"Bye, Aunt Flo!" Clara called.

Florence blew her a kiss.

"We're good people," Evie said before she reached for the door handle. "We don't deserve to be cursed."

"It doesn't matter what we deserve."

As the words left her mouth, she felt a twisting sensation at the center of her chest. A wave of dizziness washed over her, and she closed her eyes. When she opened them, she found Evie stabilizing herself against the door frame.

Before either of them could speak, a siren's wail filled the air, and a firetruck flew past the shop. Evie's phone started to ring. The color drained from her face as she brought it to her ear.

"Is everyone all right?" She nodded, quickly. "I'm on my way right now."

But when she hung up, she didn't move.

Her eyes met Florence's, round and dark and frightened. She held her hand over her chest and said, "The house is on fire."

Chapter Seven

Evie, Now

Evie had been so desperate to be right about how to break the curse that she never let herself stop to think what it might mean if she were wrong, if the people she loved were in danger. Any one of them could be next, and for the first time in almost thirteen years, fear wrapped its hands around her and refused to let go. If the house could catch fire, anything was possible.

She looked up at Florence—her older sister, her protector for most of her life—and tried, and failed, to will the desperation from her eyes and voice.

"Are you coming?" Evie asked.

Florence looked away. "Evie, I can't."

The words cut deep. Evie knew her sister wouldn't go near the house, but this was different. The house was hurt, and Evie was hurting, and this is what big sisters were supposed to do. She wanted to say, "You can't ignore this." She wanted to say, "I need you." She wanted to say, "Please."

Instead, she took Clara's hand in her own, threw her hair over her shoulder, and said, "If that's the way it has to be." Then she dropped her phone into her bag and pushed the door open once more.

"Evie, wait!" Angela said, as she came out from around the counter and followed Evie onto the sidewalk.

"You don't have to come," Evie said.

"I'm not letting you face this alone."

"She's not alone," Clara said through a hiccup of tears. "I'm here."

"And I'm here with both of you." Angela took the keys from Evie, her fingertips brushing Evie's palm. Evie gripped her hand for a moment, the metal between them, and did her best not to cry. Angela looked into her eyes, took a step closer.

"Is the house okay?" Clara asked.

Angela broke contact with Evie, then grabbed Clara's other hand.

Evie took a steadying breath and tried her best to keep her voice from breaking. "Let's go find out."

Chapter Eight

Honeysuckle House, Now

The protection candle burned in the window where Evie left it, the flickering flame reflected in the glass. The house felt every moment of it—the heat from the fire, the intentions in the wax. It was a familiar power, one that had become deeply embedded in the walls, clear down to the studs, and one that was starting to fray at the edges. As hours slipped past and October thirteenth crept closer, the magic in the walls shuddered, longing for a release that could only come one way.

The house did its best to hold on.

The Caldwells were a comfort, the way only family could be. They were joy and love and history, everything Honeysuckle House felt and longed for because of the magic in their hearts that had given it life. But Clara? Clara was special—untouched by what had come before. The house loved her desperately. It knew if she uncovered the truth, she would do everything in her power to keep the magic flowing in the pipes and wires, like blood pounding through its veins.

The house did not want to die.

The thought made the walls creak, the hallways contracting subtly like a shallow breath. Condensation formed on the glass like tears. As it thought of all the witches who had walked its halls, all the births it had witnessed and the deaths it had endured, the energy in the air shifted. Then, the black candle tipped over.

It fell off the windowsill onto the small, circular rug.

The house would've blinked, if houses could blink, stunned as it was that the candle had fallen. Whatever power had pushed the candle had not come from the house.

The fibers in the rug caught fire, and the flames shot toward the far wall as if someone had poured a line of gasoline. The house tipped over one of Evie's jars of moon water then another and another, but the fire only grew as it ate away at the wall the house had so carefully constructed the day Linda Caldwell died thirteen years ago.

The glass glowed orange as voices rose up from the front lawn. The house opened the window wide, sending in a rush of cold air that only served to fan the flames. It tried to shift the wood and plaster, to close over on itself and contain the fire, but where the flames touched the wall, the house had lost control. As it burned, the house thought back over every tragedy that had happened on its grounds, every broken body, and wished it had understood then what it knew now.

Part II
The Lovers

A reminder to follow your heart. Often represents a solid relationship—either romantic or platonic.

Chapter Nine

Regina, 1960

When the curse claimed Helen and Christopher Caldwell, no one yet knew it was a curse. It was a tragedy that almost killed their daughters the same way it took them. As their Buick collided with the old maple tree in the front yard, honeysuckle vines shot toward the car, punched out the window glass, and pulled thirteen-year-old Regina and her older sister, Violet, free. But there was no saving Helen and Christopher. Not with how the branches had gone through the windshield, through their chests, through the front seats.

When the full tree fell, crushing them beneath its weight, it was a mercy. Though the police had looked the car over and talked with their family friends—the Greys—to determine why Christopher had lost control, it had been ruled an accident, cause unknown. No one considered the deaths a result of magic.

It wasn't until thirteen years later to the day, when another person fell victim in the Caldwell home, that the reality of the situation dawned on the town of Burdock Creek. The witches were cursed. Those who grew too close to them at risk of dying.

But we're getting ahead of ourselves. The story behind the second curse year started a week earlier, as Regina Caldwell sat dipping candles in the workshop her father had built for her mother many moons ago. It was little more than a shed with windows, a worktable, and a small stove. Still, it was a part of Honeysuckle House. The water and wax were always the perfect temperature, and the magic made the room comfortable, even on the hottest days of summer. Of course, that magic wasn't much needed in October. Though the temperature had finally started to fall, the honeybees were still busy at work, their hives close enough that with the windows open, Regina could hear the steady buzz.

As much as she loved this time of year, it always brought with it the reminder of her loss. She stared out the window at the maple she and her sister had planted after the wreckage of her parents' accident had been cleared out, and her grief opened up inside her. She sat with it for a few moments, let herself sink deep down into its embrace, before she forced herself back to the present moment.

It was hard to imagine what her life would look like now if her mother and father were still in it. Likely, she and her sister would both be married, starting families of their own, letting their power infuse their homes and filling Burdock Creek with magic. With Regina now twenty-six and Violet thirty-one, almost every candle sold came with questions about their love lives. But Regina didn't have the heart for falling in love. She had considered, more than once, lighting a candle to bring a man into her life if only so she could raise a Caldwell witch of her own behind these enchanted walls. Then, just as quickly, burning another to get rid of him. But there was time for that.

These days, it was only Regina and Violet, and Regina wouldn't have it any other way. They tended their bees, dipped their candles, and sold them out of a small boutique on Main Street—Grey's Gifts. It had once been the home of their parents' store, where they'd offered candles and honey and herbal remedies. But after the accident, the sisters sold the storefront to the Greys on the condition they be allowed to continue to sell their tapers. Though Regina and Violet shared the work of dipping the candles and harvesting from their hives, Regina spent more time with the boilers and wax, while her sister worked out of the shop.

That morning, Regina tied her dark, shoulder-length curls out of her way. Water boiled beneath the pot of beeswax, and a host of dyes sat on the table in front of her.

She rolled up the sleeves of her checkered blouse, then lifted a small green bottle and added its contents to the melted wax. Then, she began the process of dipping her wicks and hanging them to dry, allowing each layer to set before adding the next, speaking power into the candles—growth, prosperity, success. Everything green represented, made manifest by the simple act of Regina willing it so. By the time the tapers were the perfect thickness, the sun had already risen high in the sky.

She brushed a loose curl from her forehead with the back of her hand before she switched to a second pot of wax. As the flames licked up around the sides of the double boiler, she pulled an unlabeled jar of herbs from the very back corner of the cabinet, a special mix she'd made for this particular spell. Witchgrass to banish, magnolia for purity, comfrey to prevent a man from stealing her sister away, nettle to keep her sister from suspecting her work, and chickweed to amplify it all.

She added a few drops of red to the pot, enough to turn the wax pink, and stirred the color into the melted yellow. While the sisters sold their pink candles to foster love, each color could also be used for the opposite purpose. It was a simple matter of cutting off the top of the candle, flipping it over, and burning it from the bottom.

"May no man love my sister," Regina said as she dropped weighted wicks into the pot, holding the string from the middle. Warmth stirred in her chest, like the first strike of a match—her intention turning to magic as it traveled from her heart to her hands to the cotton.

She lifted the wicks, paused as the first layer set, then dipped again. Wax coated the string, and the fire in her heart grew from ember to flame.

"May no man love my sister," she repeated.

The heat in her chest expanded, flickering against her ribs, so hot she swore if she pressed a hand to her heart, her palm would come away burned. She dusted the wax with the powdered herbs. Then, she continued to dip, her words infusing each layer. Once she finished, she hung the candles to dry, the room thick with magic. But it wouldn't be until she lit the wick the next morning—and repeated the phrase for the third and final time—that the spell would be complete.

A vine of honeysuckle wove through the open window and tapped her gently on the shoulder. She looked up from her work with a soft smile. Were it not for the house, she would never remember to stop to eat. But before she could turn off the stove and push up from her stool, there was a knock at the door.

"Regina?" Her sister's voice came from the other side. "I have a treat for you."

Her eyes darted to the tapers still drying only a few inches away. There was nothing unusual about making pink candles—but the herbs were a different story, something the Caldwells only used in personal spells or special orders. Regina reached for the jar and quickly stashed it in the cabinet as the door opened.

Violet stepped through, the sun shining bright behind her. Where Regina had her hair cut just above the shoulder, Violet's was cropped much closer in a pixie, the brown so dark it looked almost black in the right light. No matter how many times Regina tried to help her sister style it to give it a gamine appeal, it seemed to have a mind of its own, never quite falling in the way Audrey Hepburn's did.

Violet glanced from her sister to the slightly ajar cabinet. Regina pushed it closed and turned off the stove.

"Just finished this morning's candles," Regina said a little too brightly. But if Violet noticed the slightly higher pitch in her sister's voice, she didn't show it as she set down a slice of banana cream pie.

Violet pulled out the second stool and perched on the edge, her brown cigarette pants riding up her ankles. Her eyes fell to the now-drying candles. "Oh good! You're dipping pink. We got a special order in today from a recently engaged couple who's been having more than a little tension while they've been planning the wedding."

"And they paid you in pie?" Regina asked.

Violet laughed, shook her head, and tugged at her marigold neck scarf. "No, this is from Tillie Grey."

The older daughter of the family who owned Grey's Gifts, Tillie had long been a friend of Violet's. She was one of Honeysuckle House's few regular guests, joining the Caldwell sisters for cocktails, dinner, and even helping them harvest honey more than once. Regina didn't much care for the woman, but then, Regina didn't much care for anyone. She tolerated Tillie because Tillie was a Grey, and without the Greys, the Caldwell sisters wouldn't have made it through those first few years after their parents' deaths.

"I didn't know Grey's sold food," Regina said.

"They don't." Violet took one of the undipped wicks in her hand and rubbed the thread between her fingers. "She baked it for you."

Regina arched her eyebrows. "What's the occasion?"

Violet hesitated, her lips pursed. Then all in one breath she said, "I've invited her to move in with us."

Regina stared at her sister for a few moments, tracking the movement of her hands, the unconscious tapping of her feet, her lack of eye contact. When Regina didn't say anything, Violet continued.

"Our house is so big and empty with just the two of us," Violet said. "Tillie isn't looking to get married any time soon. There aren't many options around here for her to move out and be on her own. The way we live, forging our own path, supporting ourselves—it's a dream for a lot of women."

Regina's brow furrowed as she tried to follow her sister's logic.

"You want to turn our home into a boarding house for unmarried women?" Regina asked.

"No, not at all. It would only be Tillie . . ." Violet trailed off, a slight flush in her cheeks.

"We don't need a roommate," Regina said.

"But wouldn't it be fun?" Violet rubbed her hands through her hair, further undoing the work Regina had done on it that morning. "We could host parties, invite other women our age who aren't . . . married. Like us. We could start a social club."

Regina didn't think that sounded like fun at all. "I don't see why Tillie has to live here for that."

"You're so alone here. You don't go into the shop or even into town much," Violet said. "I think it would be good for both of us to bring more people into our lives. And I think the house would like it, too. Besides, we can always use another hand with the bees."

Regina narrowed her eyes. "How long have you been planning this?"

"I've known Tillie for a long time," Violet said.

Even longer than she'd known Regina. Her sister and Tillie were born the same year and had been childhood playmates, what with the friendship their mothers shared. Violet and Tillie had five years on Regina, and when girls are younger, five years can be quite the difference. But Regina wasn't jealous of Tillie. There was no reason to be. Tillie would never be Violet's sister. She'd never be Violet's *family.*

Not that it changed how Regina felt about the whole thing.

"What if I don't want her here?" Regina asked. Her eyes drifted to the bottles of dye. With the right candle, she'd have no trouble making Tillie back out of whatever deal she'd come to with her sister. Violet turned, following Regina's gaze.

"No spell is going to undo this," Violet said.

Regina let out a long breath and shook her head. "You should've asked me about this first." At least then she might've had a chance to talk Violet out of it.

"I'm your older sister," Violet said. "I don't have to run every decision I make past you."

"This isn't only your house. I live here, too."

"I know," Violet said. "I know. But I thought you liked Tillie."

While Regina laughed at Tillie's jokes and mostly enjoyed the records she brought with her—even if she did take a few listens to warm up to Billie Holliday—she didn't like the way Tillie captured Violet's attention, as if Tillie was the brightest flower on the vine. It wasn't that Regina minded her sister having friends. But Regina didn't see the need for them, not when they had each other, and not when Regina didn't have any of her own.

Violet opened her mouth, then closed it. "She's bringing over a few boxes tonight and the rest of her things tomorrow. She'll be staying . . ." she paused, "in the empty bedroom next to mine."

"I don't have a say in this?" Regina asked.

"Do you want to tell the daughter of the family who keeps us in business that she can't live here?" Violet asked.

"You mean she's making you do this?" Once again, Regina's focus turned toward the wax. "I'm sure I could dip a candle—"

But Violet cut her short. "No candles. I want her here, Regina. You're not the only person in my life."

The words stung, sharp and unexpected.

"And I shouldn't be the only person in yours."

Chapter Ten

Violet, 1960

Violet parked her blue 1946 Pontiac Torpedo outside of Grey's Gifts. She'd used part of her parents' life insurance policy—and a particularly strong green candle—to buy the car. Regina had tried to talk Violet into choosing a red model, but Violet wanted to make a sensible choice, and she was the one who would be driving it. Even now, Regina hadn't bothered to get a driver's license, so it was more Violet's car than her sister's.

The Pontiac was all rounded curves and silver accents, the paint in as pristine a condition as the engine thanks to Violet's regular detailing, a skill she'd learned from Barbara Hartman, the owner of the diner across the street who worked as a mechanic during the war and helped Violet land on her feet after her parents' death. Barb brought the sisters meals every day for almost a year before Violet finally found her rhythm as both older sister and stand-in mother, ready to dip and sell tapers at Grey's. These days, Violet still brought Barb a monthly candle—the color and intention directed by Violet's tarot cards.

Violet sat in the car, her stomach in knots as the door to Grey's Gifts burst open and Tillie ran toward the Pontiac, her long brown hair flying loose behind her. Her yellow blouse was tucked into a pair of dark blue pedal pushers. The cuffed hem of her pants fell just above the calf, and the fabric clung tightly to the curves of her legs. Though her mother preferred Tillie wear skirts when working the shop—an argument Violet had overheard more than once—Tillie made it clear if her mother wanted her to continue working in the shop, she'd choose what she wore, and Violet loved her for it.

Of course, Violet loved Tillie for a lot more than her fashion choices.

She turned off the engine and pulled her bag from the passenger seat before getting out of the car. Tillie grabbed her hand in a friendly gesture that was "just the way of young women," and it took everything in Violet not to pull her closer, to press her forehead to Tillie's forehead and her lips to Tillie's lips.

Violet knew she had no reason to fear her sister, but she wished their conversation had gone differently. That Regina had been thrilled to have Tillie moving in with them, that she'd given Violet the perfect opening to tell her the truth.

"How did it go?" Tillie asked.

"I told her you were bringing a few boxes today—that your parents were helping drop off the rest of your things tomorrow," Violet said.

Tillie bounced on her toes. "It's really happening."

"It is." Violet wanted nothing more than joy in that moment, but her voice came out strained.

The spring in Tillie's step slowed as she searched Violet's face. "But?"

Violet sighed, looked both ways down Main Street, and said, "Why don't we go somewhere quiet to talk."

* * *

The diner was all black-and-white checkered floors and bright red seats. The counter wrapped around the left side of the room with jukeboxes every few stools, and Elvis Presley crooned from the speakers. A few familiar faces glanced their way as the bell rang overhead. By this time in the afternoon, the lunch rush was long gone and only people like Violet and Tillie, who worked along Main Street, or the occasional housewife sneaking in an afternoon treat, stopped in. Barb raised a hand from behind the bar. Violet and Tillie waved before heading to their usual booth at the back. Thanks to the way the building angled, the table was almost out of sight from the rest of the room.

After Tillie took a seat, Violet slid in across from her, wishing she could nestle in beside Tillie without raising any eyebrows. She tugged the scarf around her hair free, pulled off her sunglasses, and carefully tucked both into her handbag.

When she looked up, Tillie had her hands pressed against the table. "Did you . . ." But before she could ask the question, Barb approached.

"My favorite customers," Barb said with a warm smile. "What'll you be having?"

"Just milkshakes today," Tillie answered.

Barb nodded as she tucked the order pad into her apron and said, "Your mother told me you're moving into Honeysuckle House." Barb's husband had died a few years after the war, and she'd never remarried. Most people commented on what a shame it was they hadn't had children before he passed, but Barb only ever nodded and smiled. Violet had seen the way she'd watched her and Tillie over the years, always giving them this particular booth, once adorning it with a vase of purple flowers and a knowing smile.

Still, Violet felt heat rush to her cheeks as she glanced around the diner. "It's a big house."

At the same time, Tillie said, "I've been wanting to move out of my parents' for a while now."

All three women laughed softly.

"Nothing wrong with having a roommate," Barb said with a twinkle in her eye, and for the first time that afternoon, Violet let herself feel the excitement of what they were doing. Soon, Tillie and Violet would be living under the same roof. They shared a look that sent heat clear down to Violet's toes.

Barb gave a throaty laugh then said, "I'll get those milkshakes for you."

As she walked away, Tillie and Violet held each other's gaze a few moments longer until Tillie leaned in and whispered, "We're finally doing it."

After this, they'd fill Violet's car with as many of Tillie's boxes as they could, then they'd be living under the same roof.

With Regina.

Violet's stomach dropped as she looked away from Tillie. The possibility in the air fizzled out, and Violet's smile slipped away. She loved her sister. She wanted more than anything to be able to bare her heart to her, but Regina had left little space for it that afternoon.

"You didn't tell her, did you?" Tillie asked.

Before Violet could answer, Barb returned with their milkshakes and a plate of fries. "On the house," she said, that same conspiratorial warmth in her eyes. Though Violet returned her smile, she'd lost her appetite.

Once she was gone, Tillie leaned forward and rested her elbows on the table. "Vi?"

Violet picked up a French fry, then set it back in the basket. She tapped her fingers against the table and avoided Tillie's eyes and took a long sip of her milkshake that tasted more like sawdust than strawberry.

"We're in this together." The softness of Tillie's voice burned right through to Violet's heart.

Violet sucked in a breath and tilted her head back, trying not to cry. Things hadn't gone at all how she'd hoped, and she still couldn't shake the disappointment she'd seen in her sister's eyes.

Tillie reached across the space between them, took a quick glance around the diner, and ultimately set her hand next to Violet's instead of on top of it. Despite the inches of distance, Violet felt the comfort and strength in the touch she didn't—couldn't—receive in the warmth radiating from Tillie's skin. She looked up at Tillie through watery eyes.

"I tried," Violet said. "But it wasn't the right time. She didn't like the idea of you moving in at all."

Tillie tapped the side of Violet's hand with her pinkie. "Sounds like you didn't let that stop you."

"Of course I didn't," Violet said.

"I'm proud of you."

Violet bit her lip to keep her tears from falling.

"Your mom would be, too," Tillie said.

Violet let out a small sound that fell somewhere between a laugh and a whimper. Helen Caldwell had seen the way Violet looked at Tillie back when they were teenagers, and though she'd warned Violet to keep it secret, she never pushed her to stop. In fact, it had been her mother who had mentioned the idea of roommates all those years ago. That had been before the accident, before Violet took over caring for her sister and their home and their livelihood.

"I'll tell Regina soon," Violet whispered. "I promise we won't have to pretend forever."

Tillie leaned in closer and lowered her voice. "So, you told her I'm moving into one of the spare bedrooms?"

A flush bloomed in Violet's cheeks, and she ducked her head with a smile that had her right incisor digging into her lip.

"Do you really think she bought it?" Tillie asked.

Violet almost hadn't believed her sister's response. She'd been so certain she and Tillie had been obvious about their feelings in front of Regina—the way they'd danced around the living room, sat long into the night curled up on the couch drinking cocktails, walked hand in hand down to sit with the bees. Violet thought Regina not only saw the love between her and Tillie but accepted it. But her sister only ever had eyes for their magic. Maybe that was Violet's fault, the way she'd poured so much time and willpower into keeping their candle business alive.

"She thought I was suggesting we turn our home into a boarding house for single women," Violet said.

Tillie clapped a hand over her mouth as she stifled a laugh. "I don't hate the idea," she whispered. "You and me creating a home for women like us."

They'd talked about other women around them, looked for signs they weren't alone, and though Burdock Creek was a quiet place, safe from the sort of hatred she knew plagued towns across the country, they still worried.

"Let's start with our future," Violet said.

Tillie sighed. "It's probably for the best you didn't tell Regina. Until we know it's safe."

"It's safe," Violet said. "Regina loves me. She wants me to be happy just as much as I want that for her."

Tillie made a thoughtful noise then popped a French fry into her mouth. Violet stirred her milkshake. She'd watched Tillie try to warm up to her sister, but Tillie was lucky to even get a smile out of Regina. Violet knew this, but still she hoped things would change.

"Did you at least give her the cards?" Tillie asked.

Violet shook her head as she pulled a wooden box containing a deck of tarot cards out of her large handbag—one of her mother's old purses that Regina had tried more than once to convince Violet to give up in favor of the smaller bags that were in style now.

Tillie had hand-painted the cards, complete with illustrations from the Caldwell sisters' home—bees, flowers, vines, and even Honeysuckle House itself. She'd made a deck for both Violet and Regina, something the sisters could share and a sign of what both Violet and Tillie hoped would become a new family dynamic. Violet had considered lighting a candle to ensure the cards would do just that, but she wanted her sister's love and acceptance without any magic pulling it out of her.

Violet handed the box over to Tillie. "I think they'll be better coming from you," Violet said.

She hoped it was true.

Part III
The Magician

The power to bring your desires into the world.

Chapter Eleven

Evie, Now

Evie had been worried about the candle she'd left burning in her room that morning, a part of her tempted to go up and blow it out, then light it again when she returned. But she'd always been able to put her faith in the house. Now, she didn't know what to think.

She held her hands tightly in her lap, her breath shallow, part of her still believing it was some sort of misunderstanding. That there was no fire at all. But as soon as Honeysuckle House came into view, Evie's delusions shattered. Flames shone inside the window above Evie's bedroom. Smoke billowed out. Evie tore at her seat belt. She threw open the door before the Jeep had come to a stop and jumped out of the car.

She ran for the house, but one of the volunteer firefighters stopped her before she could get very far—Ron Cooke, the same man who co-owned the antique shop she'd visited that morning.

"That's my house!" she said.

"I know," he said. "But you have to stay back."

How could she? Honeysuckle House was more than a business. It was more than a home. It was family.

The front door opened wide at the sight of her. Evie almost ran for it despite the warning, when Angela and Clara caught up to her. Clara barreled past, and if Evie hadn't grabbed her, she would've been through the door and into the flames herself.

"But Mommy! The house needs us!"

Tears streamed down Clara's face. Evie knelt down in front of her and pulled her close. "I know, honeybee. But the firefighters are taking care of it."

She stared up over the top of Clara's head and watched the stream of water pour from the hose and into her attic where she lit every candle and cast every spell, building this life for herself and her daughter.

Nothing had ever damaged Honeysuckle House before. Even when a heavy branch had fallen on the roof a few years ago, the house had found a way to shore itself up before the impact, and the splintered wood had slid off the shingles like it weighed little more than a leaf or twig.

After several minutes that felt like an eternity, the flames died down, leaving only smoke in their wake. Evie tucked Clara into her side and shuddered, afraid of what she'd find once they let her inside. Angela rested a hand on Evie's shoulder.

"You'll get through this," Angela said.

Evie nodded, swallowed hard, nodded again. "I wish Florence—" But her sister's name got stuck in her mouth.

"I know," Angela said. "I know."

Evie's throat tightened, and her tears started up all over again. She blinked them back and forced herself to take in the rest of the scene now that the flames were out.

The handful of guests who'd been at the bed and breakfast when the house caught fire stood on the lawn staring up at the turret. Very likely she'd have to turn them away, cancel the rest of their stays. But she could still hold the festival—the honey harvest, the candle dipping. She didn't need to have anyone in the house for that. All of her work didn't have to be for nothing.

Clara tugged at her sleeve.

"Can I go see the house now?" she asked. "The fire's out."

"We need to wait until they tell us it's safe to go inside," Evie said.

Clara stuck out her bottom lip. "But . . ."

Before Clara could argue, Ron came over to talk to them.

Clara's eyes brightened. She planted her hands on her hips, looked up, and said, "What's the damage, Ron?"

"That's Mr. Cooke to you," Evie said, though she was grateful that even in a moment like this her daughter could put a smile on her face. But when Evie spoke to Ron, she couldn't keep the fear from her voice. "How bad is it?"

"Not as bad as it looks from out here," he said, and Evie sagged forward with relief. Angela rested a hand on her back.

"The fire burned a hole through an interior wall in the turret." He nodded to the little tower Evie had made her own. "There was some damage to the floor as well, mostly cosmetic—like it shot straight for the wall and hit nothing else. Never seen anything like it."

"Is it safe to go in?" Evie asked.

He rubbed at the back of his neck and looked behind him toward the truck where the rest of his crew was packing things up. "I'm not supposed to give you an opinion, legal reasons and all that. But it looks safe to me. Hardly even a lingering smell."

Evie felt the tension drain from her shoulders. Angela took her hand and gave it a gentle squeeze. Clara ran right up the front stairs and wrapped her arms around one of the columns. "I'm so glad you're going to be okay."

"Thank you so much," Evie said. "I'll go let the guests know."

Before she could take a step, Ron held up a hand. "It might look safe to me, but I'm no expert on building integrity. You really need to have someone come take a look to be sure. You can go in to grab a few things, but I wouldn't let anyone sleep in the house tonight."

Evie nodded slowly.

"You and Clara can stay with me," Angela said.

Ron pulled a card out of his pocket and held it out toward Evie. "This is a fire remediation expert I trust out of Knoxville. Let him know I sent you. He'll probably be able to come out tomorrow to let you know if there's more damage than what we saw up there and when it's safe to be back in the house. I won't be surprised if he tells you your guests can come back as early as tomorrow night."

Evie breathed a long, slow sigh of relief.

But Ron wasn't finished. "Of course, even if he does say that, I might consider keeping your doors closed until after the festival this year, maybe let things stay in the town square. If you know what I mean."

Evie could only nod, the fight gone out of her. Even if there wasn't lingering smoke or danger, even if the house had managed to stop the flames, it had still caught fire. It had turned a pregnant woman out of her bed. As Evie looked up at it now, it stared back, haunted in a way it had never felt before. As much as Evie wanted to believe her efforts had been enough to break the curse, she couldn't take that risk. Because in four short days, there was a very real chance someone she loved would die right here in her home—if the curse didn't take her instead.

Chapter Twelve

Clara, Now

Clara slipped around the firefighters and the guests and her mom's not-so-watchful eye, wishing she'd thought to bring Ink with her, but of course she couldn't have brought Ink because her magic had summoned Ink for Aunt Florence, which meant Aunt Florence needed him more. Clara did, however, wish her aunt had come to the house with them (and Ink with her) so they could all be there together to get the news that maybe it wasn't so bad after all.

On second thought, it was probably best Aunt Florence wasn't there. Best that her mom and Angela were distracted. Because whether or not her Aunt Florence was right about the curse, the fire at Honeysuckle House hadn't been from the curse.

It had been Clara's spell, plain and simple.

She'd wanted to help her aunt and help the house, and her candle had burned so fast; then the house caught fire. There wasn't any other explanation.

With one last look over her shoulder, she turned the corner of Honeysuckle House and ran for the back door. She rushed to the handle, held it firm, and asked, "Are you alright?"

The windows slowly opened and closed in response, though Clara wasn't sure if it was a "yes" or a "no" or a "please don't worry about me." She was leaning toward the yes with a caveat about the worry.

"No matter what happened, I'm not afraid of you," Clara said. "I'm going to come inside now. Is that okay?"

Again with the windows.

"I have to worry about you. I love you, and that's what you do when you love someone."

The handle warmed beneath her hand, and she pulled open the door. The house didn't smell of smoke any more than it usually did—the lingering hint of a snuffed candle that seemed as much a part of the place as the peeling paint or the cobwebs or the collection of pretty rocks Clara had gathered from the woods out back. She took it as a good sign, a sign that maybe she hadn't done something with her magic to catastrophically ruin the place she loved most.

She left her sneakers at the door. Though they let guests walk around with shoes, Clara felt she wouldn't very much like for people to run all over her without any idea where they'd been. Then she ran through the hall to the main staircase, which she followed up and up as fast as she could, reaching the landing short of breath with her hands on her knees. The hallway rug lifted in response, gently brushing against her foot.

"I'm fine," she said. "It's you I'm worried about."

She started down the hall toward her mom's room. She pushed open the door and ascended the spiral staircase that led to the attic where her mom did her magic. When she reached the top of the stairs, her eyes welled with tears. She put her fist to her mouth and bit down into her knuckle.

There was water everywhere, soaking her mom's altar and her favorite chair and the floral wallpaper. The black candle lay overturned. The flame was out, and dried wax pooled on the ruined rug. A charred line ran from the wax to the opposite wall, which now had a doorway-shaped hole in it to a room Clara had never seen.

"I'm so sorry," Clara said through her tears. "I was only trying to help."

She started for the burned wall, when a sharp pain shot through the ball of her foot. She stopped short and stared down to find she was now dripping blood through her sock onto the already ruined rug.

She blinked back tears of pain and guilt and fear to find broken glass littered the floor, all the jars of water she and her mom set out during the last full moon, destroyed.

She started to cry louder, her gentle stream of tears now interrupted by full-on hiccups as the reality of what her spell had done sunk in. She'd never been hurt in the house before. She'd had close calls—slipping down the stairs in a pair of thick socks, reaching for a hot pan of cookies without an oven mitt—but always the house stepped in.

"I broke you," she said, throat tight.

The window opened and closed half-heartedly, as if it took all the house's energy to respond, and though Clara knew the house was trying to tell her it wasn't her fault, it didn't change the fact that, as far as Clara was concerned, it was very much her fault indeed.

"Clara?" Her mom's voice came from the room below, and that only made Clara cry harder. "Clara are you all right?"

When her mom reached the top of the landing, Clara wanted nothing more than to run into her arms and cry and cry, but with the glass on the floor, she didn't dare move.

Evie's eyes swept over the room before landing on Clara's foot.

"Oh, honeybee." Evie stepped across the glass to Clara and scooped her up, one hand under her knees.

"It's all my fault," Clara said.

"This isn't your fault." Evie pulled a chair from the corner and gently set Clara on it, away from the glass. Behind her, Angela emerged at the top of the stairs.

"Are you bleeding?" Angela asked.

"It's not me you should be worried about!" Clara managed through her tears. She threw out a hand toward the room. "I did this! I did that spell for Aunt Florence and the house and all I wanted was to fix things, but my magic burned up the rug and made a hole in the wall and now all our moon water is gone and the house is never going to be the same!"

Evie knelt down before Clara. "You didn't do this. Whatever caused this started long before you were born."

"I'll go grab some rubbing alcohol," Angela said before she disappeared back down the stairs.

Evie lifted Clara's foot, and though Clara winced, her mom's touch was gentle and cool as she pulled the shard of glass free and tugged off Clara's sock. Blood welled at the site of the wound, but not nearly as much as Clara expected.

"Something is wrong with the house, Mommy," Clara said. "The wall burned, and my foot got cut."

"That may be," Evie said as Angela reappeared. Evie gently cleaned and dressed Clara's wound as she spoke. "But it did spill our moon water trying to put out the fire—and if that's not a good use of it, then I don't know what is. And, yes, the rug and the wallpaper are probably ruined, but the house is okay. And look," Evie gripped Clara's chin gently and guided her attention to the hole in the wall. "We didn't even know there was a room back there! We've discovered something new."

Clara sniffled and rubbed at her nose. Angela handed her a tissue.

"And you get to stay with me tonight," Angela said.

Clara's eyes brightened. She'd stayed with her Aunt Florence a few times, but never with Angela.

"We'll go to the store and get your favorite snacks, and I'll make popcorn, and we can watch any movie you want," Angela said.

"But won't the house be lonely without us?" Clara asked.

Her mom's eyes clouded as she looked over the room. "It probably will be a little bit lonely," she admitted. "But the firefighters think we need to stay somewhere else tonight, and I'm sure the house understands."

Again, that window opened and closed softly.

Clara nodded, still convinced she was at least partially responsible for what happened. "Can we at least look in the hole before we go?"

Evie gave her daughter a small smile. "I suppose we could take a peek."

Clara jumped up, then winced and grabbed her foot. Evie picked her up and carried her across the room. As they approached the wall, the curtains rustled, and the glass along the floor started to move like someone was shaking the boards.

"See?" Evie asked. "The house is going to be fine."

Clara worried at her lip but gave a short nod as her mom set her down in front of the wall.

"Let me make sure it's safe," Evie said before she stepped into the hidden room. Clara followed her as soon as she was through the opening.

"Seems safe enough." Clara turned in a circle. Though her foot still stung, what she found was enough to make her forget the pain—at least for now.

It almost looked like an extension of her mom's attic room. Taper candles in all sizes and colors hung from hooks. On the far wall, a bookcase had been built into the corner, packed with books and jars full of herbs and tinctures and honey. Several journals had fallen from its shelves and lay in a heap on the floor in front of it. Next to them sat a plush chair with a high back, all dark green and tufted like the ones she saw at the antique shop whenever she and her mom delivered candles, and in front of the chair, a small table. A leather journal lay open in the center alongside a pool of wax, as if someone had walked out while they were in the middle of a spell.

Chapter Thirteen

Evie, Now

After finding her mother's journal thirteen years ago, Evie had turned Honeysuckle House upside down searching for more of her things. Where Florence had avoided any run-in with their shared trauma, Evie was desperate for an explanation, a reason for all the pain they'd gone through. Yes, their mother had hurt them. Yes, Evie still carried the effects of that hurt in the way she flinched at Florence's anger. At how she sought to make everything just right for a disgruntled guest and agonized over guiding Clara too much in her magic or too little or really at all in fear she'd get it wrong. But if she could piece together her mother's life before she had come into it, maybe she could find some sort of peace with the broken parts of her, or at least uncover enough to patch the holes.

She stared out over the room. It had been hidden just beyond where Evie worked her own magic. Had her mother cast some sort of spell to keep Evie from finding it?

Evie wouldn't put it past her. Linda Caldwell had used magic to keep the curse from Evie and Florence for years, leaving them unprepared for their father's death back in the 90s. After that, once they were old enough, the sisters had looked everywhere for answers about the magic that haunted their family. But there was little to be found beyond a few newspaper articles about the past victims—their grandmother, their great-aunt, and a woman who must've been a friend of the family long before their mother came into the world. After their mother's death, they still had little to go on with only tarot to guide them. But now? Maybe the answers Evie needed had been hiding in the house all along.

She wanted to flip through each of the leather-bound journals, to collect the crystals and cleanse them in water and moonlight, to run her fingers over the candles her mother had dipped. She wasn't foolish enough to light them, but she wondered what magic lingered in the wax.

Clara was way ahead of her. Already she'd crossed over to her mother's altar, lifted the large wooden box containing her tarot cards; the deck was a sister to Florence's, but where Florence's card backs were green, these were black. Evie recognized her mother's deck from her childhood. She'd searched for it after her mother had died, but she'd come up empty-handed.

When Evie took the cards from Clara, her daughter looked up at her, tears still glistening on her cheeks.

"What is this place?" she asked.

"It was my mother's," Evie said. "I didn't know it was here."

"Are we going to take the wall all the way down?"

"I think that's an excellent idea," Evie said.

"But not yet," Angela said as she followed them through the hole. Evie raised her eyebrows, and Angela shook her head with a smile. "I see that look in your eyes."

Evie laughed softly. She was tempted to go get her sledgehammer and have at it then and there.

"Fine," she said, "not yet."

She crossed over to her mother's altar and rested a hand on the top of Clara's head, ruffling her hair as she looked over what Linda Caldwell had left behind. The candles were curious, but Evie was more interested in the journal laying open in front of them, dated thirteen years ago. She ran her fingers over her mother's handwriting, likely the last time the woman put pen to paper.

"Is that a spell?" Clara asked.

Evie blinked away thoughts of her mother, focusing instead on the words scrawled on the open page in front of her.

Something offered
Black candle
Brown candle
Tourmaline, obsidian, and quartz
An anchor
Objects belonging to spell subjects
String
Magician card
Temperance card

Dip the candles with the intention of the spell infused into the wax. Create a spell circle, placing each crystal to form a triangle. Tie the anchor to the objects, bind them with string, and place them in the center. Make the offering. Light the candles. Use the flame of the black taper to burn the cards. Once the wax finishes melting, the spell will be sealed.

Evie looked from the book to the pooled wax to the tied objects. With Caldwell magic, candle and flame and occasionally a circle of salt were enough for most spells. This went far beyond that. Only the most difficult work required ritual.

"It looks like a spell," Clara said, when Evie didn't answer her question.

"You have a good eye, honeybee," Evie said. "I think it's a binding spell."

The anchor, the black candle, the string. She wasn't quite sure how the brown candle—a color for home—or the temperance card fit in, but the rest seemed clear. Such spells were difficult work. Evie had avoided them because to bind was to enforce your will on someone else, most often to cut a witch off from her magic. It didn't surprise her that her mother would use one, but by the look of it, this was the last spell she cast before the curse took her. Who, Evie wondered, had her mother spent her final moments trying to bind?

Clara lifted her head up, looking right at Evie. "What's a binding spell?"

"It's tricky magic," Evie said. "When you bind something, you're changing it, stopping it from doing what it wants to do."

"That's against our rules," Clara said.

"Which is why I've never taught you about them," Evie said. "My mother never taught me about them, either." All Evie knew about binding spells and other sorts of manipulative magic came from books and speculation. Spells written but never cast.

Clara looked from her mom to the table and back again. She reached for the bound objects in the center of the circle and plucked out a tarnished brass sphere with a honeysuckle engraved on the front. "This looks like the doorknob to my bedroom!"

A string had been knotted around it, tied to a pair of necklaces, each one half of a heart. They'd been a gift from Evie's father—one for her and one for Florence. They'd stopped wearing them by the time Florence went to high school. Evie thought she'd lost hers. It hadn't been in her jewelry box when she and Florence moved out of Honeysuckle House on Evie's eighteenth birthday. It seemed her mother had taken it.

Clara glanced up at Evie and asked, "Was grandma trying to bind the house?"

The pipes started to groan, a low sound that echoed through the attic.

Evie stared at her daughter, her eyes going wide as Clara's suggestion sank in. Evie had been so focused on trying to break her family's curse for the past thirteen years—and to prove her sister wrong—that she hadn't stopped to think about the possibility that it wasn't the family that was cursed at all. The house had been the one who showed Evie the journal. The house had been the one who tried to convince her she was safe within its walls.

This spell called for an anchor, and what more powerful anchor was there than two Caldwell witches? Yes, Evie knew her mother had hurt her over and over. Yes, the wounds lived on. But what if she had been on a path to redemption, to finally making things right for her family? Perhaps she *had* been trying to bind the house, and if so, what had stopped her?

Evie glanced around the room, looking for something she missed. She stepped past her mother's altar, stopping in front of the bookcase where several journals lay as if they'd only just been dumped off the shelf. There among them sat her mother's diary from 1986, the same one Evie thought she'd lost. If the journal was in this room, then it couldn't have been her mother who put it there. She knelt down and started stacking up the fallen books.

"Find something?" Angela asked.

Evie tilted her head back, but before Angela came into view, Evie's eyes landed on a broken rod and chain hanging from the ceiling, the edge of the metal jagged from where it had snapped from an old lighting fixture. The day of her mother's death flared bright in Evie's memory. The honeysuckle vines that had attacked Florence the moment they'd stepped on the property. Evie's inability to stop them. The fear that the curse had claimed her sister. And then, a crash had echoed from somewhere deep inside the house, and with it the cracking of wood and metal and glass. Evie could still hear her mother's scream if she closed her eyes. When they'd found her, her mother was already dead, her body pinned beneath the chandelier.

A sense of unease tapped its fingers along her spine, but Evie forced her voice calm.

"Mommy?" Clara asked.

"That is a very interesting theory, honeybee," Evie said slowly. "But she would have no reason to bind the house. The house is our friend."

"And our family!" Clara said brightly.

At their words, the house's moaning stopped. Though the attic grew quiet, Evie's pulse quickened.

"Right," Evie said, something in her heart breaking. Because despite everything, the house *was* their family. Even if it had deceived Evie, she couldn't blame it. She wouldn't want to be left alone, cursed to hurt the ones she loved.

"If it wasn't the house, maybe Grandma was trying to bind the curse," Clara said before she turned her attention back to exploring the rest of the room.

"Now there's an idea." Evie tried to keep her voice light and thoughtful.

Angela saw right through it. She came to stand beside Evie, close enough for her to whisper, "Are you alright?"

Evie brought her mouth the Angela's ear. "I think Clara was right."

"You can bind a curse?" Angela asked.

Evie shook her head subtly, then nodded to the ceiling directly above them. Angela glanced up at the remains of the old chandelier, then back down, one eyebrow arched. Evie dropped to her knees and lifted the edge of the rug. There, in the wood, markings as if something had crashed through once, long ago.

Evie stood and brushed the dust from her knees. She leaned in close to Angela once more. "The house kept this room from us." It had shut away her mother's spell and the very journal Evie had read that made her think her benevolence could break the curse.

"Then how are we in here now?" Angela asked.

Evie glanced at her daughter who held her mother's quartz in the palm of her hand.

"Why did you think the fire was your fault?" Evie asked her.

Once more tears welled up in Clara's eyes. "I'm sorry. I didn't know. I didn't mean to hurt the house."

But Evie took her hand and said, "Don't you see, honeybee? You made this possible. Your magic broke through whatever kept us from finding this place."

Clara's eyes brightened. "When we made the candles yesterday, I was thinking about you and Aunt Flo. I know she doesn't ever come here, and I wanted her to. You and Angela are always talking about how lonely she is, so I put all of those feelings together. I did the pink wax because you love Aunt Flo and I love Aunt Flo and everyone should love Aunt Flo, and then I added the blue mostly because it felt right."

Evie smiled softly. "Trusting your intuition."

Clara nodded emphatically. "When I lit the candle I spoke my intentions, like you taught me. I asked for the fire to bring her a friend, and after everything I heard you and Angela talking about this morning with the house . . . I asked it to show me how I could help. Then the whole candle burned, fast. Really fast. And then . . . and then . . ." She looked back toward the hole in the wall and sniffled. "I wanted to help it, not set it on fire."

"Fire is part of our magic," Evie said. "And I'm the one who left that candle burning."

"And," Angela chimed in. "From what the firefighters said, there really isn't much damage at all."

"Does that mean we can come back tomorrow?" Clara asked. "And maybe this time Aunt Florence will come!"

"We could call her," Angela said. "If anything is going to bring Florence back here, this is it."

Part of Evie knew Angela was right. The spell would be stronger with the two of them, and with the way Florence felt about Honeysuckle House, she'd have no qualms binding it. But if Evie were going to do this, she had to find a way to make sure the spell would only bind the darkness in the house—whatever it was that caused the house to kill—rather than putting out its magic all together.

No, binding the house was something Evie had to do alone.

"I'm not sure that's a good idea," Evie said.

"But that was my spell," Clara said. "To bring Aunt Florence home."

"And we will," Evie said. "I just need a little time with this to make sure she knows it's safe for her here."

"Because of the fire?" Clara asked.

Evie knelt down in front of her daughter. "I love this house as much as you do, honeybee, and so does your aunt. But when we were little like you, a lot of bad things happened to us here. She still feels those feelings when she thinks about this place."

"Do you feel them?" Clara asked.

If Evie was honest with herself, she did feel them, sometimes, when she let her mind slip back to her childhood. But it was easier not to think about those times, to turn around and walk out of the room when an unpleasant memory floated to the surface. It was something she wished her sister would do. Florence, at least, had lived thirteen years here with their father to keep her safe before the curse took him. Evie had only been seven when he died. She'd spent most of her childhood at Honeysuckle House with no one to protect her, and yet still she walked its halls. She'd reshaped it, then reclaimed it, and made it her own instead of running from what had happened.

"Not anymore," Evie said. "For me this place is full of memories of you and me and Angela and the festival. It's a place of joy, and that's why we're going to make sure nothing bad happens to it." She said the words not only for Clara, but for the house. "For now, we should probably go ahead and pack our things. Why don't you ask Angela to help you put your bag together while I finish up in here?"

"I don't need any help," Clara said. "But I did find some new rocks at the creek yesterday. You can look at them while I pack."

"I love new rocks," Angela said. Then she crouched down and said, "Hop on. I'll carry you over the broken glass." Once Clara was on her back, Angela looked over the altar one last time, her eyes meeting Evie's.

"Let's keep this between us for now," Evie said. "I don't want Florence to feel forced to come home before she's ready."

Angela hesitated but ultimately nodded. "Be careful, and be quick."

"I will," Evie said.

Once Angela and Clara disappeared through the hole in the wall, Evie reached for the journal that lay open on her mother's altar. As her fingers closed around it, a moan echoed through the room, like a heavy weight had been placed on the floor. A lamp in the corner flicked on long enough for the old bulb to shutter off with a loud pop and an explosion of glass.

"I'm going to make this right," Evie said to the house. "Whatever this curse is doing to you, I'm going to fix it."

Again the wood creaked, right beneath Evie's feet. As the floorboards shifted, throwing her off balance, her breath caught. The fire might be out, but the house still wasn't safe. Her hands went cold. Fear made its way up her spine to the base of her neck—the first time she'd felt anything like it in a long, long time.

She grabbed the stack of journals and her mother's tarot deck, and with one last look over the room, she hurried through the hole in the wall and out, out, out.

Chapter Fourteen

Florence, Now

Only a handful of customers had come in that afternoon, almost as if the shop had decided against its normal habit of enticing people off the streets. Normally, Florence would welcome the quiet. It gave her a chance to wander and see what new mysteries Ink & Pages had for her, to be alone with her thoughts. But the last thing she wanted now was space to think.

The look in Evie's eyes stayed with Florence long after the door closed behind her. It should've been easy to go with her, to hold her hand as she took in the damage—whatever that might be—to be the sister Evie needed and the aunt Clara deserved. But Florence's fear bound her to the shop.

Even the thought of going up the driveway, of seeing the front door, the yellow walls, the black-trimmed windows, made her palms sweat and her heart race and her throat close up. She wanted to tell herself it was the curse. With October thirteenth so close, she couldn't bring herself to go back there. But if that were the case, she could've visited these last thirteen years, or at the very least driven past.

The first year, she tried to stop by on Evie's birthday only to end up pulling over in a full-blown panic attack. She'd given it another shot after Clara was born and she was old enough to understand birthdays, but as soon as Florence reached the bend in the road that would reveal the old Queen Anne, her eyes spotted over and there was a roaring in her ears.

The year her mother died, the curse had almost claimed Florence instead. Her mother had summoned her and Evie home with a spell, and though Florence had tried to talk her sister out of listening to the call, Evie feared for their mother's life. When they'd arrived, the honeysuckle vines had wound their way around Florence. They'd pinned her to the ground. They'd closed around her windpipe. Then, they stopped. Like they'd never touched her at all. The curse had taken her mother instead.

But it wasn't only the curse that kept Florence from going home. She couldn't visit Honeysuckle House without being reminded of everything bad that had happened behind its walls. Though her mom was long gone, Florence's memories of her lived on—not only in her mind, but in her body. She rubbed at the scar along her forearm and wished she were stronger, or at least a little bit closer to healing.

She considered calling Evie, but after the way things had gone earlier, that probably wasn't the best idea. Better to give her sister space.

Instead, she sent a text to Angela.

Is the house still standing?

She'd hoped for an immediate response, but the message had sat unread for the past hour, twisting up her stomach even more. She stood idly scratching between Ink's ears with one hand and tapping her fingernails against the counter with the other. She needed a distraction.

Her eyes landed on the front window.

"What do you think we should put on display?" she asked Ink. "I'm leaning toward something seasonal."

The kitten blinked his eyes open and looked up at her, but he didn't speak. Of course he didn't. Her niece might have summoned him, but he was still a cat.

"Do you have any ideas?" she asked the shop.

In response, there came a thump, thump, thump of books hitting the ground a few shelves over. Ink rubbed his head against her hand before he hopped up, leapt from the counter, and trotted off in the direction of the sound. Florence followed him into the stacks, where she found a handful of paperbacks laying face up in the aisle, the same ones that were waiting for her that morning. All books about sisters.

It was just like the shop to be at once helpful and meddling—the way Florence imagined a good mother might be. She gathered up the paperbacks along with the kitten and headed over to the front window.

Ink sat atop the stack of books in her arms as she stared at the current display. A banner of fake leaves hung across the glass. Beneath it, hand lettering read, "Fall in love with reading." From the leaves they'd hung a host of romances perfect for the season. And, of course, an empty shelf for the shop to add whatever book a passerby might need.

Now, it seemed, the shop wanted her to put witchy books on display. "We need something catchy for the window," she said to kitten. "Maybe, 'Reading is magical?' Is that too corny?"

Ink looked up at her, tail twitching, and meowed in response before he started swiping his paw at one of the dangling books.

"That's not a no."

Florence shifted away from the banner, trying not to drop the kitten and the paperbacks along with him. Ink meowed in protest before leaping off the stack and slinking away to make mischief elsewhere, leaving Florence even more alone than before.

As she considered the window display, Owen appeared on the other side of glass. Their eyes met, and he held up a bag of lemons and several cans of kitten food. After everything that had happened, Florence forgot he promised to come back.

Despite the unfamiliar warmth in her chest, she willed her smile away. She was glad Owen was there, in more ways than one, but most importantly because he was in danger at Honeysuckle House. Even if she hadn't grown close to him yet, she could feel desire turning the pages of her heart, and she feared that would be enough to make him a target for her family's curse.

She reached the door before he did and held it open, the tinkling of the bell overhead mirroring an unwelcome flutter in her chest that she promptly ignored. Until she could get him to agree to stay away from Honeysuckle House, she couldn't risk even thinking how nice it was to be shorter than someone for once—by at least five inches!—or how seeing him cast an unexpected light into far corners of her heart she'd long abandoned. He smiled down at her.

Before Florence could say anything, Ink shot out the door and wound his way around Owen's legs. "I guess wet food was the right choice." He held out the bag of lemons and said, "I wasn't sure how many you needed. I figured the more the better."

Florence was starting to think there weren't enough lemons in the world to protect her family. "At this rate, my sister probably needs them more than I do."

"I can bring some back to Honeysuckle House with me," Owen said.

Florence blinked at him. "You're going back there?"

He tilted his head to the side. "Why wouldn't I?"

"Don't tell me Evie is already letting people in the house again." Florence's anger took the place of the shame that had settled into her.

"I'm not following," Owen said.

"Wait. You don't know?" At his blank look, she said, "Honeysuckle House caught fire."

Owen's eyes flashed with something Florence couldn't quite read. He covered his mouth with his hand and glanced out the shop windows as if he could see the house from there. "I heard someone talking about a fire at the store, but I didn't realize . . . Is your family okay?"

"They were here when it happened," Florence said.

"And the house?" he asked. "The bees?"

Florence hadn't even thought about the bees. At that moment, her phone vibrated. She fished it out to find Angela's name staring up at her.

The house is okay. Evie and Clara are staying with me tonight. We'll be here a little longer if you think you can manage it.

A little bubble popped up showing Angela was typing something else. Then it disappeared, reappeared, disappeared, until, finally, one last message came through.

I know it would mean a lot to Evie.

Florence stared at her phone, the anxiety that had wound itself up in a knot in her chest finally starting to unravel.

"It looks like the house is okay." Florence set the lemons down near the register and leaned against the counter for support. Then, she mumbled, "I should be there."

"It sounds like I may need to get another room for the night," Owen said. "I can give you a ride."

Florence glanced up at him. If ever there was a time to try to visit the house again, it was now. She was going to be thirty-nine in a few days. She needed to lay her old ghosts to rest.

But she couldn't do that with Owen, not with the curse closing in on her.

"I need to watch the shop," she said.

Owen took a quick look around them. The room was empty save the two of them and the cat.

"Are you sure?" Owen asked. "I'm already headed that way."

She opened her mouth and almost agreed to go with him. Then she shook her head.

"I'll put these here, then." He set the cat food on the counter. "See you around?"

Florence nodded. "Thanks for this."

His answering smile only made everything much worse. Florence watched him turn and walk away. Once he was well out of sight, she took a long, slow breath. Then, she flipped the sign to Closed and grabbed her bag, leaving her new kitten in the shop's capable hands.

The fall chill still hung in the air. Florence let a breeze blow her loose hair across her face and opened the car door. She dropped her bag in the passenger seat, then took a steadying breath before she turned the key. The rain started up once more as she left downtown and followed the winding road that would take her to her childhood home.

With each passing second, her heart rate kicked up. Her hands felt sweaty, her chest and throat and face, hot. "You can do this," she whispered to herself. As she neared the last bend in the road, her breath came in shallow gasps.

Her vision began to spot over.

Her throat constricted.

Her chest burned.

She moved the car to the side of the road and cut the engine. She dropped her head as she tried to catch her breath. Her tears fell hard and fast as rain pounded against the roof, and a sob tore through her throat.

"It's not fair!" she shouted. "I'm supposed to be past this by now!" She cried, and she cried, and she cried. The house was only a few hundred feet away, just out of sight, but she couldn't bring herself to see it. She closed her eyes tight, let the panic take her. It coursed through her hot and sharp until her breath came in shallow gasps and her whole body shook with the force of it. Then, the anger came.

"You did this to me!" she screamed as if her mother could hear her. "You made it impossible for me to go back there. I used to love that house. Now I can't even look at it!"

She slammed her fist into the steering wheel, and the horn blared. "Dad is dead because of you. You kept us here. You knew what could happen to him, to any of us, and did nothing to stop it."

Her voice had gone hoarse, but still she carried on.

"I'm supposed to be free from you. You're gone, and I'm glad. I've been glad since the day it happened and I knew I'd never have to hear your voice again. You'd never get another chance to twist me up inside and make me doubt who I am and who I've become. You'd never get to hurt me. But here I am, still hurting and still broken and still unable to be who I need to be for Evie."

Florence threw back her head and screamed. Everything she'd done to protect her family had been for nothing. She was as lost as she'd always been, still living in her mother's shadow.

As she sat in her car on the side of the road weeping and raging and feeling more alone than ever, something warm brushed the fabric of her skirt. Then, a gentle kneading. She blinked her eyes open and swiped at her still-falling tears to find Ink—who she thought she'd left back at the bookstore—had crawled halfway out of her canvas bag and set to making biscuits out of her thigh.

He looked up at her through wide yellow eyes and meowed softly. Florence laughed through her tears and dropped her hand to scratch between his ears. He immediately butted his head against her palm and started purring. Though Florence worried after her niece and her magic and what it might mean for the curse, she found herself grateful for Clara's spell.

She lifted Ink and held him to her chest as she looked out over her steering wheel, where she knew, just beyond the trees, Honeysuckle House waited for her. Ink rubbed his head against her chin, and she wept into his fur.

Part IV
The Five of Cups

A symbol of loss and grief and regret.

Chapter Fifteen

Florence, 1999

Unlike most twelve-year-old girls, Florence had never particularly cared for her birthday. It came every October, and every October her mom became stormy. At the slightest provocation, Linda would yell, slam a door, and fly out of the room, only to come back hours later and hold her children close and whisper apologies into their hair. Florence's father would wrap his arms around them all and tell Linda they'd make it through this.

Florence knew this time of year was hard for her mother. Her own mother, Florence's grandmother, had died the same day Florence was born. But Florence thought, maybe one day, her birthday would change things. That her mother would celebrate Florence, who was right there in front of her, not mourn the grandmother Florence had never met.

That had yet to happen, so Florence would rather skip the whole affair if it meant Linda Caldwell stayed closer to overcast than full-on thunder. Her dad, at least, had a constant sunny disposition, and birthdays only made him shine brighter. Most years, Florence tried her best to mirror his enthusiasm, but this year was different. As soon as October rolled around, Florence had felt an unease start in the center of her chest—where she most often felt her magic—and with each day that brought her closer to turning thirteen, it grew worse, like she had become the sky in the moments before a lightning strike.

When her father gave her a crisp ten-dollar bill to spend however she wanted after the bus dropped her off from school, and with it, permission to ride into town on her bike with Evie at her side, she couldn't help but smile a little.

The cool fall air rushed against her as she pedaled toward Main Street, her sneakers a blur of blue and her flannel puffed out behind her. She held onto her backward ball cap with one hand and gripped the handlebar tight with the other.

"Florence!" Evie cried. "You're going too fast!"

She slowed her speed and turned, circling back to where she'd left Evie several yards behind, her training wheels moving as fast as they could to keep up, and her cheeks pink with the effort.

"Don't worry," Florence said as she brought her bike alongside her little sister. "I won't leave you behind."

"I can't go as fast as you," Evie huffed.

Florence reached across the space between them and adjusted the sunflower on the front of Evie's denim hat. "Once we get you out of those training wheels, I'll be the one asking you to wait up."

* * *

The sisters bought as much candy as they could with ten dollars, then took their bounty to the little park off Main Street. The sweetgum trees looked like bonfires with their orange-red leaves, providing cover for the cardinals that flitted from branch to branch, their song the perfect backdrop for a perfect day.

Angela already sat under one of the trees with a blanket spread out for the three of them. She leaned back against the trunk and crossed her ankles, the soles of her combat boots facing skyward, and the orange of her dress matching the leaves overhead.

Florence's mom had homeschooled her and Evie most of their lives, but last fall, her dad had insisted they send Florence to school to be around kids her age. She mostly hated it. The other kids were nice enough, but no one seemed to want to get close to a witch. But after

Angela had gotten a bad grade on a test, Florence offered to study with her and dipped her a candle to help her focus. They'd been inseparable ever since.

Evie let her bike drop to the ground with a crash before jumping on the blanket, landing on all fours, and pulling her backpack free. She managed to unzip it and dump the candy out before Florence had even finished carefully resting her bike against Angela's.

"I got two pink ring pops and a blue one because I remember you said you liked the blue one, but if you'd rather have the pink, you can have mine," Evie said all in one breath.

"Blue is perfect," Angela said, as she took the offered candy ring. Then she jumped up and grabbed Florence in a fierce hug. Sometime between April and September, Florence had grown six inches and now towered over Angela, all elbows and knees.

"Happy birthday!" she said into Florence's side.

"Almost birthday," Florence said. "I wish you could come over tomorrow and celebrate."

Evie shook her head. "Mom's in one of her moods." It was a phrase she'd picked up from their father. "Doubt it'll be over by tomorrow."

"I don't know why my mom's so worried about it. If there really was—"

But whatever Angela said was lost on Florence as her ears started to ring. When she looked back at Angela, her mouth was still moving, but Florence couldn't make out the words. She'd gotten used to her hearing going in and out over the years—a trait she and her sister shared.

She stuck a finger in her ear, thinking maybe that would help even though it never did, to find Evie was shaking her head.

"—you'd tell me," Angela finished. "Wouldn't you?"

"Tell you what?" Florence asked.

"Did you hear anything I said?" Angela asked.

But Florence shook her head. "Ears were ringing."

Angela pursed her lips. "They seem to do that every time I bring it up."

"Bring what up?" Florence asked.

"I know I hardly mention it," Angela said. "All the kids at school whispered about it when you started. The first time I asked you about it, I thought maybe you were acting like you couldn't hear me because you didn't want to talk about it. But tomorrow's the thirteenth."

"My birthday," Florence said.

"Yes and . . ." Angela trailed off. "I think maybe your mom doesn't want you to know. Could she do something like that? Light a candle to keep you from hearing something?"

Florence nodded without hesitation. "She muffled my ears once. Said I was listening to something I shouldn't have been." She still remembered the sensation, even more she remembered the conversation. Her father claimed Linda had used her magic on him—to do what, Florence didn't know. She'd leaned too far over the stairs, and her mother had seen her straightaway. She hadn't been able to hear right for a week. "It wasn't like the ringing though. I don't think the magic works that way. She'd have to keep doing it."

"Maybe she has," Angela said.

"You could ask her," Evie suggested, still not fully aware how the wrong question could send their mother over the edge.

"Maybe after my birthday," Florence hedged.

Angela opened her bag and took out a small box that she handed to Florence.

"My mom helped me pick it out."

Inside Florence found a necklace—a black leather cord with a small dark crystal hanging from it.

"Tourmaline!" Florence said. Though her mom sometimes used crystals in her spell work, Florence had learned more about them from Angela than she ever had from her mother. Angela had bought a guide about them at the book fair, and she'd been obsessed with them ever since.

Angela pulled a cord from around her own neck and fished a matching stone from beneath her shirt. Florence pulled hers over her head and tucked the crystal under her shirt to rest beside the half of the heart necklace she shared with Evie.

Beside them, Evie pouted. "What about me?"

Angela met Florence's eyes with a grin and an arched eyebrow. Florence nodded.

"It's not your birthday, is it?" Angela asked.

"No," Evie said with a sigh and a matching frown.

"Don't worry," Angela said. "Mom got one for you anyway." She pulled out another small box and Evie squealed with delight.

"I thought these might help with your mom," Angela said. "And with the thing you never seem to be able to hear me talk about."

"The thing that's keeping you from coming over tomorrow," Florence said. She worried at her lip. "Maybe there's a way around it. Could you write it down?"

Angela pulled a notebook out of her bag and flipped to an empty page. She started to write, but when Florence looked over her shoulder, all she saw were smudge marks. She shook her head.

"Evie?" Florence asked.

Her little sister looked up from the necklace she hadn't stopped turning over in her hands. "Hmm?"

"What does that say?" She pointed to the notebook.

Evie frowned. "Doesn't say anything."

"Let's try something else," Angela said. "It rhymes with . . ." she paused and tapped a finger against her lip. "Purse."

"Nurse!" Evie suggested.

"You think my mom wouldn't let me come over because of a nurse?" Angela asked.

"If it was a scary nurse," Evie said. "It's going to be Halloween soon."

Florence pursed her lips, then, starting with the beginning of the alphabet, made her way through the consonants. "Burse . . . curse. Oh! Curse?"

"Yes!" Angela said.

"There's a curse?" Florence asked. "At . . . my house?"

"On—"

Again with the ringing. Florence shook her head. "I think you might be right."

"What's a curse?" Evie asked.

"It means something bad happens," Florence said.

"Bad things happen all the time," Evie said. "Like mom forgetting you at school or getting mad about the broken flowerpots or yelling when I got honey stuck in my hair."

"Not those kind of things," Florence said. "Curses are much worse."

"She cut off all my hair," Evie said. "I guess curses must be pretty bad."

"It's like in Sleeping Beauty," Angela said. "If the princess pricked her finger on a spindle, she'd fall asleep forever."

"The wicked grandmother did that to her," Evie said.

"Godmother," Florence corrected.

"Do we have a wicked godmother?"

Florence considered the question. Her mother had never spoken to her about curses. "Not that I know of," Florence said. "But I think they work like spells."

"So someone cast a curse on us—"

All at once, both Evie and Florence clapped their hands over their ears, the ringing worse than it had ever been. After a few moments, it subsided. That was when it hit Florence. She'd learned about curses from books.

"Tell it to us like a story," she said to Angela.

"You really think that will work?" Angela asked, doubtful.

Florence shrugged. "It depends on what my mom wanted the spell to do when she made the candle."

"Make sure you start with 'Once upon a time,'" Evie said as she tried—and failed—to put her necklace on. Angela leaned over and took it from her. She unclasped it and brought it around Evie's neck.

"Once upon a time," Angela said, "there was a family of witches who could cast spells with candles. They had a magical house at the edge of town. Though they were powerful, their magic wasn't enough to protect them from bad things happening. Once every thirteen years, someone they loved died at that magical house."

As the words sunk in, Florence's heart stuttered.

"I don't like this story," Evie said. "It doesn't have a happy ending."

"Is it true?" Florence asked.

"In the story, it's been happening since . . ." Angela paused. "The forties."

Florence tried to think back to what she knew about the Caldwells who came before her. Her grandmother had died thirteen years ago, the same day Florence was born, but before that? Her mom didn't talk about it.

If Florence's family really was cursed, there were only four people she loved—her mom, her dad, her sister, and Angela.

"Your mom's afraid it will be you," Florence realized.

When Angela nodded, Florence took her hand and gave it a squeeze.

"In the story, does it always happen at the house?" Florence asked.

"It does," Angela said.

"Then we can't be home tomorrow." If all the deaths happened at Honeysuckle House, she thought, then being somewhere else might keep them safe.

"Maybe you can get your dad to take you somewhere," Angela suggested.

"What about Mommy?" Evie asked.

Florence and Angela shared a look that was a mixture of fear and resolve, and Florence had never felt as seen in her life as she did in that moment.

"We'll try," Florence said.

As hard as Linda Caldwell was, Florence loved her mother. She certainly didn't want her to die, but she'd kept the truth of the curse from her, and, as far as Florence knew, she had no plans to take them away from Honeysuckle House—to protect them. If getting her father and her sister to safety meant leaving without her mother, then that's what she would do.

Chapter Sixteen

Evie, 1999

At seven years old, there were a lot of things Evie didn't yet know about the world or herself or her family. But there were a few things she knew for certain.

She knew Florence was her favorite person and the worst part of the day was when Florence left for school and Evie was stuck at home learning from her mom.

She knew her dad loved her more than he loved anyone else except for Florence and her mom, but he told her more than once that with them it wasn't a competition because he loved them all equally.

And she knew she loved her mom even when her mom was sad or angry or didn't want to talk to anyone, which was more days than not, and if there was anything Evie could do to make her happy, she'd do it. Because that's what daughters did.

When they got home and found their mom crying while eating the first piece of the cake she'd baked for Florence's birthday, Evie ran right to her, wrapped her arms around her waist, and leaned her head into her back.

"Don't be sad, Mommy."

Her mother only ever ate sweet things when she was very sad or very angry, and Evie hoped it wasn't the latter.

Linda stiffened at Evie's touch, then relaxed into her hold. She was a tall woman, so tall that, even seated, Evie only came up to her shoulder, and when Evie hugged her, she could wrap her arms almost all the way around her thin frame. Evie pressed her face into her long brown hair—just like Florence's and not at all like Evie's short blonde waves—and took a deep breath that smelled of candle smoke and sadness.

She glanced back at her sister, who stood frozen in the doorframe, eyes shifting from Linda to the cake. Evie was still learning to read. It took her a moment to realize the frosting said, "Happy Birthday Florence" because the "day" and part of Florence's name were missing.

"Where's Dad?" Florence asked.

Her mother didn't turn around, didn't look at them. She only took another bite and said, "He's taking a nap."

Florence's brow furrowed.

"I didn't know Daddy took naps!" Evie said.

"He doesn't," Florence replied.

"He had a long day at work," Linda said.

"But he was here when we left to get candy," Evie said.

"And he doesn't work on Tuesdays," Florence added.

Linda set her fork down. "All I know is he was tired." She pushed the plate of cake away.

Evie considered this, and, after everything Florence and Angela had talked about that afternoon, a thought occurred to her. "Did you cast a spell on him like you did on us?"

Across the room, Florence took a sharp breath.

Her mother turned around in her seat, forcing Evie to let her go and take a step back. Her eyes had a dark look to them as they slid over Evie slowly, a quick flick to Florence, then back to Evie.

"What did you say, sweetie?" her mom asked.

A cold feeling washed over Evie. She still hadn't quite gotten a hold of her mother's moods the way Florence had. But another thing she knew for certain was Linda Caldwell didn't use nicknames for her children, not unless something was wrong. Not unless she was about to turn into needles and thorns and broken glass.

Evie crossed her arms, holding herself close, and swallowed, trying to figure out where she went wrong.

"She didn't—" Florence started, but Linda held up a hand, stopping her short.

"I was speaking to your sister."

Evie decided the best course of action was to simply repeat herself. "I asked if you cast a spell on him like you did on us." Her mother stared at her, and in the ensuing silence, Evie's stomach turned over, forcing out more words. "The curse," Evie said, her ears ringing with the word. "Why didn't you want us to know about it?"

Evie expected a shout, but her mother's voice came out low and soft and somehow that was so much worse. "He told you?"

What Linda did next happened so fast that Evie felt it before she processed it. One minute, her mother was sitting in the chair in front of her, the next, she was standing in front of Evie with her hand in Evie's hair, her mouth twisted in anger. There was a sharp tug at Evie's scalp. She had to rise to her tiptoes to follow. She cried out, tried to twist away, but any move she made sent pain through her head.

Florence was on them within moments.

"Let her go!" Florence shouted as she pushed against their mother.

The floorboards rocked beneath their feet. Linda lost her grip on Evie, but not before she took a fistful of Evie's hair with her. Evie scrambled back behind her sister.

"Run," Florence said.

Evie turned and started out of the kitchen, Florence on her heels. She shot out the door and down the hallway. Her heart raced, her scalp burned, her eyes stung. She took one look over her shoulder. Their mother was only a few steps behind them when she grabbed for Florence.

"Florence!" Evie shouted.

Linda gripped Florence by the arm and threw her against the hallway wall. Florence ricocheted off the plaster, sending a family photo to the floor. Glass shattered. Evie reached for her sister. At the same time, the rest of the frames fell from the walls. They landed between her mother and Florence—none of them quite hitting Linda, but in that moment, Evie wished they had.

Evie grabbed her sister's hand, and together they rounded the corner to the stairs. With each step they cleared, the house flattened it out, giving their mother no purchase to follow. They ran for Florence's room. As soon as they made it through the door, Florence slammed it shut and turned the lock. Then she pulled Evie close, holding her tight as they stared at it.

Within a few moments, their mother was pounding on the other side. The handle rattled, and Evie trembled against her sister's arms. Linda's voice came through the wood muffled.

"Let—me—in," she huffed, voice strained as though each word was an effort.

Honeysuckle vines peeked under and through the seams of the door. What Evie couldn't see was the wall of greenery the house had summoned up on the other side. No matter how many vines Linda tried to tear free, more kept coming, blocking her from her daughters.

Chapter Seventeen

Florence, 1999

Florence and Evie stayed behind the wall of honeysuckle for the rest of the evening and into the morning. They had peeked through the keyhole more than once, but they couldn't make out much of anything through the vines. A bruise bloomed on Florence's shoulder where she'd collided with the wall, and every time she noticed the patch of red on Evie's scalp, her heart caved, the sadness and anger all too much. It was the first time Linda Caldwell had ever laid a hand on her daughters. Yes, there'd been the time with the broken flowerpots. But that had been Florence's doing, Florence's fault in the first place, the sort of discipline good girls needed. Until tonight, all of her mother's violence had been secondhand. Now, they'd crossed some sort of bridge, and Florence didn't think there was any going back.

She and Evie ate the rest of the candy for dinner, played all the board games Florence kept in her room, and then Florence held her sister until she fell asleep. All the while, Florence kept her attention on the hallway, listening for every creak of a floorboard or opening of a door.

Part of it was fear that after their mother had given up and trudged away, she'd return. Another part of it was hope her father would wake to get a glass of water or a midnight snack and Florence could tell him everything. Then she could convince him to get in the car and drive far away so they'd be safe.

By the time morning broke through the curtains, Florence still hadn't slept. The window opened, but not even the crisp air and golden sunlight streaming through the maple leaves outside were enough to ease her dread.

She released her hold on her sister and slowly slipped out of bed, before pulling on a pair of loose jeans and a flannel. She gently pushed against Evie's shoulder. Her sister's eyelids fluttered open, and she stretched her arms above her head.

"Happy birthday!" After a few moments her eyes darkened. She took a sharp breath and glanced at the door. "Mom . . . ?"

Florence shook her head. "She hasn't come back. Get dressed and wait here."

Evie scrambled out of bed wearing one of Florence's T-shirts. She shook her head. "I'm coming with you."

"You'll be safer here." Florence had been wracked with guilt all night that she hadn't gotten to Evie fast enough, that she hadn't predicted what her mother was going to do. That it hadn't been *her* hair Linda ripped out by the roots. She couldn't let something like that happen again, not today. Not ever.

But Evie wouldn't hear it as she wriggled back into yesterday's dungarees. "I'm not staying."

Florence knew there was no point arguing with her. With a heavy sigh she said, "Let's find Dad and get out of here."

"Because of the—"

Florence clapped a hand over Evie's mouth gently. No time for ringing ears.

"No one is going to die today," Florence said.

Evie nodded once, determined. Florence took her hand and started for the door. The vines poked through the gaps around the hinges. Florence rested one hand on the knob. It warmed beneath her touch, and one of the vines crept across the wood to brush against her knuckles. A honeysuckle flower bloomed.

"I think the house is wishing you a happy birthday," Evie said.

Florence felt a sad sort of warmth in the center of her chest. She leaned her forehead against the door and tried her hardest not to cry. "Thank you," she murmured.

She swiped at her tears, picked the flower, and tucked it behind her ear. "It's okay," she said to the house. "You can let us out."

The vines receded, and a few seconds later, the lock turned. The door opened slowly enough to creak, but it didn't make a sound. Florence stuck her head out. She peeked down the hallway to find her father making his way toward her, two duffle bags in hand.

"Dad?" Florence whispered.

He held a finger over his lips.

Evie ducked underneath Florence's arm and ran for him. She wrapped her arms around him, and he rested a hand on the top of her head. She winced, retreating from his touch and revealing the dried blood from the night before. His brow furrowed as he looked up, meeting Florence's eyes. She gently gripped her own shoulder.

"Did your mother do this?"

She nodded, her tears once again threatening to spill over as her throat constricted and her whole chest went hot.

"She threw Florence against the wall," Evie said before she buried her face into his side.

"We found out about . . ." Florence paused. "Today. And her spell to keep it from us."

Shame flashed across her father's face, and he pulled Evie closer to him.

"I'm sorry," he said.

"You knew?" Florence asked, the heat growing into something like betrayal. She clenched her hands into fists.

"She thought it would be better for both of you if you didn't. The way this town talks . . . I agreed with her. At least until you were ready." He shook his head. "We can talk about this later. Let's get to the car. I wanted to go last night—we'd been talking about it all week—but . . ." He looked over his shoulder.

"She stopped you," Florence said. "Why?"

Robert shook his head. "I don't know."

He gestured for her to follow. Florence ran toward him, and together, the three of them made their way to the stairs then down and out the front door. Robert opened the trunk of their hatchback and tossed the bags in. He slammed it shut, turned to his girls, and grabbed them in a hug.

"Let's go celebrate your birthday," he said to Florence.

She bit her lip and nodded, unable to speak without crying.

"Is Mommy coming?" Evie asked.

"Not this time, sweetpea," Robert said as he opened the back door for her.

"My necklaces!" Evie said. Florence had taken them off and put them on the nightstand while Evie was sleeping, afraid they would get tangled up in her hair.

"We can get them tomorrow," Florence said.

But Evie shook her head. "I need them. The crystal is supposed to protect us." She started toward the steps, when Florence grabbed her by the hand.

"We can't go back in there."

"I can't go without them!" Evie protested.

"Where are they?" Robert asked.

"On my nightstand," Florence said, "but—"

"I'll be quick." He kissed her on the forehead, then made a run for the house.

Florence stared after him, her stomach twisting as he started up the steps. She held her breath, waiting to see him appear through the window on the second-floor landing. When his face shown through the glass, she exhaled and gripped Evie's hand tighter. He raised a hand to wave.

"Look, Evie," Florence said.

Evie glanced up and waved back, but as Robert turned to go down the hall, something in his face changed.

He tipped toward the window, slowly at first, so slowly Florence didn't realize what was happening until he collided with it. Wood snapped and glass shattered around him. He fell through and onto the top of their covered porch. As his body met shingles, Florence pulled Evie's face against her, never once taking her own eyes off her father. He rolled down the roof, turning over and over and over.

Florence wanted to scream for him to stop. To catch himself. To do anything other than fall off the edge. But it was too late. The honeysuckle hung limp. The gutters offered no help as he slipped over the side. He landed in the yard with a thud, his neck bent and his arm pressed behind his back.

Florence stood there, staring at his lifeless form. The world slowed around her.

Evie squirmed free from her arms. "Daddy!" She ran for him. She dropped to her knees beside him and pushed against his shoulder, but he didn't respond.

Still Florence couldn't move.

It wasn't until Evie started to cry that Florence felt her own tears falling, the shock of them enough to propel her forward. She knew he was gone—the curse had taken him—but she crouched next to her sister. She pressed her ear to his chest, and when she didn't hear anything, she pressed fingers against his neck where his pulse should've been. She was met with cold skin and not a single flutter of movement.

She stood.

Then, she ran.

Back to the house, up the porch. The door swung open before she reached it, and she took the steps in twos all the way to the third floor. She didn't even hesitate at the door to her parents' room or at the base of the spiral staircase that led to the one place in the house she was never allowed to go.

When she reached the top of the landing, she found her mother standing at her altar, her back to Florence, two candles burning before her. Florence's racing heart slowed. Though tears still fell, every piece of her that felt like it was threatening to burst apart over the past few days stilled, and a sort of numbness settled in.

"You're too late," Florence said, voice flat, heartbroken. "That black candle won't protect anyone. Dad's gone. You made him sleep so we couldn't leave and the curse took him and it's all your fault."

Linda turned, eyes bright with anger. She crossed the space between them and grabbed Florence by her forearms. "Everything I've done has been for you and your sister. Everything!"

When Florence tried to pull back, her heel almost slipped from the top step. Linda's nails dug into Florence, drawing blood as she stopped her fall.

"Do you think I wanted it to take your father? Do you think I wanted any of this?" She looked down at where her fingernails pierced Florence's skin. She gripped tighter, her lips pressed in a thin line. It wasn't until Florence cried out that Linda pulled back, eyes wide as if seeing Florence for the first time. "Oh, baby," she said. "I'm sorry. I'm so sorry."

Then she pulled Florence to her chest and started to cry.

Chapter Eighteen

Florence, Now

Florence did not make it to Honeysuckle House the day it burned. As soon as she had her breathing under control, she wiped her tears and drove in the opposite direction, afraid her sister would see her sitting helpless on the side of the road. She'd gone home; taken Ink up to her apartment, where she washed herself clean of the lines of mascara making marks down her cheeks; and drank a cup of chamomile tea. Then, because she had no excuse not to, she went back downstairs to the shop and reopened the doors.

She hadn't heard a word from Evie, and that was just as well. After her panic attack, Florence wasn't sure she could handle any further reminders of what she stood to lose when her birthday rolled around.

Things at the shop were even slower than they'd been before Florence left. Not a single customer came in search of a book. At five minutes before close, Florence took a deep breath and reached for her phone. Nothing from Evie. But with her sister staying at Angela's, there was still a chance Florence could be there for her, even if she knew it would likely end in another fight. That was a risk she was willing to take if it meant keeping her sister alive. As she walked toward the door to flip the sign and lock up for the evening, she started to type out a message to Angela.

Have you had dinner yet?

She erased it.

How much does Evie hate me right now? If I bring over some kind of dessert do you think she'll talk to me?

She rested one hand on the door as she looked the message over before she erased that one, too.

Room for one more for dinner?

With a small nod, she hovered her thumb over the send button, but before she could hit it, the door opened under her hand. She let out a surprised yelp, and her phone slipped from her grip, hitting the floor. She looked up to find Owen standing in front of her.

"Sorry, I didn't mean to scare you," he said. "I tried waving through the glass, but you didn't see me." He knelt down and picked up Florence's phone then handed it to her.

"I was about to close up," Florence said.

"Mind if I grab a book before you do?" As if on cue, a paperback fell off a nearby shelf. He grinned. "Maybe that one?"

"You don't even know what it is yet," Florence said.

Owen shrugged. "I've yet to have a book fall at my feet in this shop that I didn't love."

"Even the rom-coms?" Florence asked.

"Especially the rom-coms," he said.

She laughed, gave the wall by the door a little pat, and said, "All right, let's ring you up."

Owen jogged toward the book laying face up in front of one of the end caps. Ink had already beat him to it and sat swiping at the spine with his paw. Owen scratched him between the ears before he held up the paperback, revealing one of Florence's favorite magical realism novels about the Flores sisters—three witches in a small Appalachian town.

"I know what you're doing," she murmured under her breath to the shop. The bell over the door tinkled in response, and it took everything in her to suppress her smile.

"What was that?" Owen asked.

"Just that I love that book," she said.

"Then I'm definitely buying it."

Her lips curled upward against her will as she went to meet him at the register.

"How was the house?" she asked.

"You couldn't even tell it burned."

Florence worried at her lip. Evie, eternal optimist that she was, would probably take it as a sign that her efforts to break the curse had worked and there was nothing to worry about.

"And the festival?" Florence asked. "Is it still on?"

"The grounds seemed fine. The bees weren't at all bothered when I went to check on them," Owen said. "Though I hope Evie would've told me if she was planning to cancel. There aren't any vacant rooms left in town, so I'll be spending the night in my car, which is why I need reading material." He held up the book.

Florence looked from Owen to the book and back to Owen. Something in her almost offered up a spot on her couch, but if Evie really was going to move forward with the festival, that would put Owen at Honeysuckle House on the thirteenth. She didn't want to endanger him anymore than she already had.

"If I had a spare room . . ."

Owen held up his hands. "Oh no, I didn't mean . . ." He shook his head. "If the car ends up not working, I can drive the hour to Knoxville and grab a room there."

Florence flushed and rubbed at the back of her neck. "Maybe you should get a second book. Just in case."

"Not a bad idea," Owen said. He did a quick turn toward the shop, when the lights winked on and off in the far corner. "What's back there?"

Florence followed his gaze. It was past the children's book section, where she most often found Clara disappearing when she came to visit the shop.

"Picture books," Florence said.

This time, all the lights in the shop winked out except for those in the children's corner, including the power to the register. Owen and Florence stared at each other in the dark, his pupils growing as he took her in. Florence was the first to break eye contact.

"I better go check the breaker," she said, even though she knew the shop was up to something. "You can take the book and pay for it later."

"Picture books aren't really my thing, but maybe they could be. First books start falling at my feet every time I come in here, now the lights are leading me to the back of the shop. I'm starting to think this place has more in common with Honeysuckle House than you let on."

Florence winced, and Owen responded with a grin. He set the paperback down on the counter and headed off in the direction of the lights. Florence followed, her unsent message to Angela forgotten.

"It's much safer here than at Honeysuckle House. Or it should be," she said, making a dig at the shop.

Owen glanced over his shoulder. "No attics catching on fire?"

"Not yet," Florence said.

They rounded the corner past the wall of children's characters, the lights leading them beyond the last shelf. Owen stopped short, and Florence had to come up beside him to see what he was staring at.

In front of them stood an open door that usually lay hidden behind a shelf of books. Today it had transformed into a small room, complete with a daybed, a kitchenette, and a love seat situated in front of a coffee table, where a pot of tea sat with steam rising from the spout.

Florence held a hand over her face. She'd told this man she didn't have a spare room, and now the shop made her out to look like a liar.

"I didn't know this room was back here," Owen said.

Florence had tried to keep from oversharing when it came to Owen, but this was something she couldn't simply explain away. With a heavy sigh she said, "It usually isn't, but it seems the bookstore doesn't want you to spend the night in your car."

And Florence had learned, long ago, when the shop wanted something, it was better not to get in its way.

Chapter Nineteen

Evie, Now

After her tenth text from Florence earlier that day, Evie had silenced her notifications. While she understood her sister had a difficult time coming to the house, Evie had survived the same trauma. Were their roles reversed, she'd have been there for Florence in a heartbeat. She tried to remind herself that it was better Florence hadn't been there, better she knew nothing of Evie's discovery.

Not that it changed the way Evie felt about her absence.

Evie sat on Angela's couch with a slice of pepperoni pizza while they watched a movie of Clara's choosing. Clara curled up between the two of them and gave a steady stream of commentary throughout the film. As much as Evie tried to respond to her daughter thoughtfully, her thoughts kept straying to her mother's journal, her mind picking apart the spell as best she could without the pages sitting open in front of her.

Angela reached an arm behind Clara and gently tapped Evie's shoulder.

"You okay?" she mouthed.

"Distracted," Evie murmured.

"Soon," Angela whispered.

When the credits finally started to roll, Evie wanted nothing more than to tuck Clara in and start working through the spell. Only after she made sure Clara brushed her teeth and they read one of Clara's favorite picture books together did Evie finally get the chance.

She sat on Angela's couch, going through each line of the page from her mother's journal. She flipped through her newfound tarot deck to discover it was missing both the temperance and the magician cards. She reached for Clara's bag, which she'd left beside the couch, and fished out her sister's deck. She rifled through it until she found the temperance card. It was exactly as she'd remembered it. A woman stood inside the workshop behind Honeysuckle House, where the Caldwell witches dipped their candles. Honeysuckle vines twined around a shelf full of powdered herbs and candle-making supplies. She held a bottle in each hand. Melted wax flowed between them. This card had made Evie certain sharing her magic would protect her family.

"Any luck?" Angela asked as she brought Evie a cup of tea. She sat close enough to Evie that their shoulders almost touched.

"Not yet," Evie said. "I can't believe the house burned. We're just as cursed as we were thirteen years ago. I'm sure Florence is sitting in her shop thinking she was right, ready to say 'I told you so.' But for all we know, her decision not to use her magic is the reason this happened."

Angela rested a hand on Evie's shoulder, and Evie leaned into her touch.

"Better we know now than in four days," Angela said. "At least there's still time to do something."

"If I can figure out this spell and direct the binding magic to stop whatever is affecting the house, we might have a chance," Evie said.

"Anything I can do to help, I'm here," Angela said. "And I know it doesn't feel like it, but Florence is, too. Maybe if you show her the spell—"

"She made her position clear this afternoon. I have to do this on my own. Knowing her, she'd tell me to burn Mom's journal and keep everyone away from the house until after the thirteenth."

"Maybe she's right," Angela said. "The way your mom treated you and Florence? You can't trust her."

"I have to do *something*," Evie said.

"Cancel the festival," Angela said. "Close the doors until the curse day has come and gone. Stay here, with me."

"If leaving was enough to stop it, my mom and my grandma would've left when Florence was born. My mom wouldn't have kept us in the house the year my dad died. He tried to leave, and the curse took him."

It was something Evie had thought about a lot over the years. Her memories from childhood were hazy—full summers nothing more than an impression—but her mind had preserved the day her father died like a film. When she closed her eyes, she could still feel the pain in her scalp, the way his arms had felt around her in the hallway the last time he held her, his glassy eyes looking skyward. Something had shifted deep inside Evie that day, like the space where her power sat tucked up under her heart had caved in on itself, going cold.

If she hadn't demanded he go in and get her necklaces, maybe they would've made it out.

It didn't make sense for their mother to keep them in the house, to cast a spell on her father. Not unless she really was trying to protect him.

"Our best chance is to finish what my mother started," Evie said.

"Maybe she's not the only one who can give us answers." Angela leaned forward and spread the stack of journals out across the coffee table. She picked up the oldest-looking book and flipped it open.

Evie leaned closer to Angela, looking over her shoulder. The inside cover of the journal read: *Regina Caldwell, 1960. Return if found.*

"That's my grandmother," Evie said.

Angela tilted her head to the side as she counted on her fingers. "It's also a curse year. You and Florence always said if you knew how the curse began, you'd have a better chance of breaking it."

"But it started thirteen years before that," Evie said.

"Still," Angela said. "Clara's spell opened that room for you. There has to be a reason those diaries were hiding in there."

Angela leaned forward and opened the rest of the journals. Every single one was from a curse year:

Violet Caldwell's Thoughts and Spells. 1960.
Regina Caldwell. 1973.
My Diary by Linda Caldwell. 1973.
Regina Caldwell. 1986.
Property of Linda Caldwell. 1986.
Linda Caldwell. 1999.

"There's not enough time to read all of these *and* figure out my mom's spell," Evie said.

"We could give a few to Florence." Angela quickly flipped through the pages until she got to the back half, which was full of spells. Toward the end, one was dog-eared. She opened to that page to find a list that mirrored the one Evie had found in her mother's journal. A few items had been crossed off, and the brown candle was missing, but it was clear the two were related.

"This is almost the same spell," Evie said, taking the journal from Angela. "It looks like my grandmother tried to do what my mother was doing."

"But I thought they didn't know there was a curse until after the second victim," Angela said.

"What if she realized it, but she was too late to stop it?" Evie said. "Maybe if I compare the two spells . . ."

"Before you do that, you have to do something about the house," Angela said. "It turned that woman out of her bed. It caught fire. It's not safe to bring your guests back."

Evie hated to admit it, but Angela was right. "I know," Evie said. "I can't let the guests come back. At least until I can complete the spell."

Evie took a long drink of her tea then leaned her head back against the couch. "I really thought we were safe—that sharing my magic with the town was all it would take. But now that the house has burned, I don't know what to think. I could lose Clara or Florence. Or you."

Angela took Evie's mug and set it on the coffee table. Then she took Evie's hands in hers. "Or we could lose you." Heat spread from Evie's fingers, up her arm, and into her throat.

"I know. You all care about me, too." Evie stared at their joined hands, afraid to look up and into Angela's eyes. Afraid to find out if this thing Evie had felt burning between them was all in her head.

"It's more than caring about you," Angela said, voice low.

Angela, who had driven her home when Honeysuckle House caught on fire. Angela, who had been at her side when Evie was all alone as a young mother. Angela, whose very presence lit Evie up inside. For years, Evie had done her best to ignore her growing feelings for the other woman—all for the sake of her sister. But if Florence couldn't be there for Evie, then what reason did Evie have to stay away from Florence's best friend?

Angela rubbed her thumb along the side of Evie's hand. Then, she reached over and tilted Evie's chin toward her. Evie's eyes drifted up until they locked on hers.

"Aren't you afraid of the curse?" Evie whispered. "That if I . . . if we . . ."

"Terrified." Angela pressed a hand to her chest, and the fear in her eyes made Evie want to rage or weep or scream. This was why her sister had kept everyone at arm's length. Because every person she loved was at risk, and she decided it was better to never know them, to never love them, than to be the reason they lost their life.

Evie didn't want to live like that. She *couldn't* live like that. But she couldn't hurt Angela either. She started to pull back, but Angela brought her other hand to Evie's cheek. Evie's lips parted, a surprised gasp slipping through.

"I'm scared the curse might take you from me, or me from you," Angela said. "But that doesn't change how I feel about you. How I think you feel about me."

They sat like that, suspended for what felt like hours, this ember that had been smoldering between them for years finally flickering to life. Slowly, Evie threaded her fingers through Angela's. She pushed forward at the same time Angela did, and they met in the middle. When their lips touched—soft and supple and sweet—the flame became a fire.

Evie's mouth parted, making way for Angela's tongue. It glided against Evie's before sweeping her mouth. Angela pressed her hand to Evie's shoulder, gentle at first, until they were falling. Evie on the couch, Angela on Evie. Chest to chest, heart to heart. The journal and the cards and the curse forgotten.

Angela's twists fell forward, curtaining Evie as she looked up into Angela's eyes. Evie loosened her grip on Angela and brought her hands to either side of her face. Then she lifted her head from the couch and deepened their kiss.

When they finally broke apart, Angela held herself up with her hands on either side of Evie while Evie came up onto her elbows. She stared into Angela's eyes, the pupils so wide it was hard to see where the black ended and the deep brown began. Evie reached up and brushed her thumb over Angela's cheek. Angela leaned into her hand, and her eyelids fluttered softly.

"I've loved you for a long time," Evie whispered. The words settled over them both, and Evie knew she had to find a way to keep Angela safe.

Chapter Twenty

Honeysuckle House, Now

If houses had fingers, then Honeysuckle House could've counted the times it had spent the night alone on one hand. There was the time Regina had lit a red candle, put on a matching shade of lipstick, and left in a car she'd purchased sometime after Violet had left Burdock Creek. Linda had been born nine months later.

Before that, it had only been left behind once, when Helen and Christopher took their daughters on holiday after the war, and the house didn't much like to think of that trip. It had been so excited to see the Buick pulling up the drive that it hadn't noticed the car was going too fast, its tires swerving out of control. Of all the deaths, that one the house should've been able to prevent, but it wasn't fast enough. The house had never really gotten the chance to say a proper goodbye to the first witch who had given it life.

Now, Honeysuckle House sat staring out over the fall leaves. Dusk had long since turned to dark. Inside, it felt empty and alone. It creaked the floorboards and rattled the pipes in an attempt to block out the silence, but it didn't help. Every sound it made was a reminder of the sounds it lacked.

Laughter.

Whispers.

Footsteps on stairs.

With a heavy sigh and a settling of wood and plaster, the house closed the shutters and turned out the porch light.

Part V
The Ace of Swords

The start of a new journey that brings clarity or truth.

Chapter Twenty-One

Regina, 1960

Whenever Regina needed to calm her mind, she turned to the bees. The workshop sat several hundred feet behind the house, and the apiary another several hundred feet behind that, before the meadow gave way to the creek bed and the water to the mountains.

They had a total of fifteen Langstroth-style hives, each stacked three boxes high. Regina sat on the clover a few feet from the bees. Their steady hum filled any empty place in her heart left behind by her parents, a soft, lulling sound she could lose herself in. She held out a hand as one of the worker bees came to investigate. It landed lightly on the base of her palm, small legs tickling Regina's skin. Another came to join it.

Regina's eyes trailed from the gentle insects to one of the hives, where tens of thousands of sisters like these worked to fill comb with nectar, to feed their young, and to tend to their queen, when Regina heard a high-pitched buzzing. She shook the bees from her palm and stood to investigate.

There at the edge of one of the hives, far from where she should be, stood a queen, her long abdomen reaching beyond the length of her wings, her antennae twitching as the other bees of her colony clustered around her. Their urgency almost looked as if they were coming to her aid, but Regina knew better. Her heart raced, part terror, part anticipation. There was nothing she could do to stop what was about to happen. But she couldn't look away.

Bees pressed in on the queen, their buzzing loud and insistent and almost enough to drown out the queen's piercing cries. But not quite. They crawled over top and underneath, pulling her this way and that. They tore at her thorax, at her abdomen, at her wings. Though she struggled to escape them, they were too many. They pressed in until Regina couldn't see her anymore, covered as she was by the wriggling bodies. Regina picked up the ball of bees and held them in the palm of her hand. Their humming made her skin tingle, but they didn't seem to notice her.

Regina stood there mesmerized as the queen's high-pitched cries slowed. Then, all at once, it stopped. The bees pulled back from the ball they'd formed as if nothing had happened. The queen's body sat there, lifeless and mutilated, in the middle of Regina's hand.

She'd been young the first time she'd watched a hive decide their queen was no longer viable. When she'd told her mother about it, Helen had been worried Regina had to see it that way, all by herself. She'd explained that nature could be harsh, brutal even. But these things had to happen.

It was a lesson that had stuck with Regina.

Now, she turned the conversation with Violet over in her mind as she turned the queen's torn and lifeless body over in her hand. Maybe it wouldn't be terrible having a roommate, another person to take care of the house, the bees, the land, the way the workers took care of each other. Violet was right, the house *was* quiet. But Regina preferred the quiet. It was why she rarely left Honeysuckle House, why she didn't have any friends of her own. Were she a bee, she wouldn't live in a hive at all. She'd be the solitary kind.

At least she wasn't losing her sister to a man.

The sound of tires on gravel pulled Regina from her thoughts. She knelt before the hive and dug her fingers into the earth, deep enough to place the queen's body in the dirt. Then, with a long breath, she made her way around the workshop to find Violet and Tillie opening up the back doors of the Pontiac, which was full to the brim with boxes.

As if sensing Regina's approach, Violet turned. Her eyes lit up, and her look of love warmed Regina. She picked up her pace as she approached the car. Violet set down her box and wrapped Regina in a hug. Regina breathed her sister in—all rosewater and Appalachian forest.

When Violet pulled back, she gripped Regina's arms lightly, and Regina wondered if she'd ever seen her sister so happy. The thought both softened her and twisted something deep in her belly. She tried her best to ignore it. If this didn't work out, she could always light a candle, whether Violet approved or not.

"Do you have a few minutes to help us put these in m—" she stopped short. "In Tillie's room?"

As much as Regina didn't want Tillie there, she nodded. She could do this for Violet.

Tillie pulled a box out of the back and offered it to Regina. "Thank you for welcoming me into your home." Though Tillie's voice was bright, her smile bigger than Regina had ever seen it, there was a slight narrowing of her eyes, a hesitation in the way she stood.

Regina took the box, maybe a bit forcefully, but she smiled back, her mouth tiring quickly. "It's a big house." She turned and carried the box up the front steps.

When the door opened for her, she frowned. Part of her had hoped the house would share her sentiments and refuse to let them in with Tillie's things. As if sensing her mood, the house cradled her first step over the threshold, the hardwood soft underfoot, a bit like a hug or an apology, and she relaxed the tension in her shoulders. Violet and Tillie followed her with boxes of their own. Regina took the stairs up to the second story, one floor below her own room. The lights turned on overhead as they went down the hall, and the door to the guest room that never saw guests creaked open.

The bed sat fresh and clean, the window cracked, a soft fall breeze fluttering the curtains.

Behind her, Regina heard her sister murmur, "Thank you."

Regina set the box down and, with a touch of bitterness in her voice, said, "It seems the house is happy to have you."

Tillie arched an eyebrow.

"It's always loved her," Violet said warmly as she bumped Tillie's shoulder with her own. "Come on, let's get the rest of the boxes."

After two more trips, the only things they had left were Tillie's houseplants: a fiddle leaf fig that came up to Regina's hip, a parlor palm, and three philodendrons in macrame hangers. Regina lifted two of the philodendrons, while her sister wrestled with the fig.

As Regina made her way toward the stairs, Violet paused and said, "This will be perfect in the front sitting room."

"And we can hang one of the philodendrons in the kitchen and another in the bedroom!" Tillie said. "Maybe the third in the library upstairs?"

"The palm would fit well there, too," Violet said. "Let me drop this one off. I'll take one of those philodendrons, Regina."

Regina stood there, a plant hanging from each hand. She'd resigned herself to Tillie taking up a spare bedroom, but in her head, Tillie would be in her room. There would no trace of her anywhere else—more of a boarder than a proper roommate. But Tillie's plants taking up residence in Honeysuckle House meant Tillie herself taking up residence in a much bigger way than Regina had let herself come to terms with.

Regina set the plants down and crossed her arms. "I thought Tillie's things would go in Tillie's room." Regina made no effort to mask the bite in her voice.

Violet winced, and Tillie gave Regina a long look that edged on a glare before she took a step toward Violet. They stood side by side, shoulders touching. Violet leaned into Tillie, and all at once the feeling Regina had earlier that afternoon came back to her, like somehow she was losing Violet to Tillie, that if she let this continue—whatever this was—things would end with Regina alone, the only family she had left taken from her by this other woman.

"I suppose I shouldn't be surprised," Regina said. "Your parents take the shop from us, and now you're here taking the house."

"You sold the shop to my family," Tillie said.

Regina started to speak, when Violet cut her short.

"Why don't we put the plants down and take a break?" Violet's voice was soft and gentle, a tone Regina had only heard from her sister the few times their bees had swarmed and then that first day after their parents' deaths. Though Regina prickled that Violet was so clearly trying to calm her, she also found her stomach starting to unknot.

"I'll mix us some Manhattans," Violet said. It was Regina's favorite drink.

Before Regina could argue, Violet had gone through the open archway to the sitting room and set the fig down in one corner. Regina hated to admit it was a perfect fit. Even Honeysuckle House seemed to like it, as the record player started up, one of Tillie's albums somehow already on the turntable. The soft jazz set Regina further at ease.

While Violet went to the bar cart, pulled out a bottle of Bonner Bourbon, and started mixing drinks, Regina took up a spot on the green velvet sofa she'd purchased after a particularly successful spell had brought in an abundance of candle orders last year. Tillie stopped in the middle of the room, one arm across her chest, the other limp at her side as she glanced between the sisters.

"You have to admit, the fern does fit this room perfectly," Violet said.

Regina shrugged but accepted her Manhattan all the same when Violet crossed the room to hand it to her.

"I can finish making those," Tillie offered.

"Wasn't there something you wanted to show Regina?" Violet asked.

Tillie's eyes brightened. "You're right," she said. "I have something for you, Regina. For both of you, actually. I'll be right back."

She hurried out of the room, and as soon as she was gone, Violet sat down beside Regina and leaned her head against her shoulder. "Thank you for going along with this. It means a lot to me. Imagine getting to live with your best friend."

"I already do." But what Regina wanted to say was, "I thought *I* was your best friend."

"And now you can have one more." Violet hurried to her feet and back to the bar cart.

Regina studied her as she poured the other two drinks. She hadn't seen Violet like this in a long time, a mix of nerves and a quiet sort of happiness that had disappeared in the wake of their parents' deaths and Violet's new responsibilities. They'd settled into a rhythm over the past thirteen years, one that eased Regina's heart despite the deep grief that still lived there. Now, Violet's eyes were bright, her smile brighter—like a girl in love. But that was impossible with the spells Regina had been so careful to cast. She sipped her drink. The hint of guilt she carried because of said spells eased as she realized her sister never needed love to find happiness.

Tillie reappeared with two wrapped boxes in her hands. She set them on the table. Violet handed her a Manhattan, and Tillie took a long drink, almost draining the glass. Regina smirked, glad she'd made it clear who was in charge here.

Violet took up the spot beside Regina on the couch. Tillie set her drink on the table, grabbed the boxes, and offered one to Regina and one to Violet before sitting at the edge of their yellow lounge chair.

"It's a housewarming gift," Tillie said.

"Shouldn't *I* be the one giving *you* a gift?" Regina asked.

"I'm open to that," Tillie said with a laugh, "but since you're welcoming me into your home . . ."

Regina tore through the tissue paper with the tip of her fingernail. Beside her, Violet struggled with the tape thanks to her always-short nails. Regina leaned over and pulled it free. Her sister smiled, and they opened their gifts the rest of the way to reveal two wooden boxes.

Regina slid the cover off hers and found a deck of cards nestled inside. The backs were a rich, deep black with a candle in the center. She glanced over at Violet's, a mirror of her own but in green. She lifted the first card and flipped it over to find a woman standing on a front porch, honeysuckle-wrapped columns on either side of her, in much the same pose as the fool card.

"Tarot?" Regina asked.

"For your magic," Tillie said. "Both of you. I painted them myself."

Regina held the card up in front of her and traced the tip of her finger over the steps, the vines, the door in the background.

"Is this . . . ?"

"Honeysuckle House," Tillie said.

Regina glanced up from the card to find Tillie's eyes earnest, a small smile on her face. She tucked a loose strand of hair behind her ear.

"They're a matching set," Tillie said, with a nod toward the deck in Violet's hands.

"They're beautiful," Regina said, surprise in her voice. She'd never received such a thoughtful gift. She pulled the full deck from the box and held them gently in her hands. A window opened and closed, and she glanced toward the wall with a grin. "I think the house likes the way you've painted it."

Tillie flushed, then finished her Manhattan. "Go ahead," she said. "Pull a card. Both of you."

Regina nodded slowly as she wondered if her sister was right, if the house had been lonely with just the two of them.

"You first," Violet said.

But Regina shook her head as she started to shuffle her cards. "Let's do it at the same time."

After the deck was fully incorporated, Regina fanned it out in front of her. She held a hand over the cards until she felt a warmth in her palm that ran all the way up her arm to the center of her chest, so much like the heat she felt when preparing a candle. She let it sit there, flames brushing up against her heart for a few seconds, a reminder of her power.

"Ready?" she asked.

Violet nodded, and they flipped their cards.

"Oh!" Violet said with a soft gasp. Regina glanced at her sister's card before looking at her own. In the center, two hands had been lovingly detailed. They held each other, nails cut short and painted bright red, a six along the top. Regina tilted her head, trying to make sense of the image.

"The lovers?" she asked. It was different than the illustration on the Rider-Waite-Smith deck Regina used.

The card most often represented romance, but that was impossible. Regina had made sure of it, which pointed to only one thing: platonic soulmates. It had to be about Regina and Violet. For the first time since Violet broke the news about Tillie, Regina felt the fear in her heart melt away. She looked up to find her sister's eyes locked on Tillie's, her cheeks flushed. Tillie bit her lip.

"Regina . . ." Violet started, but as she looked away from Tillie to the card Regina had revealed, she stopped short.

"So Violet will be lucky in love," Tillie said, a smile in her voice, when Violet stilled her with a hand on her knee.

Both Tillie and Regina followed Violet's gaze, and Tillie let out a soft, "Oh."

Regina lifted her own card to get a better look at it. Vines entwined the carefully painted heart. Three sharp thorns dug in deep, dripping with blood. This might not be the exact illustration she'd grown up on, but Regina knew right away what card she held: The three of swords. A sign of betrayal, heartbreak, or both. The last time she'd pulled this card had been the night before her parents' accident.

She traced a finger over the vines, wishing the card would tell her more. Regina didn't put her heart at risk, she'd made careful work of that over the past thirteen years. But betrayal? She looked up at her sister.

"I suppose it's a good thing I'm not in love." There was only one person Regina loved, and she knew her sister would never break her heart.

"It doesn't have to mean future heartbreak," Violet said. "It could be pointing to a past loss."

Regina nodded slowly. In a few days it would be thirteen years since their parents' death—half of Regina's life spent without them. She couldn't imagine a worse heartbreak.

Chapter Twenty-Two

Regina, 1960

After Regina pulled the three of swords the night Tillie moved in, her mind was a mess of worry and overthinking. She made herself a cup of tea, lit a blue taper, and went to bed early, not even bothering to wash her face or wrap her hair. In the candle smoke, the house had conjured up images of a young Regina and Violet tending to the hives with their mother and father. It was a nighttime ritual the house had begun not long after her parents died, give Regina a chance to see her parents' faces and hear their voices again thanks to the house's magic. Those quiet, easy moments brought Regina peace, but tonight that wasn't enough. She lay beneath her quilt for what felt like hours, the soft music winding its way up the stairs, but sleep wouldn't come.

The walls creaked in her bedroom, as though the house sensed her unease, and when she finally sat up in bed, giving up on sleep altogether, the bedside lamp switched on.

"What should I do?" The question was for the house as much as herself.

Her new deck of cards sat open on the bedside table—not on the dresser where she'd left it. A slow smile spread across her face. She lifted the box and flipped it over, depositing the deck in her hand.

"You always know exactly what I need."

The curtains fluttered at the compliment.

She hadn't taken the time to look at the cards closely, had been almost afraid of them after her draw, but the beautiful thing about tarot was the deck always offered clarification. Before she pulled another card, she fanned the cards face up in front of her, marveling at Tillie's work. Regina might not care much for the woman, but she couldn't deny her talent. The care she'd taken into hand-painting the cards and the detail were unmatched. Regina imagined Violet running her fingers over the same cards, the decks now yet another thread in the magic that bound them together.

The blue candle still burned where she'd left it on the windowsill, wax spilling down the edge and pooling at the base. She'd dipped the candle specifically to help with sleep—she had a full stock of them thanks to the nightmares that plagued her, reminding her of every detail of her parents' deaths—but blue also fostered intuition. It brought clarity, and clarity was exactly what Regina needed.

She shuffled the cards, taking care not to bend the backs. Then, with a deep breath, she spread them out on the quilt. As she lifted one, her bed frame rattled, the floorboards shook, and it slipped from her hands. She narrowed her eyes.

"I thought you wanted me to do this."

The window cracked open, and a breeze stirred the hair around Regina's face. She reached for the card she'd dropped. Once again, the bed began to shake, but this time she held tight.

"You don't want me to have this card?"

The window opened and closed in response.

"Unfortunately for you, this is the card I drew."

She flipped it over, but before she could make it out, the lamp turned off.

"You can't stop me from seeing it."

She reached over and pulled the chain on the lamp, but it didn't react. With an annoyed sigh, she slipped out from under the quilt, several cards falling from the bed and landing on her rug, their shadows just visible in the moon and candlelight. She crossed the room to where her candle burned. The curtains stirred, as if to put out the flame, but Regina snatched the candle holder away from them before they could. She lifted first the candle, then the card. The warm yellow light cast the depiction of Honeysuckle House in a soft glow. At first, Regina smiled, seeing her front porch so lovingly detailed, but the longer she examined the artwork, the more her unease grew, until it threatened to choke her, much like the vines climbing the columns on the card—each one studded with thorns. Seven of them. A warning of deceit. A call to be cunning.

Her mind skipped to Tillie, this invader in her home. Tillie, whose father had been trying to buy her family's shop the day of the accident, who had been upset when the Caldwells wouldn't budge. Tillie, whose family now owned the very storefront Christopher Caldwell had refused to sell.

Regina tapped a finger against the card, unsure what to make of it, why the house didn't want her to see it. But she knew one person who could help her sort it out. She set the candle back on the window-sill, slid her feet into her slippers, and hurried toward her sister's room.

Chapter Twenty-Three

Violet, 1960

Violet stared after Regina as she left the sitting room, tarot cards in hand, worried how she might interpret the three of swords. She should've told her about Tillie that afternoon, should've explained when Regina put up a fight about the plants, should've confessed the truth the moment she'd pulled the lovers card. But Regina had a look in her eyes that gave Violet pause. Regina had never given Violet any reason not to trust her, but this felt different. For so long, they'd had no one but each other. Violet had never brought home anyone aside from Tillie, and she still remembered that first time almost seven years ago.

They'd finished up their late lunch at Barb's. At some point what had started as a way to pass the time on particularly slow afternoons at the shop had become a tradition. Each time, Violet found herself wishing she could reach across the table between them and take Tillie's hand—ask if their years of companionship and their conversations about music and literature and life meant as much to her as they did to Violet. More than once she entertained the idea of lighting a blue candle to draw the truth out of the other woman, but Violet feared what the truth might hold. That what they shared was no more than a common friendship between young women.

As Violet took the last sip of her milkshake, Tillie pulled a faded book out of her handbag. She set it on the table between them, the spine facing Violet so she could see the title—*Orlando* by Virginia Woolf. They'd discussed Woolf before, usually sticking to her safer works, always carefully skipping over this particular novel, which in itself had been an awakening to Violet the first time she'd read it. Her eyes flitted up to Tillie's, searching them for meaning she wanted desperately to find.

"You've read it?" Tillie asked, a slight tremor in her voice.

"It's a favorite," Violet whispered, praying for Tillie to understand her meaning.

Tillie's lips curved up. She flipped the book open to the very back, where a flower sat pressed between the pages. A violet.

"I picked this back in the spring," Tillie said, voice low. "It reminded me of you."

Violet took in the delicately pressed flower, the curve of the still-green stem and leaves, soft and full as they led up to deep purple petals parted like lips whispering secrets. Where two of those petals met, were Violet to lift them gently, carefully, she would find the bright yellow stamen perfectly preserved beneath, an invitation to the promise of sweet nectar.

"It's beautiful." Violet breathed the words more than she spoke them.

She reached across the space between them, setting her hand on the book. Tillie, too, reached for the novel. The tips of their fingers met, and heat shot up Violet's arm all the way to her heart, where it settled in, warming her chest and her stomach and licking its way up her throat. Her cheeks flushed, and when her eyes flitted up to Tillie's, she found her own desire mirrored there.

"Do you—" Violet started.

"Maybe we could—" Tillie said at the same time.

They both laughed, but neither moved their hands from the book.

"Would you like to come over for . . ." Violet paused. "A drink?"

Tillie's scarlet lips parted, and Violet couldn't tear her eyes from them.

"A drink would be nice," Tillie said, a little breathless. "I can bring a few records. And we can . . ." she trailed off. "Listen to them together."

That night had been the first time they'd danced—the first time they'd kissed—but it hadn't been the last. Now, Tillie was here, in Violet's home with her records and her plants and her clothes and they were finally, finally building a life together.

Once Regina was gone, Tillie jumped up from the chair and took the spot next to Violet. She reached for Violet's hand and held it gently in hers.

"Do you need to go after her?" Tillie asked.

But Violet shook her head. Since their parents' deaths, Violet had always put Regina first. It was time to live her life for herself.

"It can wait for morning. What do you say we hang up those philodendrons in the bedroom?" Her lips quirked up.

Tillie's flush was all the answer Violet needed.

* * *

When they made it up to Violet's room, the house had already pulled Tillie's portable record player from her boxes, and Billie Holliday's voice sang softly through the door.

"Have I mentioned how much I love this house?" Tillie asked.

The hallway light flickered.

"I think the house loves you, too." Violet cracked open the door to find her bedroom lined with candles—not the enchanted ones the Caldwell sisters made, but decorative pillars of all sizes, casting the room in a warm, yellow glow.

Tillie gasped, and Violet felt a smile spread over her face. Here, they were safe. Here, they were accepted. Here, they were home.

Violet took her by the hand and tugged her into the music and candlelight, closing the door behind her with her foot. She rested her free hand at Tillie's waist and started to dance as the soft, slow jazz washed over them. Violet stood a few inches taller than Tillie so when Tillie leaned into her, the tip of Tillie's forehead pressed against

Violet's cheek. The warmth of Tillie's skin through the soft fabric of her shirt blazed hotter than any magic Violet had ever burned into the world. If the intention she poured into her candles were spells, this love—this woman—was sorcery.

"Everything I have is yours," Violet murmured as they swayed to the music.

Tillie nestled closer, singing along with Violet. Her mouth moved against Violet's skin with each word, and every brush of her lips sent a tremor through Violet. She gripped Tillie's waist tighter, held her body closer. As the song came to an end, Tillie pulled back, the dark of her pupils impossible to distinguish from the honey brown of her eyes.

Tillie rose up on her toes, and Violet ducked her head. Their lips met in the middle. This was all Violet needed. The heat of Tillie's touch. The softness of Tillie's mouth, the sweet taste of cherry and whiskey still fresh on her tongue. She cupped Tillie's face gently in her hands. Tillie wrapped her arms around Violet's neck. Violet broke their kiss and began to trail her lips along Tillie's chin, down her neck, to the edges of her collarbone, only just visible beneath her blouse—living for every sound she drew from Tillie's throat. She undid the first button, then the second.

Before she could reach the third, the candles blew out.

Tillie laughed softly, "Message received, house." She ran her hand through the back of Violet's hair, brought her lips to Violet's throat. As much as Violet wanted to sink into her touch, she stilled.

More than anything, the house used light to communicate. Lights on were a greeting or a direction. Lights off were a warning. The lamp at Violet's bedside flickered on and off.

On and off.

On and off.

Then, the door opened.

"Violet, I drew another card and—" Regina stopped short. The glow from the hallway spilled into Violet's room, falling on her and Tillie—their embrace, Tillie's state of undress, the mess of Violet's hair. The hall bulbs winked out, but it was too late.

Tillie started to pull away, but Violet reached for her hand and kept her close. She wouldn't live her life in hiding, not in her own home.

"There's something I should've told you a long time ago," Violet said. Then to the house, "It's okay, you can turn on the lights." Her bedside lamp flickered to life, followed by the floor lamp in the corner beside her two lounge chairs—where she and Tillie planned to hang one of the philodendrons—then, finally, the hall lights.

"You love her," Regina said. Where Violet had hoped to see joy and acceptance in her sister's face, she was met instead with narrowed eyes. But they widened again so quickly Violet wasn't sure if they'd ever narrowed at all. Regina held a hand up over her mouth as she glanced between them.

Then, "You lied to me." Her voice had sharpened to a point, and Violet winced.

"I never lied to you," Violet said.

Tillie wrapped an arm around her waist, and Violet leaned into her touch.

"You told me she would be a roommate," Regina said, as if Tillie wasn't standing right there with them. "Every time you've brought her here, every drink, every record. How long?"

Violet hung her head, shame spreading in her chest.

"Seven years," Tillie said. "Seven beautiful years." Her words buoyed Violet.

Though they'd been close for far longer, it wasn't until that day in the diner that they'd taken things a step further than friendship, and Violet's only regret was it hadn't happened sooner.

"Why did you hide this from me?" Regina asked. "We're sisters. You're all I have, Violet. You're all I've ever had."

"I wanted to tell you," Violet said. "So many times I tried, but . . ." She shook her head, still not wanting to admit her fear, to find herself proven right.

"You were afraid I wouldn't accept you," Regina said.

Violet sighed, nodded.

"I love you. There's nothing you could do to change that. I take no issue with women loving women. I just didn't realize . . ." Regina started, stopped, not really looking at Violet anymore, her eyes focused on some middle distance between them.

Violet felt Tillie let out a long breath beside her, and Violet, too, found her sense of relief to be a physical thing. She pressed closer to Tillie and tried not to cry.

"I thought you didn't bring men around because of the candles," Regina said more to herself than to Violet, "but it's always been this way. I should've seen it."

At her words, Violet's chest went cold. The hairs on her arms prickled.

"What do you mean, 'the candles'?" she asked.

Regina blinked, a flush creeping into her cheeks. After a few seconds she started to speak, slowly, "I lit candles to protect you. You know how men can be."

Violet's body went cold. "You tried to keep men away from me."

"Not that that's a bad thing," Tillie said with a light, uncomfortable laugh.

"For your own safety," Regina said, as if it were obvious. "With you working in town, I didn't want you to get hurt."

Violet's memory went back to the workshop that afternoon, the single set of pink tapers she'd walked in on her sister drying. Pink was not a color for protection. Before she could say as much or even follow the thought to its conclusion, Regina started talking again.

"Should I make some black candles for you both, for us?" Regina asked. "With Tillie living here now, if people knew . . ."

"We've been careful," Violet said. Their town had no history of violence against women like Violet and Tillie, but McCarthyism had only ended a few years ago. Violet still remembered the news, the call to report any suspicious activity. Love, it seemed, was dissidence.

"A spell couldn't hurt," Regina said.

"Violet's been lighting them for us," Tillie said.

"Good," Regina said with a nod. "Good." Then, she offered a light smile that didn't quite reach her eyes. "Welcome to the family, Tillie." She held her arms open, and both Violet and Tillie stepped into them.

The lights in Violet's room let out a soft buzzing, almost too high-pitched to hear, but Violet felt it right where fear had pooled in her stomach at the mention of the candles. When she pulled back from her sister's hug, she said, "You know I love you, Regina."

"Of course I do," Regina said. "I only wish you'd told me sooner. You were right. It'll be nice to have someone else in the house. We'll have to celebrate tomorrow."

And with that, Regina kissed first Violet on the cheek, then Tillie, before she disappeared down the hallway. Violet took a few steps forward and braced herself against the doorframe as she stared after her sister.

Tillie came up behind her and rested a hand on Violet's shoulder. "That went better than I expected."

A small, thoughtful noise slipped through Violet's lips. She reached her hand up to grip Tillie's. "I think my sister has been casting spells on me."

As if in confirmation, all of the lights down the hall glowed a touch brighter before they flickered off and then back on.

"To protect you," Tillie said. "It sounded good-natured."

Violet shook her head. "I think she was trying to keep me from falling in love."

Part VI
The Three of Swords

A sign of betrayal, heartbreak, or both.

Chapter Twenty-Four

Florence, Now

Florence sat inside the room the shop had prepared for her and Owen, cradling a cup of tea in her hands that was still steaming from when she poured it from the pot. She closed her eyes and let herself savor the marshmallow and cinnamon taste, giving her a chance to sit in this moment for a few seconds longer before she shared her family history with a stranger who had somehow begun to melt the ice around her heart in the few short weeks he'd been there. When she finally opened her eyes, she found Owen staring at her intently, his mug untouched.

"It's delicious tea," she said. "You shouldn't let it go to waste."

He slowly lifted the cup to his mouth and took a sip. Though they were both on the love seat—and though Owen took up a fair share of it—he'd managed to keep a sliver of space between them, just enough that should Florence lean slightly to the left, their thighs would brush. As it was, she could feel the heat from him even more than the warmth from the tea. He took another sip, watching her all the while.

"It tastes like s'mores," he said. "Where'd you get this?"

"I've only ever found it here, when I need it the most."

"I'm guessing this is like Ink and the books falling off the shelves," Owen said.

At the mention of his name, Ink leapt onto the coffee table, circled the teapot, then lay down with his back touching the warm ceramic. Florence scratched between his ears.

She avoided Owen's eyes as she said, "The bookshop is enchanted."

"I gathered as much." Owen leaned forward, bringing his profile into Florence's peripheral vision. She glanced at him, and his lips tilted up in that smile she'd been trying so hard to ignore.

He rested a hand on the table. Ink's tail flicked against it before the kitten resituated himself with his head up against Owen's knuckles. When Owen obliged by scratching him, Ink began to purr.

Florence sighed. It didn't help that her kitten liked him.

"I need you to know I only brought you back here—I'm only going to tell you what I'm about to tell you—because I don't want you to get hurt."

A furrow appeared in Owen's brows. "You think *I'm* in danger?"

"Let me back up." Florence set her mug on the table and twisted to face him, their knees touching. She almost pulled back but realized that would be more obvious than staying there with the warmth of his leg against her tights. She planted her hands on her thighs, took a deep breath, and did her best to distill her family's tragedies into as comfortable a package as possible to keep this man safe.

"My sister and I are witches." She paused, looking for some sort of reaction. When all Owen did was nod, she swallowed and nodded in return. "Right, so. The house, my bookstore, they're sort of a byproduct of our magic. Well, that's what we thought, but I haven't used my magic in thirteen years because I thought, foolishly, it would put an end to the curse, so I guess we were wrong. Basically, when we call somewhere home, it comes to life."

As if in response to her words, the string lights overhead twinkled on and off, and the tea in Florence's mug warmed where it sat on the table, steam rising from it once more.

Owen nodded slowly. "Well, I suppose I should say it's nice to meet you, Ink & Pages."

The lights shined a little brighter, before dimming once more to a softer, more intimate glow, limning the brown of Owen's eyes with gold. Florence traced the depths of his irises with her mind, and only when he cleared his throat did she notice she'd leaned even closer to him. She bit her lip. He glanced down at her mouth then back up, his cheeks growing darker.

The floorboards beneath the love seat shifted. Florence's side lifted up, and she tumbled into Owen. Her face collided with his chest, his flannel shirt soft against her skin and his body solid and warm. She pushed herself up, using his bicep as leverage, and found herself face to face with him. Heat rushed first to her neck, then her cheeks, and all the way down to her fingertips. His gaze flitted to her hand on his arm, her leg still partly over his thigh.

Despite her desire to push closer, to go back to where she'd fallen, Florence pulled back as if burned.

"I'm sorry," she said. "The shop . . ."

"Is enchanted." Owen's voice came out lower than she'd ever heard it, and it sent even more heat through her.

"It has a mind of its own." A strand of hair had fallen loose from her braid, and she brushed it back behind her ear and readjusted her glasses.

"How does that relate to keeping me safe?" he asked.

"I'm not making much sense," Florence said, voice rushed, grateful to be back to the topic at hand. "I've never really had to explain it to anyone, and certainly not with the shop . . ." She gestured helplessly.

"Dropping you in someone's lap?" Owen offered.

Florence let out a choked laugh. "Right, that."

She reached for her tea, anything to occupy her hands and her mind and her heart. She'd only come into this room to protect Owen—even if her shop had other plans.

"The point is, the Caldwell curse isn't some story my sister uses to bring in guests. Every thirteen years, someone we care about dies there."

Ink stood from his spot on the coffee table and hopped onto Florence's lap. He tried to wedge himself between her and the edge of the love seat, forcing her closer to Owen. She took a deep breath. She was almost done explaining. Then she could get Owen to promise not to go back to Honeysuckle House—to leave Burdock Creek and never look back—and her heart rate would go back to normal.

"You can't stay in the house," she said. "You can't even be there on the thirteenth. If something happened to you . . ." She shook her head. "I can't have that on my conscience."

"But the festival," he said. "Your sister hired me for a job."

"You'll find other jobs."

He leaned forward, his hands on his knees. Then he tilted his head and glanced at her sidelong. There was a certain heat in his eyes. "You said the curse only takes someone you care about. And you said I'm at risk . . ."

That was enough for Florence. She stood so fast her knee bumped the coffee table. Owen leaned forward and steadied it before the tea-pot could tip over, but Florence was halfway to the door before she even realized it.

"Florence!" he said. "Wait!"

She looked back at him, her hand on the doorknob. The lights brightened overhead. "I need to go. I shouldn't have come here at all. I've already put you in enough danger. Don't go back to Honeysuckle House."

She turned to go, opening the door.

"I already knew about the curse," he said. "After this conversation I can now say I've been warned away from Honeysuckle House and its witches by everyone who owns a business on Main Street."

That stilled her, but it didn't surprise her, even if it stung. She didn't look back at him, only said, "You could've saved us both a lot of time."

"I think the curse killed my great-aunt. Tillie Grey."

Florence braced herself with a hand against the door. When she turned to look at him, he was holding out an old photograph. As tempted as she was to walk away, she couldn't ignore this. With a steadying breath, Florence crossed the space between them and took the picture from him.

It was torn down the middle. The remaining part showed two women standing in front of a brick building, smiling as they stared at each other instead of the camera, their hands just touching at the pinkies. One of them looked like she could've been Florence's twin, were Florence's hair a lot shorter. From their clothes, Florence would've placed it in the early 1960s. She flipped it over. On the back, it read: *Tillie & Violet.*

Florence had only seen a few photos of her great-aunt—her mother had never kept them on display, but the house would occasionally hang them up of its own accord—but this was the first time Florence had seen Tillie outside of a grainy photo of her obituary on the library's microfiche. Of course, Florence knew Tillie by name. Her research on the curse had made it clear Tillie was one of its early victims, but Florence had never been able to piece together how she was connected to the Caldwells enough that the curse would take her, beyond a long-standing friendship between the families. Looking at the photograph now, it was obvious. Her great-aunt had been in love with the woman. The way they stared at each other, like they had their whole lives ahead of them, sent a wave of sadness through Florence.

"She's why I'm here. My grandpa . . ." Owen paused, his voice catching on the words. "He had dementia. Tillie was all he would talk about at the end. He kept this photo of her at his bedside. I came to Burdock Creek hoping to learn more about my family history. I needed a way to stay here for more than a few days. When I saw the advertisement for a beekeeper, it felt like it was meant to be."

"Why didn't you tell me sooner?" Florence asked.

"I've tried asking you to coffee more than once," Owen said with a small smile.

At his words, Florence felt a twisting in her stomach. She'd thought this man had wanted to take her out, but he was just looking for answers. She'd let herself build up a picture of him in her head that wasn't true and put him in danger because of it.

"I didn't realize . . ." She paused, trying to keep the disappointment out of her voice. "Does Evie know?"

Owen shook his head. "I didn't know Tillie was connected to your family when I first got here. Nothing my grandpa said about her over the past year made sense, and he never talked about it with my dad when he was younger. When I started asking around about my great-aunt, people told me she was one of the curse's early victims. I wanted to talk to Evie about it, but I overheard her telling Angela how tired she was of trying to convince people she'd broken the curse. I was afraid she might fire me if she knew the truth, so I started coming around here."

"I'm sorry to disappoint you," Florence said. "I might be a Caldwell witch, but I don't know much more about the curse than anyone else in this town."

"But you gave up your magic because of it," Owen said, confusion clear on his face.

"Evie and I did a tarot reading after our mother died," Florence explained. "I drew temperance reversed and the hermit. It was a sign that our magic was out of balance, and a call to put it aside for good."

"It sounds like Evie interpreted it differently," Owen said.

"She thought we needed to use our magic more, to make it available to everyone in town," Florence said bitterly. "Maybe one of us was right and our efforts canceled each other out, or maybe neither of us were. But the tower card you pulled? The house catching fire? The curse is coming, and now we'll never know if we could've stopped it. The best I can do is try to keep everyone away from the house. We're out of time and we're out of options. Maybe if I had more to go on than a few tarot cards." She shook her head. "I don't even know how the curse started."

"What if you did?" Owen asked. "Could you undo it then?"

"I don't know," Florence said. What was the point wondering? The town's accounts of the curse had done little to tell her what had happened behind the walls of Honeysuckle House. She turned the photograph over in her hands, looking for any other secrets it might be hiding. "There's no chance you have the other half of this, is there?"

Owen frowned and shook his head. "I thought maybe if I could figure out where it was taken that I'd be able find more information about Tillie, but I haven't had much luck with that, either."

All at once there came a thump from behind the couch, and with it the cracking of glass. As Florence and Owen turned to look over the back of the sofa, Ink hopped up to investigate. A picture frame lay face down on the ground behind them. They shared a look of confusion and excitement that had Florence wanting to reach across the space between them and take Owen's hand. She resisted the urge and instead jumped up and followed the cat. Owen had the same idea, and they met behind the sofa, crouched down facing each other. Florence turned the frame over, careful not to touch the broken glass. It was a photo of her grandmother, and on the door behind her was a sign that read *Grey's Gifts*.

"I remember seeing that picture in the hallway at Honeysuckle House," Owen said, "where your sister has photos of all the Caldwells who died. How did it get here?"

Florence was less concerned with the how and more interested in the why.

"Ink & Pages and Honeysuckle House have always been connected, ever since the shop came to life," she said. "I don't fully understand it, but I think it's like me and Evie. We're family. There's a part of us that will always be tied together."

"So it's able to pull things into the shop," Owen said. "Like your tarot cards."

Florence nodded. It wasn't only things from Honeysuckle House; the shop had a tie to Evie and Clara as well. If something was connected to one of them, the shop could use it to cause mischief.

Owen took a closer look at the photo. "Is that . . . ?"

He flipped the frame over and started to remove the backing; the lights glowed brighter overhead. When he pulled the picture loose, he found half of it torn. He stared at it for a moment then stood quickly and grabbed the photo of Tillie and Violet from the couch. When he held it up to the one of Regina, it fit perfectly.

"The other half," Florence gasped. She leaned closer to Owen, so close their shoulders brushed and her mind tripped back to her hand on his bicep after the shop had dropped her in his lap. She shook the thought away.

"This photo was taken here," Florence said. "Right out front. The bookshop used to be *Grey's Gifts*."

"What does it mean?" Owen asked. "Why would my grandfather have this, and why would your grandmother be torn out?"

Florence shook her head. "I don't know. My mom rarely talked about her mother, and she never mentioned Violet."

"Maybe they had a falling out?" Owen asked. "Like you and Evie?"

"It's possible," Florence said. "But that doesn't help us understand why the curse started. If we're going to solve this, we need to go back before Regina and Violet. We need to know what happened to my great-grandparents. I've asked around before, but it was seventy-eight years ago. There aren't many people still alive who are old enough to remember the details. It was a tragedy—that's all they could tell me."

"We could go to the library, see if there are any old newspaper clippings," Owen said.

Florence shook her head. "I've tried. There's nothing pointing to any sort of magical cause. It was a car crash."

"There might be a police report," Owen suggested.

"But it was an accident," Florence said.

"It's still worth a try."

Florence nodded slowly. They didn't have much else to go on, and if Owen really wasn't interested in her, then maybe Florence could get her own feelings in check to keep him safe.

Chapter Twenty-Five

Florence, Now

The sun had set by the time they stepped out of the shop, and the rain was coming down in sheets. Though Ink made to follow, as soon he stepped one paw on wet pavement, he turned around and went right back inside. If it weren't for the urgency, Florence would've done the same. At least the shop had left two umbrellas by the front door.

"I'll drive," Owen shouted over the downpour. He pressed the button on his keys, and the truck parked right out front beeped in response. They made a run for it.

"Thank you for doing this," Florence said, a little breathless, as she slid into the passenger seat.

"It's part of my family's history, too." Owen wiped his wet hands against his jeans. "Too bad the café's closed or we could make a copy of the police report and read it over there."

"Something else to discuss over coffee," Florence said with a touch of sadness in her voice. She pulled off her glasses to clean the rain from her lenses.

"I'm not sure that would count as me taking you out, but the way you've avoided my offers, it might be the only way to get you over there."

Florence slid her glasses back into place and looked up at him. "I thought you were only asking me to coffee to talk about your aunt."

"I did want to ask you about her, yes, but that wasn't all it was."

Florence flushed, and despite the risks, she couldn't help the way her heart warmed.

* * *

Florence had never had a reason to go to the police station—she wasn't particularly fond of law enforcement—but if their website was to be believed, they were open to the public at all hours. After she and Owen made another dash through the pouring rain, she was pleased to find the doors unlocked and an older man sitting at the front desk.

Florence shook out her umbrella and turned.

"Please leave your umbrellas by the—" the police officer cut himself short. "Florence Caldwell."

"Yes, hello," she said, her eyes landing on his name tag. "Officer Rollins."

He crossed his arms as he glanced from her to Owen. "The thirteenth isn't for a few more days."

"Don't worry. If I were reporting another death, I'd call it in," she said wryly. He'd taken her call when her mother died and let her mother's body sit inside Honeysuckle House until the fourteenth, too afraid to send any of his men on a curse day.

He broke eye contact and started shuffling a few papers on his desk. "What brings you in?"

"I was wondering if there was a report filed for the car accident that killed Helen and Christopher Caldwell," she said.

That got his attention. The officer looked back up at her, eyebrows raised. "Those files haven't been digitized. I'd need the exact date—" he cut himself short.

They stared at each other in silence for a few moments until Florence tilted her head to the side and said, "October 13, 1947."

"Normally I'd need you to fill out a couple of forms," he said, still not moving from behind the desk.

"I'm trying to stop it from happening again," Florence said.

"And a police report is going to help you do that?" the officer asked.

"Where are the forms?" Owen cut in. "We'll fill them out while you get the report."

Officer Rollins narrowed his eyes at Owen. "Aren't you the beekeeper Evie Caldwell hired to work the festival?" He glanced at Florence. "Here I thought you were the sister who *wasn't* dragging people into your family's mess."

"Tillie Grey was my great-aunt," Owen said. "I dragged myself into this. Now about that paperwork?"

Rollins gave a long, drawn-out sigh before he pulled out a form from behind the desk and handed it over, then disappeared without another word.

"What was his problem?" Owen asked.

"My sister has done a lot to change the way this town thinks about our family, but there are still plenty of people who don't want anything to do with us," Florence said. "It's easier to keep us at an arm's length than worry about becoming the next victim."

They hadn't even finished filling out the form by the time Rollins returned with a file box marked *Caldwell*. There were several dates scrawled across the front.

"This is everything we have on the deaths," he said.

"That was fast," Owen said. "You made it seem like it was going to take a while."

The cop raised his brows. "You want this or not?"

Florence finished the form and handed it over. Rollins led them to an interrogation room. He flipped the light switch on, casting them in the harsh glare of fluorescents, and Florence found herself wishing she was back at the bookstore with a cozy lamp and a squashy chair. Rollins dropped the box in the middle of the table with a grunt.

"Don't take anything out of the station."

With that, he left them alone. As soon as the door closed behind him, Florence opened the box. Inside she found six file folders, all so thin she doubted they were going to be much help. Still, she pulled them out and opened the first one, labeled 2012.

Inside she found a police report detailing her mother's death. Florence's witness statement had been typed up alongside Evie's. The case was labeled closed and cleared. Cause of death: Accidental injury. Behind the report were the photos the officers had taken. Florence fanned them out on the table and stared at them for a few moments.

Her mother's body lay on the floor of her bedroom, neck twisted at an angle, eyes open and unblinking. A metal chandelier pinned her to the ground. Blood pooled from where its iron spikes had driven through her arms, her stomach, her chest.

"You shouldn't have to see those," Owen said.

Florence blinked up at him, surprised to find tears on her eyelashes. She brushed them away. "I already saw it in person."

"That doesn't mean you need to relive it."

Florence shook her head slowly as if she could dislodge the grief that had pushed its way out of the hole where she'd tried to bury it. When Owen reached for the photos, she didn't stop him. He carefully put the report and the images back in the folder, then set it off to the side.

Florence took out the rest of the folders in order. They were much the same as her mother's. A few short pages detailing the scene of the death. A ruling of accidental injury. Photographs she'd rather not be looking at but couldn't seem to tear her eyes away from.

Her father, dead on the front lawn.

Her grandmother, neck broken at the base of a spiral staircase.

Her great-aunt, impaled on a loose floorboard.

Tillie Grey, drowned in a bathtub.

Like the others, the case had been closed, the death marked accidental. Unlike the others, Tillie's folder had a little more weight to it. Someone had actually investigated Tillie's death, with both Violet and Regina listed as possible suspects—the only two people in the house when it had happened. There were no markings on Tillie's body to suggest anyone had held her down, and Violet and Regina claimed to have been together in another room when the drowning occurred. On the final page of notes, a single line: *Thirteen years to the day after the deaths of Helen and Christopher Caldwell.* The first time the town pieced together what had happened, the reality of what the Caldwells faced.

Florence handed the folder to Owen and picked up the final case in the box: her great-grandparents, pinned by the limbs of an old maple tree then crushed beneath its weight.

She lifted the black-and-white photo. The bodies were barely visible beneath the fallen leaves, the blood a dark shadow. Honeysuckle vines wrapped around the car.

The report was short, an attempt to understand what had caused Christopher Caldwell to lose control of the wheel. The car had been so damaged by the falling tree, there was little to be gleaned from it. The windshield, shattered. The roof, caved in. The brake fluid reservoir, pierced by one of the branches.

There were statements from each of the sisters. Together, they told the same story. The Caldwells had gone for a weekend trip with the Greys. They'd returned early after an argument between their father and Tillie's. Christopher Caldwell had been driving fast, complaining how the entire vacation had been a ruse, another attempt to get them to sell their shop. Though Helen had tried to calm him down, tried to convince him to pull over and let her take the wheel, Christopher had refused. They'd gone around the curve to Honeysuckle House too fast, and instead of slowing and turning up the drive, they'd careened into the yard, colliding with the tree. When questioned about how they escaped the car, the girls said the house rescued them, pulling them free with its vines.

After she read each page, Florence snapped a photo then handed the report to Owen. By the time they finished, she let out a long groan, planted her hands on the table, and dropped her forehead to meet them.

"This doesn't make any sense," she said. "The way I learned the story, the tree fell on the car. But this report makes it sound like the car hit the tree *first*."

"Why is that a problem?" Owen asked.

"The curse takes someone every thirteen years, and it always does it at Honeysuckle House. But if the car lost control *before* it was on our property, then it couldn't be the curse, could it?" She tapped her fingers against the table. "I hoped we might find something that would point to why the deaths happened, how the curse started. But out of all of these, this one actually reads like an accident report."

Owen reached for one of the pages and set it in front of them. "Except for this," he said as he pointed to the paper. "They tried to find why the car lost control, but it was inconclusive. There wasn't any brake fluid in the reservoir."

Florence shook her head. "That's because of the tree."

"It says it *might* have been caused by the tree," Owen said. He picked up the page and read, "Brake fluid reservoir was empty at time of investigation. Tree pierced the reservoir, but it's impossible to determine amount of fluid prior to accident."

"You think someone tampered with the brake fluid?" Florence asked.

"I'm not sure what I think," Owen said. "But it seems like someone else may have had that thought. Why else would they feel like it was important to include the argument with my family?"

Florence tapped the tip of her finger against her nose as she connected the pieces of Owen's theory. She flipped through the report and pulled up the transcript of an interview with William Grey. "They even talked with your great-grandfather because he wanted my great-grandparents' shop."

"If the police couldn't determine when the brake fluid was emptied, then it could've happened before they crashed into the tree," Owen whispered.

They sat in silence as the realization hit them: Florence's great-grandparents may not have been killed by the curse at all. They may very well have been killed by Owen's family.

Owen dropped his head into his hands. "I wanted the truth," he said, "but I didn't want this."

Florence reached out a hand toward him, almost rested it on his back, but stopped herself. "Do you really think it's possible? Would your great-grandfather have done something like that?"

He glanced up at her. "I never knew him."

"Let's say this theory *is* right," Florence said. "How would a murder lead to the curse? I could understand it if maybe it was *your* family that was cursed, but if they really did kill my great-grandparents, they got away with it."

"Tillie died," Owen reminded her.

"Because a Caldwell loved her," Florence said. "There has to be more to it—something we're not seeing."

"I know you gave up your magic," Owen said. "But maybe it's time for you to pick up your tarot deck again."

Chapter Twenty-Six

Violet, 1960

Though Violet tried to put her worry aside, her unease only deepened. She held Tillie close, her chest pressed against Tillie's back, trying to let the soft sound of Tillie's breath and the slow beating of her heart lull her to sleep.

But sleep wouldn't come.

A few hours before dawn, Violet slipped from beneath the sheets and donned a robe over her striped pajamas. The door opened without a sound, and the floorboards kept quiet as she snuck out of the house and into the night.

When she reached the workshop, she kept the lights off, letting the soft glow from the burner guide her work, afraid her sister might look out the windows and come to investigate. While she waited for the wax to melt, she opened the cabinets, unable to see much in the dark.

"I need wormwood, basil, and oregano," she whispered.

The jars inside shuffled around each other until three moved to the front. She gave the cabinet a gentle pat and said, "Thank you."

She set to grinding a teaspoon of each with a mortar and pestle. She rolled her shoulders back and wiggled her fingers, but before she could start to work, the door creaked open behind her. Violet jumped up, surprised the house hadn't warned her. When she turned around, it was to see Tillie silhouetted by the moon, and she breathed a sigh of relief.

"I thought I might find you here," Tillie said.

"I couldn't sleep. I didn't want to wake you."

Tillie crossed the space between them and wrapped her arms around Violet's waist.

"We're in this together." She looked around Violet's side at her setup. "I don't know what I can do to help, but I'm here."

"That's more than enough." Violet pressed her lips to Tillie's and lingered in the soft quiet of the moment. She wouldn't let anything come between their love, and she knew Tillie wouldn't either.

"Sit with me," Violet said as she made room on the bench. Though they'd been together for seven years, Violet had only brought Tillie into the workshop a handful of times—mostly to pick up candles to take back to the store. She'd never had a reason to show her the process.

"You can help me make them," Violet said.

"Will that work?" Tillie asked.

"If anything, it will make the spell stronger," Violet said. "I've never experienced more magic than when I'm with you."

Tillie leaned her head against Violet's shoulder and whispered, "That may be the most romantic thing you've ever said to me."

"Imagine what I'll be saying thirty years from now," Violet said.

They kissed once more. Then, they got to work.

Violet gathered two sets of string, four weights, and black dye. If Regina really had used her magic against Violet, then Violet didn't doubt she'd do it again. She hoped four candles would be enough. If she lit one daily, her sister would find her magic useless against Violet's, and she'd give up. If she didn't, then Violet would simply make more.

Once the wax melted down, she handed one set of weighted wicks to Tillie and held her own above the boiler. Tillie mirrored her. With her free hand, Violet threaded her fingers through Tillie's.

"May our love be protected," Violet said.

"May our love be protected," Tillie repeated.

Violet felt that first stirring of power in her heart. The heat built in her chest, and she and Tillie dipped their strings at the same time. Wax dripped from the wicks as they lifted them from the boiler. Violet released her grip on Tillie and sprinkled the first layer with herbs.

Then, she rejoined hands, and they held the wicks aloft for a few moments to let them dry.

"May our love be protected," Violet said again. And, again, Tillie repeated her, the fire inside Violet growing stronger as it worked its way from her heart to her shoulders to her arms, and clear down to the tips of her fingers.

As they lowered the candles into the wax, the magic flowed from Violet's fingertips brighter than she'd ever seen it. Instead of the usual soft glow, the early layers of wax looked almost orange beneath its light, as if the candles were already burning.

"It's beautiful," Tillie breathed.

"It's never been like this before," Violet said, pulling up on the string.

"What's different?"

Violet rubbed her thumb along the side of Tillie's hand. "You're here."

They continued that way in companionable silence. Dipping and pausing and dipping until the candles had formed and dawn waited at the doorstep. When they'd finished, she hung the candles from her hooks. She emptied the boiler of the wax, scooping what little remained into a small jar should she need to pull from it later. Then she filled the inner pot once more, this time mixing sun-bleached wax with pink dye.

"More?" Tillie asked.

Violet shook her head. "A little something extra."

Once the wax had melted, she handed Tillie a set of the tapers. She held Tillie's hand and dipped them once more into the wax. This time, she only lowered them part of the way, so the bottom half of the candle was pink, and the top black. Tillie followed her lead. Violet dropped one of the tapers into a glass of water to set the wax.

Now finished, the two women took the candles and made their way back inside. Violet positioned one of them on the small table in the bedroom sitting area. She struck a match, and the wick caught flame as the sun started to rise.

Chapter Twenty-Seven

Regina, 1960

Over the next few days, Regina feigned happiness for Violet and Tillie while she tried, three separate times, to use her magic to come between them. The first attempt had been the morning after she discovered them in a state of undress, when she'd found them drinking coffee in the kitchen. Judging by the bags under their eyes, they hadn't slept any better than Regina had.

"I thought I might make dinner for all of us tonight," Regina said as she poured herself a cup. "We didn't get to celebrate Tillie moving in properly."

Violet's eyes narrowed. Regina avoided meeting them by pouring milk into her coffee, adding a spoonful of sugar, and stirring three times clockwise.

"You don't make dinner," Violet said.

Her sister wasn't wrong. It wasn't that Regina didn't know how to cook. She'd learned from her mother when she was a girl, but after their parents' deaths, Violet had taken on all the responsibility herself.

"It's a special occasion," Regina said. "I was thinking beef stroganoff."

"That sounds delicious," Tillie said.

"It's Violet's favorite." Though she didn't mean for it to, Regina's voice had a bit of a malice in it.

"You never told me that," Tillie said.

"I don't have it often," Violet said. "It makes me think of my mother."

"Now you can reclaim it," Regina said with a forced lightness. "And think of Tillie instead."

Violet made a thoughtful noise as Regina watched her over the rim of her coffee cup.

* * *

After Tillie and Violet left, Regina got to work. She started with the same spell she'd used to keep her sister from loving a man. It had worked perfectly well for years. Regina simply hadn't been broad enough with the types of people her sister might come to love, so she expanded her wording. As soon as she finished, she took the candles into the house, set one up in her favorite spot in the attic, and prepared to light it.

But the moment she tried, the window opened, and a breeze blew out her match.

"Not this again," she said.

Her lamp flared brighter, as if to say, "Yes, this again."

"I can't have Tillie stealing my sister away from me," Regina said. "Whether you like her or not."

She walked over to the window and slammed it shut. Then, she struck another match. The window opened a crack.

"Don't you understand?" Regina asked. "If it weren't for Tillie's family, we'd never have lost Mother and Father. They took us on that stupid trip so they could convince Father to sell his shop. If we hadn't been out with them, then he wouldn't have been driving so fast. He wouldn't have lost control, and he wouldn't have hit the tree."

The lights flared brighter, curious.

"Lucky for the Greys I suppose. If they hadn't died, Violet never would've sold the store," she paused, a new thought taking form. "Maybe a little *too* lucky."

She'd said something similar to Violet the day Tillie moved in. But the more she thought about it, the more she wondered. Her father hadn't been the most careful driver, but he'd never been reckless. As riled up as he'd been, he wouldn't have rounded the corner so fast if he thought he wouldn't be able to stop.

"For all we know, Tillie's father did something to the car, and now you're playing music so Violet can dance with his daughter."

The light dimmed, and the window closed.

"That's better."

Regina lit the candle. But as it started to burn, the taper melted in a way Regina had never seen before. Rather than a steady burn, the flame flitted this way and that, sending uneven rivulets of wax down the edge.

"Is this your doing?" she asked the house.

The light flickered off. No.

"I'll light another just in case."

* * *

That night at dinner, Regina sat with an untouched plate of beef stroganoff in front of her. She'd expected Violet to come home without Tillie thanks to her magic. When she'd heard their laughter from the kitchen, she thought maybe her spell simply hadn't taken hold yet. She'd almost run up to the attic to see if her candles had finished burning, but she didn't want to arouse Violet's suspicion. Instead, she'd dished up their plates, poured them each a glass of wine, and set the table.

As Regina brought her fork to her lips, a record started spinning in the other room, the lights dimmed, and Regina lost her appetite.

"Tillie and I were talking at work today," Violet started to say, her voice a little hesitant.

Regina sat up straighter, thinking this was the moment she'd been waiting for.

"What do you think about adding a few more hives to the apiary?" Violet asked. "We're always running out of candles at the shop. With more bees, we'd have more wax so we could dip more candles."

Regina slumped back in her seat. "That's an idea," she said. Then, she drained her drink.

* * *

She tried another candle the next morning, only to find it melted wrong. At dinner, things were much the same. Regina sat, moving rice around on her plate, trying not to show her disappointment at the happiness between Violet and Tillie.

"I got everything to make waffles in the morning," Violet said. "Just like Mom used to."

Regina blinked a few times as her sister's words sank in. She glanced at the wall calendar hanging from the side of cabinet, and the date stared back at her. Tomorrow was October thirteenth. With everything that had happened, she'd almost forgotten the anniversary of her parents' deaths.

She pressed a hand to her chest, taking pause at all the pain she'd felt over the past few days. Her fear over losing her sister had shadowed every waking moment. She wondered if she'd had it wrong. If it had simply been her grief sneaking up on her and finding a new way to express itself.

"Do you want me to take off work tomorrow?" Violet asked. "I could stay home. We could play a few games of backgammon out by the bees. Drink a Manhattan before noon."

"I can pick up lunch at the diner on my break," Tillie offered.

The sound of Tillie's voice snapped Regina out of the moment.

"I'll be fine," Regina said. "It's been thirteen years."

"That doesn't mean the pain's gone," Violet said gently.

"No," Regina agreed. "But I've learned to live with it."

Violet made the same breakfast every year to mark their parents' deaths, and every year Regina found comfort that she didn't have to live with this grief alone. But now, as Tillie wrapped an arm around Violet, Regina realized for the first time that she *was* alone, and if things continued this way, it would never be just her and Violet again.

After dinner, Regina had gone straight for the attic and lit her fourth and final taper. As the flame blew toward one side, the wax dripped off the edge while the rest of the candle remained unaffected by the heat. She started to wonder if somehow she'd done something wrong while dipping them. But, no, that wasn't possible. If there was one thing Regina excelled at, it was magic.

Only Violet was better, simply because she was older. As a Caldwell aged, her magic grew stronger. That was when the realization hit her. If her own magic wasn't working, it must be because Violet was countering her spells. Regina thought she'd been so careful. She welcomed Tillie in after she learned the truth. She made them dinner. She suggested they all spend time together.

She played back the last few days in her mind. She'd let slip about the candles she'd made to keep men away from Violet, but that shouldn't have mattered. Her sister had always trusted her, had always believed Regina only wanted the very best for her. And that was true. Every spell Regina had cast on her sister's behalf had been for her own good. For her own happiness. Violet might have thought she was in love with Tillie, but she'd never find the sort of happiness in love that she would find in a life spent with her sister.

If Violet truly was countering Regina's magic, there was little Regina could do about it. Her sister had left Regina with only one choice: She had to find another way to get rid of Tillie.

Part VII
The Seven of Swords

Suggests a need for resourcefulness and strategy. May point to deception.

Chapter Twenty-Eight

Florence, Now

When Florence and Owen got back to the bookshop, there was already a hot pot of tea waiting for them. Florence immediately went to it and poured herself a cup, trying to center herself. As much as she'd come to fear her own magic, the day's events made it clear that giving up her power had been for nothing. If they wanted answers, the cards were the only hope they had.

"I can't believe I'm actually going to do this," Florence said. "But we're out of options."

"Unless the shop has some way to let us look into the past," Owen said.

"It used to be Grey's Gifts, but that was before it became like a home to me—before it came to life," Florence said. "It's possible the woman who sold me the shop still has something from back then. It's a long shot, but it's worth a—"

Before Florence could finish her sentence, the lights flickered off, plunging her and Owen into darkness. Florence yelped and stepped a little closer to him until their shoulders touched. The bulbs came back to life a few moments later. Neither of them stepped apart.

"What was that about?" Florence asked.

The coffee table began to shake. In the middle of it sat an ordinary candle—the sort they sold at the home décor store just a few shops down the block—and beside it, a book of matches.

"That wasn't there before, was it?" Owen asked.

Florence shook her head. "You want me to light this?"

The bulbs glowed brighter.

Florence sat down on the couch and stared at the wax. It wasn't a spell candle, so there was no danger in it. And she *had* come back to the shop for the sole purpose of a tarot reading. Still, the thought of setting wick to flame sent a burst of fear through her.

Owen sat beside her.

"Lighting this candle will help us somehow?" she asked.

Beneath her, the sofa gave an impatient shake, threatening to tip her into Owen once more.

"Alright, alright." Florence picked up the matches, her hand unsteady.

"Do you want me to light it?" Owen asked gently.

"Would you?"

When she gave him the matches, their fingertips brushed for just a moment. Their eyes met, and Florence almost gripped his hand and held him there. Instead, she let go.

Then, Owen struck a match.

As soon as he lit the candle, an unnatural breeze blew through the room, putting out the flame and sending up tendrils of smoke from the still-red wick until the wisps coalesced into shapes. As a picture began to unfold, unfamiliar voices filled the room, and Florence watched the past play out before her.

Chapter Twenty-Nine

Regina, 1960

On the anniversary of her parents' death, Regina road her bicycle down a side road that provided alleyway access to the Main Street businesses. She needed to go to Grey's Gifts, and she needed to do it without her sister seeing.

Like his sister, Joshua Grey worked at the shop. While Tillie oversaw the sales floor alongside her mother, Joshua managed inventory and shipments, which meant he could often be found at the loading dock or in the small office at the back of the store. There was no guarantee he would be there, but Regina had burned a gold candle for luck before leaving the house. She had no doubt she'd find him exactly where she needed him.

Regina leaned her bike against the brick wall and pulled off her leather gloves. Then she started up the back steps. When she reached the door, she pressed the button next to a sign that read *Ring bell for deliveries.*

She stepped back and waited. A few moments later, a man with a stunning likeness to Tillie stood in the doorframe. He had the same mousy brown hair and piercing honey eyes. But where Tillie only had an inch on Regina's five-foot-four, Joshua towered over her—well over six feet tall. Regina squared her shoulders and crossed her arms. Were anyone watching the two of them, they would've sworn Regina was the one looking down at Joshua, not the other way around.

"Regina," Joshua said, a softness to his voice. "Violet's out front, why did you—"

"I'm not here to see my sister." Regina cut him short with a certain urgency in her clipped and whispered words. "We need to talk."

Joshua's thick eyebrows rose on his forehead. He grabbed a nearby brick and wedged it in the door, then gestured for Regina to lead the way down the steps. He followed her into the loading area.

"What's this about?" he asked.

The most Regina ever said to Joshua since her parents' deaths was a professional hello the few times they'd run into each other in town or when Violet had called asking her to drop off candles she'd left at home.

"Violet and Tillie." Regina paused, weighing her words. As soon as she outed them, there was no going back. Regina wanted nothing for her sister as much as she wanted her happiness. For a moment she wondered if Tillie could bring joy into Violet's life in a way Regina couldn't. But, no. It had always been the two of them, and that had always been enough.

Regina took a quick look around them, but the alley was empty. Still, she lowered her voice further and gestured for Joshua to come closer. He bent over, dipping his head so she could whisper into his ear.

"They're not just roommates."

Joshua's eyes narrowed, and the doubt Regina had about telling her sisters' secret melted away. She was right. This was exactly what she needed to get Tillie out of their lives for good. When he didn't respond, Regina continued.

"I don't think anyone else knows," Regina said. "But with them living together in our house, it's only a matter of time."

Joshua straightened as he looked Regina over. "Are you threatening my sister?"

Regina's eyes widened. She forced an innocence into them that she didn't feel. Unfortunately, her voice betrayed her. "Not any more than I'm threatening my own."

"I see." Joshua's voice was both protective and sad. "Violet told me they'd be safe with you."

As Regina processed his words, something cold wound its way around her heart. She'd been so certain Tillie's family didn't approve of two women in love—why else would Tillie have needed to hide away at Honeysuckle House?

"I'm worried what would happen if word got out," she said.

"And how exactly would word get out?" Joshua asked.

"They live together. It would only take the wrong person to question that, which is why you need to convince your sister to leave. What they're doing is dangerous."

"No one has any way of knowing what goes on behind those walls unless someone were to tell them," Joshua said, an underlying accusation in his words.

Regina placed a hand on her hip and tapped her foot against the pavement. Charming people had never been her area of expertise. That had always been Violet's talent. Regina never saw a need for it, not when she could get what she wanted with magic. It was why she'd burned the candle this morning. This conversation should've been going differently, but it seemed whatever magic her sister had done to counter Regina's was more encompassing than she anticipated.

But Joshua didn't know that.

"I don't think I've been quite clear in my meaning." Regina's voice took on a sharper edge. Her eyes narrowed, and she imagined herself every bit like the wicked witches she'd read about in fairy tales. "You need to get your sister out of my home."

Joshua took a step back, and Regina smirked, satisfied by the fear in his eyes.

"I see," he said.

"I certainly hope you do."

Chapter Thirty

Violet, 1960

Violet stood out front at Grey's rearranging one of the candle displays when Joshua came in from the back, flipped the sign to closed, and locked the door.

"Is it already five?" Tillie asked as she glanced down at her watch.

Violet had known Joshua as long as she'd known Tillie. He was the first person they told about their relationship, not because Tillie had unflinching trust in him, which she did, but because he brought it up. His kindness and excitement mixed with the protective way he had looked over his shoulder to make sure they weren't overheard had endeared him to Violet.

The way he moved now, quick and precise, and the stormy look in his eyes—so much like his sister's when something worried her—had Violet on edge.

"Joshua," Violet asked, "what's wrong?"

At the same time, Tillie said, "I think my watch stopped." She looked up from her wrist, eyes flitting between Violet and her brother. Slowly, she dropped her arm to her side.

"It isn't five o'clock, is it?" she asked.

"Your sister just left," Joshua said.

Violet glanced out the front window. "I didn't see her."

"She came through the back. To see me."

Violet and Tillie shared a look.

Joshua ran a hand through his hair. "She told me about the two of you."

Violet held a hand over her mouth.

"She wants you out of her house," he said to his sister. "She threatened your safety."

Violet closed her eyes and rubbed at the space between her eyebrows. She'd heard from her own sister's mouth that she'd cast spells on Violet. Though Violet had dipped candles to protect herself and Tillie, she didn't want to believe it was true, that any of it was necessary.

Part of her wondered if it was her fault. Had she been more like their mother, more prepared to raise a thirteen-year-old girl, maybe Regina wouldn't have turned out this way. Their mother had only ever taught them kindness. She'd fostered their magic within the gentle warmth of her love, making certain to remind them every spell ought to leave the world better than they found it.

Violet had done her best to hang on to her mother's teachings after the accident, to make up for the lost love of their parents. She never pushed Regina to make friends or go out with boys from school or venture far from Honeysuckle House. She'd made Regina dependent on her, then she'd taken that stability away.

Tears stung Violet's eyes. She leaned her head back and tried to will them away as a small hand slipped into hers. Her eyelids fluttered open. Tillie stood beside her.

"This isn't your fault," Tillie said.

A choked cry caught in Violet's throat.

"If I'd told her sooner . . ."

"It would've been the same," Tillie said. "Her candles . . ."

Violet squeezed her hand.

"Maybe there's some sort of magic you could cast to keep her from telling people," Joshua suggested.

Violet never used her magic to control a person. Yes, she'd countered her sister's spells, but her words? Her autonomy? But with Tillie's safety at stake, that might have to change.

"No," Tillie said. "You can't keep that up forever. We'd never be able to live our lives the way we want to."

"You could leave," Joshua said. He, too, had tears in his eyes.

"And go where?" Violet asked.

"Maybe he's right," Tillie said. "We could travel north, to a big city. Find somewhere to lose ourselves."

But Violet wasn't ready to give up her home.

"She doesn't get to win," Violet said. "I'm going to talk to her."

"And if that doesn't work?" Tillie asked.

"Then I'll do what your brother suggested," Violet said. "If Regina came here, it was a last resort. She always turns to her magic first."

"Our candles," Tillie said.

Violet nodded. "Regina's magic isn't as strong as mine. If she's not willing to change, then she's the one who has to leave. Not us."

"I don't want you to have to fight her for the rest of our lives," Tillie said.

"Whether we stay or go, Regina won't give up," Violet said. "Not unless I make her."

Chapter Thirty-One

Florence, Now

The smoke and sound faded, leaving Florence and Owen in the quiet of the bookshop, staring at the space where they'd witnessed Regina's betrayal unfold. Florence blinked a few times as she tried to parse what they'd seen. She didn't even know the shop could communicate to her through smoke—Honeysuckle House certainly never had.

She tilted her head back and looked up at the string lights. "Did you see this happen?"

The lights brightened.

"But you weren't mine yet." Those conversations happened long before Florence's magic had brought the shop to life. None of it made sense.

She lifted Ink from her lap and stood before walking over to the wall and placing her hand on it. There was still so much Florence didn't know about her magic, so many things her mother had never taught her that she and Evie were forced to piece together themselves.

Owen followed a few steps behind. "I'm no witch, but I've always thought places held memories."

Again, the lights brightened.

Florence laughed softly then leaned her forehead against the wall. "You surprise me every day, shop."

"If the shop was able to show us what it's seen, does this mean Honeysuckle House could show us what happened there?" Owen asked. "To your great-grandparents?"

Florence opened her eyes and turned back around to face him as his words sank in. The house had heard her and Evie discuss the curse at length after their father's death. Not once did it reveal a single moment of their ancestors' past or even present a photo the way the shop had.

"I think so," Florence said. "But it hasn't . . ."

"Ink & Pages didn't until you asked," Owen said with hope in his voice.

It was a fair point, but asking Honeysuckle House meant going to Honeysuckle House, something Florence was still unable to do.

"Let's try tarot first," she said. "Do you have a deck? I had Angela take my cards so I wouldn't be tempted to use them."

As she said the words, a thud came from behind the couch once more. Ink leapt off the sofa and went in search of the sound. Florence followed, and when she reached him, she found the shattered glass from earlier was gone. In its place sat a wooden box—the same one the shop had pulled from Honeysuckle House that morning. Ink rubbed his back along the side of it.

Florence glanced up with a small smile. Though she had let few people into her life over the past thirteen years, the shop had always been there. It knew her almost as well as she knew herself, but nothing it did was ever simple. Yes, it had called Florence's cards to her so she might find a friend—or something more—in Owen, but it also knew she would need them.

When she bent down to pick up the box, fear flickered in her heart. For so many years she'd avoided her magic, afraid that even laying a finger on a tarot card would be enough to tip the balance and put her family in danger. She still didn't quite know what to make of the last reading she'd done. The hierophant reversed, the hermit, temperance reversed. She'd been so certain what the cards meant, but if her suspicions were right, then neither Florence nor Evie had read them correctly.

Gently, she picked up the box, the worn wood familiar beneath her fingers. She traced the honeysuckle vine carved into the front, and a soft sort of sadness settled over her. She stood and made her way back to the couch, cradling the box between both hands. When she sat back down, she stared at it for a few moments before, slowly, she lifted the lid, revealing the green card backs. It had been so long since she'd touched them, since she'd sought solace and answers and insight from the magic inside herself. She tipped the cards out of the box and felt the weight of them in her hands. She flipped the first card, expecting to find the tower where Owen had left it but was instead greeted by the magician. She tapped a finger against it before incorporating it back into the deck. It seemed someone had used her cards.

Then, she started to shuffle. The way the cards moved, it was as if she'd never stopped reading them. With each swish of paper, power sparked in her heart like the first strike of a match, until her whole body buzzed with it. She spread the cards in an arc on the table in front of her.

Once she finished, she looked up to find Owen watching her with the hint of a smile. She forced herself to look back down.

Florence used to turn to the cards daily, her own sort of introspection, a ritual tying her to the world around her. With her magic, tarot showed her what she most needed to see and, when asked, provided insight into what was to come. If her power could pull the future from a deck of cards, could it also connect her to the past?

"I need to know more about what happened to my great-grandparents. I need to understand how the curse started. Where should we look?" As the question left her lips, her magic curled around her heart, all heat and smoke and flame. She gasped at the feeling of it. It had been so long since she'd experienced its warmth that she'd almost forgotten how it felt. She held her hand over the cards moving slowly from one end of the arc to the other, but nothing happened.

She flipped her palm over and stared at it, the warmth in her chest flickering as if about to go out. Her throat tightened. Had she waited too long? Had her magic given up on her because *she* had given up on it?

"What's wrong?" Owen asked.

Florence glanced his way. "It's not working."

"Has that ever happened before?"

She started to shake her head, when she remembered how her protection candles had come out all wrong thirteen years ago. "Right before my mother died. It must have something to do with the curse." Which meant it wasn't her at all. Despite their erratic magic, she and Evie had managed to make the candles. They'd just had to put more energy and more focus into the process.

She closed her eyes, shook out her hand, and tried again. There! A tingle as the warmth made its way down her arm and into her palm. She flipped the card to find four candles in four corners.

"The four of wands," Owen said.

It was the same card he had drawn for her that morning.

The message was clear.

"We have to go to Honeysuckle House." After her failed attempt that afternoon, she didn't think she'd be able to do it on her own. "I'm going to need your help."

"To go to your sister's house?" Owen asked.

Florence took a sip of her tea, stalling. Talking about her past, about the way it still had its claws in her life, was something she didn't do with anyone but Angela. And while she didn't owe him a reason for needing his help with this, Florence found something inside of her wanted to open up to Owen.

"I can't drive there on my own," she said. "I've tried. I never make it past the last bend in the road without a panic attack."

"Oh, Florence," Owen said softly. "I'm so sorry."

She waved a hand, trying her best not to feel anything, but shame crept in. "It's been almost thirteen years—I should be able to go back there."

"Is it because your mom and dad died in the house?"

"The curse almost took me thirteen years ago instead of my mother." She could've left it at that. It would've been enough, but it wasn't the full truth. "But before that, a lot of horrible things happened to me there. My mom was a difficult person."

That was letting Linda Caldwell off too easy. Florence had no reason to protect her, not now.

"That's understating it, actually. My mother was abusive. Emotionally and physically and magically." As she spoke the words, her anger shifted into something both softer and sharper. Her heart clenched, and her throat tightened. She brought a hand to her cheek and found herself crying.

"Sorry," she said. "I wasn't planning to go into my past."

"Don't apologize," Owen said. "I'm here to listen, if you want to talk."

To Florence's surprise, she found she did.

Part VIII
The Four of Wands

Represents celebration and completion. May point to some sort of homecoming.

Chapter Thirty-Two

Evie, Now

The morning after the fire, Evie left Clara with Angela. They stood outside on the steps of Angela's two-bedroom Craftsman, Clara insisting Evie bring her along to check on the house. Evie hadn't made it very far in her grandmother's journal, not after what happened between her and Angela—a thought that sent heat all through her. Though she was tempted to spend the day reading, she had a meeting with the fire remediation expert. More than that, she wanted to prepare the binding spell. But if she was going to find a way to make it work—and a way to do it without harming the house in the process—she couldn't have Clara hanging around.

"It's been alone all night," Clara said, throwing up her hands. "It needs me."

"You'll get to check on it soon, honeybee," Evie said. "But if the damage is worse than we thought, I need to make sure you're safe."

Clara crossed her arms and frowned.

"You can play with Ink when we get to the bookstore," Angela reminded her.

"Ink!" A smile spread across Clara's face. Then it disappeared just as quickly, as if she couldn't decide between her desire to hold the kitten and her worry over the house. "But how are we going to bind the curse together if I don't go with you?"

Evie hated lying to her daughter. She'd followed along with Clara's idea that the spell had been meant to bind the curse only because she was afraid of what the house would do if it knew her plans. But if she told Clara the truth, Evie had no doubt Clara would want to be there, and Evie wouldn't risk her safety.

"Your mom isn't going to do the spell today," Angela said, shooting Evie a meaningful look, one filled with love and worry. Evie reached for her hand and gave it a squeeze, then she knelt down beside Clara.

"We're going to take things one step at a time," Evie said. "But right now, you need to make sure Aunt Florence is taking care of the cat you conjured for her."

"Yes, well, he might need another friend," Clara said. "Will you tell the house I'm worried about it and I love it and I'll be home soon?"

"Of—" Evie started, but Clara cut her short.

"And give it a hug from me? The second porch column on the left. It likes hugs there the best. Oh, and give it this." She produced a small black pebble from her pocket, one of the many she'd gathered at the creek earlier that week.

"Isn't that your favorite?" Angela asked.

Clara nodded gravely. "This way the house will know I'm coming back."

* * *

Evie's meeting didn't last long. The damage was superficial, not enough to warrant closing the bed and breakfast, but she would still be able to get her insurance to cover the cost to tear down the burned wall and repair the damage if the house didn't end up taking care of it on its own. With the exception of a few flickering lights and creaking floorboards, Honeysuckle House had mostly behaved through the whole process. When it was done, Evie had thanked the man and sent him on his way.

Then she turned her attention to more pressing matters.

She still hadn't fully puzzled out the spell, but that didn't mean she couldn't get her preparations underway. She'd always trusted her magic and intuition to guide her, so if she made the candles, then perhaps that would be enough.

She set up her double boilers and got to work. Normally, she talked through her spells aloud with the house as company. But she couldn't let it know she planned to bind it.

"With the curse coming, we'll need extra protection," she said while the water heated. "And after the fire, I want to make sure you're safe, too, so I think we'll do a black candle and a brown candle." Though her grandmother's spell had lacked the brown candle, she opted to follow her mother's work instead, assuming her mother had been building on what hadn't worked for her grandmother.

Before she put the wax in to melt, a slip of paper fell from the ceiling, floating slowly until it landed beside Evie, face down. An old photograph. She flipped it over to find herself and Florence standing side by side in front of Honeysuckle House on Evie's eighteenth birthday. The day they finally escaped their mother.

Evie's throat grew hot with the memory, and tears pooled in her eyes. She quickly brushed them away.

"I'm not bringing Florence into this," Evie said. "She made it perfectly clear she wants nothing to do with the curse or you or any of us."

The flames on the stove turned off, and Evie sighed.

"You have made your point," she said. "You and Angela both." Evie didn't blame either of them. She wanted Florence there, too. She'd wanted her there for years—the two of them, together, putting an end to their family's tragedies and building a new life.

She turned the knobs to bring the flame back, but the starter wouldn't click.

"I thought you wouldn't want to be alone after the fire," Evie said. "But if you won't let me do this, I'll pack up and dip these candles at Angela's."

The walls shifted like a sigh, and the burner came to life. At first, the flame was small, then it flared bright and hot, coming around the side of the pot and threatening to singe Evie's shirt.

"Too much!" Evie said. The walls shook a little before the flames went back to where Evie wanted them. "Much better, thank you."

Evie wanted to tell the house she was trying to save it, but she didn't know if she could trust it. And if it came down to it—if she had to choose between the house and Clara—she knew what choice she would make.

Instead, she said, "Thank you."

Once the wax melted, she poured enough black dye into the first pot for one candle. With her weights tied to both ends of the string, she dipped one side in the darkened wax. She thought of the temperance card in her mother's spell. A call for balance. She wanted to remove whatever malevolence her mother had discovered in the house, the magic that caused it to hurt instead of help. If she could redirect it somehow, tip the scales in favor of good, perhaps it would be enough.

"An offering," she whispered, more breath than words, thinking about everyone she wanted to protect from the curse—her daughter, her sister, Honeysuckle House. Then, her mind stuck on Angela. Memories from the night before brought heat into her cheeks. "Please let this work."

The familiar spark of magic in her heart flickered erratically, like a match that wouldn't light, and she couldn't seem to direct it into the wick. She lifted the string from the boiler to find not even a drop of wax had clung to the cotton.

She brushed an errant lock of hair out of her eyes with the back of her free hand and huffed a breath. "I told you I'd leave if you didn't let me do this."

The stove creaked in response, low and sad.

"This isn't you?"

The window opened then closed.

Evie narrowed her eyes. The curse, then. That would make completing this spell more difficult, but Evie wasn't going to give up.

After her fourth try, her intention took hold. With each dip of the wick, her power went into the candle. It took longer than she expected, and the wax bubbled in some places, but the first candle was complete.

On the other side of the wick, she dipped the brown candle. This one, too, took time. But after a few tries, her magic flowed from her heart to her fingertips and into the wax. "For Honeysuckle House," she whispered, loud enough to pass her lips but not loud enough to be heard.

"May my magic be good, my loved ones be safe, and my work be a blessing." The words brought tears to her eyes. She'd said them with every spell since her mother's death, each time hoping her benevolence would undo the work of the Caldwell family curse, never realizing the problem may lay in the house itself, not her family. But as far as Evie was concerned, Honeysuckle House was family, too, and she'd do whatever she could to fix it.

Chapter Thirty-Three

Florence, Now

Florence and Owen talked late into the night, and at some point they both drifted off to sleep on the couch. When Florence woke, it was to the smell of freshly brewed coffee and sunlight streaming through a window that didn't exist on the outside of the building.

She opened her eyes to find herself lying against Owen's chest, his arm over her, a cozy blanket thrown over them both, her glasses askew. She nestled into him and found he smelled of woodsmoke and honey. She smiled softly and almost closed her eyes again, when she realized how close to him she was.

She sat up, fast, and fell off the couch.

"Are you okay?" Owen rubbed the sleep from his eyes. When they landed on Florence, they widened as he realized where she'd been.

"I'm sorry," she said.

"No, I'm sorry," he said. "We must've fallen asleep and . . ." He shook his head. "I should've offered you the bed."

Behind them, Ink lay in the middle of said bed, curled up in a ball.

Owen stood and offered Florence a hand. She looked up at it, considered not taking it, then realized she was already in much too deep for that to make any difference. Owen helped her to her feet, then looked around the room.

"When did you make coffee?" It was clear from the furrow of his brow he was trying to piece together if Florence had gotten up, brewed coffee, then slipped back under his arm.

"I didn't," she said.

Understanding dawned in his eyes. "The shop."

Florence nodded.

"Thank you," Owen said, a little too loud.

"It can hear you just fine," Florence said.

He ducked his head and laughed. "Let me try again," he said. "Thank you."

The lamps glowed a bit brighter, and Owen's eyes glowed right along with them. He headed over to the kitchenette.

Meanwhile, Ink stood up from his spot on the bed and did a long, slow stretch. Then, he hopped down, trotted over to Florence, and started meowing at her feet. She bent down to pick him up before he could claw his way up her skirt.

"Coffee?" Owen asked.

"Please," Florence said, still unsure how she'd ended up in this room with a man she wouldn't even let herself look at for longer than a few seconds for fear she might cause his untimely death.

Owen poured two cups of coffee and brought them over. He eyed the couch with color in his cheeks before he offered one to Florence without sitting down. She, too, avoided the couch. Instead, she set Ink on her shoulder and took the coffee from Owen.

"I'm going to take this upstairs and get changed. Then we can head over to the house."

"I need to grab some clothes out of my car," Owen said.

Rather than think about Owen changing his clothes, Florence took a sip of coffee on her way to the door. When she pulled it open, she found Angela and her niece standing on the other side.

"Florence?" Angela asked.

"Angela!" Florence said, her throat growing hot. She tried to shut the door behind her, but it was too late. Owen took up the full frame, and there was no way she could hide him.

"Owen?" Angela asked.

"Angela," Owen said with a small smile.

"You're the reason I couldn't get into my reading room!" Clara crossed her arms.

Florence held out the kitten as a peace offering, and her niece readily accepted him.

"Isn't that what you were wearing yesterday?" Angela asked.

"It is," Florence said.

Angela's eyebrows shot high on her forehead. Her lips curved up in a smile that quickly disappeared. "But the curse . . ."

"You don't have to tell me," Florence said.

"I will not be going to Honeysuckle House on the thirteenth," Owen said.

"What about the festival?" Clara asked at the same time Angela said, "Have you told Evie?"

"I'm hoping to talk your mother out of the festival," Florence said.

"How?" Clara asked as she buried her face in Ink's fur.

"We'll explain it all soon," Florence said. "But right now, we're headed to Honeysuckle House."

"You're actually going over there?" Though there was surprise in Angela's voice, she nodded, as if she was relieved.

"With Owen's help," Florence said. "I tried yesterday, after you texted me."

Angela took Florence's hand. "You could've called me."

But Florence shook her head. "Evie needed you."

"And now she needs you," Angela said.

"And me!" Clara said.

Angela rested a hand on Clara's shoulder. "I think this is something Florence has to do on her own."

* * *

Florence traded yesterday's skirt and sweater for jeans and a long-sleeved T-shirt. She undid her braid and replaited her hair into twin pigtails, one of which she tucked behind her ear as she and Owen followed the familiar road to Honeysuckle House. She leaned forward in the seat, her hands on her thighs. Each turn of the tires over pavement made her heart race a little faster.

"You okay?" Owen asked as they left the town center behind.

"Not in the slightest." Her legs shook.

"Do you want me to pull over?"

"The only way I'm going to be able to do this is if you do it for me."

"Maybe it would help if you closed your eyes," he suggested.

Florence glanced sidelong at him. She couldn't quite parse how she'd gone from avoiding this man to putting her panic attack in his hands. After his tarot pull, she'd planned to do everything she could to make sure whatever the cards meant, they didn't involve her. Now she was sitting in the passenger seat of his truck, entrusting him with some of most shattered pieces of her heart.

As they approached the familiar curve in the road, Florence braced herself with her hands on the dash, her breath coming out staccato. Her eyes started to spot over. Owen reached a hand across the space between them and gripped her scarred forearm gently.

"Close your eyes," he whispered.

Florence listened. She pressed her eyelids shut so tightly white burst across her vision. She dropped her hands from the dash, letting Owen thread his fingers through hers.

"Count your breaths," Owen said. "One."

Florence inhaled.

"Two."

Florence exhaled.

"Three." In.

"Four." Out.

The truck slowed to a stop.

"Open your eyes," he said.

Florence leaned back in the seat and slowly fluttered her eyelids open. Honeysuckle House stood before her. She gasped at the sight of the leaves littering the yard and the honeysuckle circling the columns beneath the front porch. Walls that once gleamed softly in the sun now absorbed the light instead of radiating it. Her breath caught in her throat, and when she finally managed to release it, it came out as a sob.

Sitting there in the car, a pang of loss and nostalgia hit Florence square in the chest. If she closed her eyes, she could remember the light in her father's smile when she brought him a fistful of chrysanthemums, their petals wet from the first fall rain. She could feel the warmth coming off a hot pot of wax as she dipped the wick for a candle all her own. She could hear Evie chasing her across the wraparound porch, their laughter strong and bright and pure until the moment they ran into their mother's potted herbs, sending the terracotta tumbling.

That, of course, brought the rest of the memories—the after. Because in the Caldwell house, there was always an after.

A flower patch razed as a reminder only her mother could take from that which she'd planted. The sensation of hot wax on skin, a punishment for making a candle not meant for her mother's magic. The mended pots stained red and the resulting scars from gluing them all back together under her mother's watchful eye. No gloves, no help, only blood and tears and lessons learned. When her father saw her ravaged fingers, she knew better than to tell him the truth of what happened.

But in every memory, the house had been on her side. Windows whispering hello through fluttering curtains. Floorboards creaking with love, always ready to catch her footfalls. Honeysuckle locking her away safely when she needed it most. She hoped it would help her again now and show her what she was missing about her family's past.

She reached for the truck's door handle to find Owen already on the other side of it.

"You're very good at this," she said.

"I dated a guy in my twenties who had complex PTSD," he said. "I'm sorry this place does this to you."

Florence blinked up at him as his words sunk in. She'd never thought her inability to come home was a result of trauma—that was for people who survived sexual assault or mass shootings or war. A single incident that changed your life forever. What had happened to her wasn't one moment of darkness, one act that separated Florence's life between before and after. It came in minutes and hours and days. One moment, her mother would tell her the world was a better place because she was in it, the next that her family would be better off without her—if only the curse had taken Florence instead of her father or her grandmother. It was the shift from a tender brushing of Florence's hair to a sharp tug, making Florence's eyes sting. It was a warm cup of chamomile to help Florence sleep, offered with love in her mother's eyes, then the hot water pouring down her throat as Linda pushed the cup into her face after her first sip.

Of course it was trauma.

She held her hand over her mouth and blinked back tears.

"Florence?" Owen asked.

"I never realized it was PTSD. I thought . . ." She shook her head, not sure what she thought. That the memories were too much. That she wasn't strong enough. That she was broken beyond repair, and somehow she was to blame. But if it was trauma, then it wasn't her fault at all.

"You still want to do this?" Owen asked.

"I have to," Florence said.

He offered her a hand. She placed her palm in his and let him pull her to her feet. As soon as she stepped on her family's land, the vines around the porch railings trembled then grew, extending past the front steps, crawling across the freshly fallen leaves, and stopping at her feet. Florence almost jumped back at their approach. Flowers tilted up at her like little faces. They rose higher, but when they reached out to touch her, Florence pulled away. The vine drooped, then turned back the way it had come, guiding her to the house.

She placed her foot on the first step. The front door creaked open, the hallway light soft and warm on the other side. Despite her fear, despite what she had to do, she placed a hand on the nearby column and pressed her forehead to the wood. She stood that way for a few seconds, just her and the house and Owen, wishing more than anything this could be a safe place once more. Not only for her, but for every person she might someday let into her heart. Tears spilled down her cheeks. Beneath her feet, the floorboards shifted, lifting her a bit higher and pushing her closer to the column.

She turned to Owen. "Thank you. I didn't think I'd ever be able to make it back here."

"I'm sorry it had to be for this," he said.

The door opened wider, and Florence bit her lip to keep herself from crying any more than she already was. It didn't work.

She leaned her head back so she could see Owen better. She hadn't realized how close they were standing, and in the light spilling through the open door, she could see that gray speckled his beard and honey threaded through the brown of his eyes. She still feared for him, still worried the curse might find a way to take him, but now that she'd let her heart open to him—now that he'd seen the truth of it and somehow showed it to her—she found she felt safe standing beside him.

She took his other hand and gripped it softly.

"I have to do this next part alone," she said, a tremor in her voice. "I know your great-aunt died here, but this is between me and Evie."

"I'll wait out here until you need me."

"You don't have to do that," Florence said. "I don't know how long I'll be."

"I'll go check on the bees," he said. "Start getting things ready for your sister—since I won't be here for the festival."

Florence released his hands and turned toward the front door. She squared her shoulders and, with a deep breath, crossed over the threshold.

She took a halting step and stopped, one hand on the banister. It warmed beneath her touch. She rubbed the wood gently and reminded herself while her memories were true and awful, they were in the past. Florence was in the present moment. Her mom was gone, and the woman wouldn't ever be able to speak a harsh word or lay a heavy hand on her again. The thought brought a weight to her chest, a mixture of sadness and relief. She'd lost so much time because of what her mother had done. But those days were gone. Florence was finally moving forward, and she wouldn't let her mother's decisions keep her from the people and places she loved ever again.

Chapter Thirty-Four

Evie, Now

Evie stood in the old attic room in a pair of jeans and a loose gray T-shirt; she'd pulled her hair back beneath a scarf to protect it from dust and plaster. She lifted a sledgehammer, holding it with both hands, and prepared to swing.

"You're taking a wall down?"

Evie whirled around to find her sister standing at the top of the spiral staircase. Were it any other house, she'd have heard Florence coming, but even with everything that had happened, it seemed Honeysuckle House still enjoyed surprises.

"You're here?" Evie asked, shock clear in her voice.

"I should've been here yesterday," Florence said.

"You should've," Evie agreed.

Florence opened her mouth but waited a few moments to speak. Finally, she said, "I'm here now."

She took a few steps forward until she was right next to Evie, her height forcing Evie to lean her head back to see her. Evie did her best to look like she was staring down her nose at her all the same.

Florence held a hand over her mouth as she surveyed the damage. "This room isn't how I remembered it."

"That's because there's a hole in the wall," Evie said as if it were obvious.

Florence cut her a look. "No, I mean . . ." She stepped back and turned in a slow circle. "It felt smaller the last time I was up here. I thought it was because I was older; before Mom died, I hadn't been in this room since Dad . . ." she trailed off, not finishing the sentence. "Mom must've put this up after that." She rested a hand against the damaged wall. Then, she ducked down and stepped through it.

It took Evie a few moments to process what her sister was saying. She set the sledgehammer down and followed after her. Already, Florence stood at their mother's altar, staring at the small table where Linda had done her spellwork. Evie had no memories of it. The only thing she remembered about this room were the warnings to not go in, and after that first time her mother grabbed her by the hair, Evie always listened to her sister's warnings. At least, she had when they were kids.

"You mean you knew this was here," Evie said.

"I've only been up here twice," Florence said. "Once with you."

The day their mother died.

"The answers we needed to end the curse were hiding in plain sight, and if you'd come by Honeysuckle House even once, you could've told me the room looked wrong. We could've broken this wall down and put an end to all of this. We could've been a family."

"What do you mean, the answers to end the curse were right here?" Florence asked.

This was Evie's chance to tell Florence what she found, but she didn't know if Florence would see things her way. Evie wanted to bind the darkness in the house while protecting the part of it she loved. But the house had attacked Florence thirteen years ago. Evie knew her sister had never looked at it the same way since, and if she knew what Evie had discovered, she'd want to raze Honeysuckle House to the ground.

Evie dodged Florence's question by waving a hand as if to encompass the whole room.

Florence reached for one of the crystals on the altar. "It looks like Mom was in the middle of a spell." Then, she paused and glanced back at Evie. "Wait, did you just admit you didn't break the curse with all your candles?"

"It's kind of hard to pretend otherwise," Evie said. As much as she wanted to believe her work would've broken the curse had Florence been at her side doing the same thing, the binding spell suggested neither of them had been right about that tarot reading.

Florence set the crystal down and turned back to face Evie. "Does that mean you're canceling the festival?"

"For now." Evie took a deep breath. Florence may have been gone for years, but she'd finally come home. This was their chance to work together. Evie tried to center herself, to convince herself Florence might actually help her if she told her the truth.

"I'm so relieved," Florence said. "I thought I was going to have to drag you from here kicking and screaming so you wouldn't be in the house on the thirteenth."

Evie rolled her eyes. "I'm not a kid anymore, and we don't even know if that would keep us safe. We weren't able to leave when Dad died."

"Because *you* wouldn't leave without your necklaces," Florence said. As soon as the words left her mouth, the color drained from her face, but the damage had been done.

Evie's heart clenched, and tears welled up in her eyes.

"You think I don't blame myself for that every day?" Evie's voice cracked. "But it wasn't my fault, not really. We found ourselves back here when Mom died, too, remember?"

"Because you wanted to make sure she was alive," Florence said.

Evie crossed her arms. "Is that why you came? To blame me?"

"I came here *for* you. For us. For Clara," Florence said. "Time's running out, and my way of trying to stop this curse didn't work. I was hoping the house could show us—"

Evie cut her short. "At least you admit it."

"Maybe it would have if you'd listened to me!" Florence said.

Evie shook her head. "Maybe if *you* had been here, things would be different. But you were so afraid of us getting hurt, you couldn't see you were the one hurting us."

Florence reared back as if slapped. "Everything I did was to keep you safe."

Fear gripped Evie's chest at the familiarity of her sister's words. She shook it off, trying not to think about how much Florence looked like their mother, as she took a step forward and pointed directly at Florence. "Everything you did was to keep *you* safe so when the curse rolled around, *you* couldn't be blamed for anything going wrong."

Hurt flash across her sister's face, and though Evie felt it, too, like a knife twisting in her gut, she stood her ground.

"I tried to come yesterday. I got in the car and almost made it here before I had to pull over because of a panic attack. I did that for you. Because I knew you needed me."

"Don't try to act like you're the only one who came away from our childhood damaged. *I'm* the one Mom grabbed by the hair. It started with *me*." Evie pointed at herself, driving a finger into her own chest.

"It started long before mom put her hands on you." Florence steadied herself with one hand on the wall, and Evie wanted to throw her out then and there for trying to find comfort in the place she'd abandoned. "I protected you from that, Evie. *Me*. And if you think for one second I don't blame myself for not being there fast enough to stop Mom that day, then you don't know me at all."

"Maybe I don't," Evie said.

Florence shook her head, and when she spoke, her voice came out so soft it sounded broken. "I thought we could do this together, but I was wrong. I'm not going to let you yell at me when I'm trying to help." She stepped past Evie toward the hole in the wall.

"Fine!" Evie called after her. "Go. Run away like you always do."

Florence paused before she turned back to face her. "This time, I'm not running, Evie. You're pushing me."

Evie crossed her arms. "Maybe you deserve to be pushed."

Florence opened her mouth as if to speak, then thought better of it before she slipped through the hole and headed down the spiral staircase. Evie tried her best to ignore the house creaking its boards and rattling its pipes in protest.

She stepped up to the window and crossed her arms as she watched her sister emerge from the porch below. Florence stalked toward Owen's truck. Evie turned away from the window and lifted the sledgehammer before she approached the damaged wall.

Chapter Thirty-Five

Honeysuckle House, Now

Honeysuckle House felt the weight of each blow of sledgehammer on plaster. Could a house wince, it would've. It had wanted more than anything to stop the sisters from fighting, to enclose all their anger and fear in honeysuckle the way it had protected them when they were children. To wrap them in the soft warmth of a fall fire or a hot cup of tea.

Instead, it had been helpless to intervene. Its magic was out of control, and every ounce of the house's strength was focused on keeping anyone else from getting hurt.

As Evie tore down the wall the house had so carefully erected thirteen years ago, it tried to hold itself together, to keep her from causing any more damage beyond what Clara's spell had done. It wanted her out of that room and far away from what her mother had left behind.

Part IX
The Tower

An undoing. A breaking of foundations.

Chapter Thirty-Six

Clara, Now

Clara had never been happier to be back at Honeysuckle House. After the fire man—the man who knew about fires, not the man who fought them—had told them it was safe, Clara had begged her mom to let her come home. And while her mother wouldn't commit to a full night in the house, she did agree to let Angela bring her by that afternoon with a promise for tomato soup and grilled cheese with honey if Clara was good while she stayed with Angela at the bookshop.

And she had been good. So good Angela got her a hot cocoa from across the street and let her pick out a book.

She flipped through it now as they made the drive to Honeysuckle House. Ink—who sat in her lap because she couldn't simply leave him behind at the bookstore without any family there to take care of him—stared intently at each page.

"That can't be good." Angela said from the front seat.

Clara looked up to see Owen's truck driving toward them, her aunt in the passenger seat.

"I thought she'd still be there when we got home," Clara said. "That we'd all get to eat dinner together." She'd wanted to be the one to add honey to Aunt Florence's grilled cheese, to flip it on the frying pan and convince her to come back for sandwiches again sometime soon.

"That was the plan," Angela said.

"They started fighting again, didn't they?" Clara leaned her head back against the headrest and sighed deep and long like she'd seen her mom do every time she talked about her aunt.

"Your guess is as good as mine," Angela said.

"But what *is* your guess?" Clara asked.

Angela glanced at her in the rearview mirror. "They started fighting."

"I took Ink," Clara said. "Is Aunt Flo going to be okay without him?" The truck drove past, and Clara turned around in her seat. "Should we follow them so I can give him back to her?"

"Is that what you want to do?" Angela asked.

Clara shook her head and held Ink to her chest. "I want to see the house." She wanted *him* to see the house.

"Then I'll text her and let her know we have him," Angela said.

As Angela pulled her car up the drive, Clara pressed her hands against the back seat window and peered up at Honeysuckle House, looking for any sign it was getting worse. Ink climbed up the side of her seat and smushed his nose against the glass.

"That's our house," she told him. "It's like the bookshop, but older. I think you'll like it."

He meowed, and though she didn't speak whatever language it was cats spoke, she decided he agreed with her.

"It's been sick," she told him. "But it seems okay from out here. I won't be able to tell for sure until we're inside though."

"I think it's going to be just fine," Angela said.

But Clara wasn't so sure. The curse had the house acting all wrong, and she was afraid it might never get back to its usual self.

The car rolled to a stop. Clara unbuckled her seat belt, pushed the door open, and jumped out of the car. Ink hopped out beside her and followed her up the front porch steps. She wrapped her arms around her favorite column.

"I hope you weren't too lonely without us," she said.

The floorboards shifted beneath her feet, a gentle up and down that made Ink jump back and give a little hiss.

"Don't worry," she said. "The house is saying hello." She kept one hand on the column and dropped down into a crouch. "See?" She held out her palm to the kitten, and he took a few tentative steps forward, eyes on the planks that had moved only moments before.

He twitched his tail, then, when he was certain the porch wasn't going to move anymore, he trotted to the column and rubbed his back against it. Clara scratched between his ears and pressed a cheek to the wood.

"I missed you," she said. "Mom says everything will be back to normal soon."

Overhead, the porch light flickered.

Before Clara could ask what the house meant, Angela caught up to her.

"I'm going to go check on your mom and get started on dinner," she said. "Any special requests?"

"Extra honey, please!" Clara said. "Oh, and put aside some goat cheese for Ink. I think he'll like it." The kitten meowed, and Clara nodded. "Just as I thought."

Angela laughed lightly, then disappeared through the front door. Clara pushed herself to her feet and made to follow after her into the house when Ink squeezed through one of the railings, leapt off the porch, and started through the clover toward the workshop. She stood, torn between following after him—afraid of losing him, especially after she took him out of the bookstore—and wanting to go inside and make sure the house knew how much she loved it.

"Ink!" She called. The kitten looked back at her, twitched his tail, then continued through the yard. "We have to check on the house!" He didn't respond, intent on whatever mission he'd set off on.

One of the floorboards shifted beneath Clara, tilting her toward the edge of the porch, away from the house. She gave the railing a squeeze and said, "I'll be right back."

She ran toward the steps and chased after Ink. By the time she caught up to him, he'd reached the workshop. Clara bent down to scoop him up, but before she could, the door creaked open, and he slipped through.

Kittens, Clara decided, were a lot more work than she realized.

She followed him inside, planning to tell him as much, when the bulb brightened overhead. Ink sat back on his haunches, low to the ground, his back legs wiggling. Clara grabbed him before he could leap onto the table. He let out a small yowl, then settled into Clara's arms.

"This is where we make our candles," she told him. "This is how I brought you to us!"

He leaned his head to the side.

"Just like these here." Clara lifted him from under his front legs, bringing him close to two candles that sat drying on the rack. She, too, took a closer look. One was black and one was brown. Both were a little lopsided.

"Mom must've been in a hurry when she made these," Clara said. "Her candles are usually perfect." She set Ink on the tabletop and brought the tip of her finger to one of the candles. It gave a little bit beneath the pressure, the wax not yet set.

Ink reached a paw out toward the tapers, about to swat at them. Clara grabbed him around the belly and pulled him back. He gave a disgruntled meow.

"We can't mess with Mom's magic," she said. "Especially if she's trying to stop the curse." The thirteenth was the day after tomorrow, so there wasn't much time left to do it.

She gently deposited Ink on the ground and brought her stepping stool over in front of the stove.

"But that doesn't mean we can't give her a little help."

She turned on the double boiler and started a candle of her own.

Chapter Thirty-Seven

Florence, Now

Florence sat in the front seat of Owen's truck, fuming. After so many failed attempts, she'd finally made it home, only to have her sister drive her away. She almost asked Owen to stop and turn around so she and Evie could sort this out. But there was no point. Evie wasn't going to help her put an end to things.

"I cannot *believe* her," Florence said. "I came to fix this, to break the curse, and all she wanted to do was tell me how I failed her."

Owen tapped his hands against the steering wheel, stealing glances at Florence. "Did you ask the house about your great-grandparents?"

Florence turned back in her seat, watching the house disappear behind them. "I never had the chance. And now we have nothing."

"It's not nothing," Owen said gently. "Your shop helped us figure out where that photo was taken, and it showed us something that it thought was important enough for us to know. We just have to figure out why."

"Where the photos were taken . . ." Florence trailed off. With everything that had happened, she'd forgotten about the tie to Grey's Gifts and the idea she'd left half formed the night before. She pulled out her phone and started to dial.

"Who are you calling?" Owen asked.

"The woman who sold me the bookstore," Florence said, hope taking hold once more.

After a few moments a person picked up on the other line. "Hello? Florence?"

"Mary Louise," Florence said with a certain softness in her voice. Before she'd used her inheritance to purchase the shop, Florence had worked for the woman for almost nine years, starting as a teenager and eventually becoming a manager. She'd kept her distance these past thirteen years to protect her from the curse, but it didn't change how much Mary Louise meant to her.

"To what do I owe the pleasure?" Mary Louise asked. "Are you finally going to stop by for a game of backgammon?"

Florence could hear the smile in her voice.

"Unfortunately, this isn't a social call," Florence said.

"No worries, my dear." Sadness had crept into Mary Louise's words; Florence wished things had been different. "What do you need?"

"I know this is a long shot," Florence said, "but do you have anything from the bookstore from before your family opened up shop?"

The older woman laughed softly. "That was a long time ago. I was only twelve when my parents moved to Burdock Creek and bought it."

Florence tried to keep the disappointment from her voice as she said, "Sorry to waste your time."

"Now wait a minute. Just because I was taking a trip down memory lane, doesn't mean I can't help. I never came across anything from the owners, but I *did* receive a letter back in the 70s addressed to their son."

Florence's heart stuttered. "Is there any chance you kept it?"

* * *

Florence and Owen sat inside the sitting room of a small colonial home. Lace doilies covered almost every visible space, and a very old, very tired-looking dachshund lay snoring in the middle of the room.

A warm, elderly voice came from down the hallway along with a significant amount of rummaging. "Are you sure I can't get you something? Coffee? Tea?"

Despite Florence's efforts to hold Mary Louise at an arm's length, the woman would come in from time to time to pick up a book and drop off cookies or brownies or cake. Apparently, retirement brought with it a lot of baking.

"We're alright," Florence called. "Just in a—"

"—hurry, I know." The older woman stepped into the room with a yellowed envelope in her hands. She had silver hair that hung in a long braid down her back and eyeglasses perched on the tip of her nose. Her deep crow's feet spoke to years of laughter. "I can't believe I still have this. My husband was always trying to talk me into getting rid of my old files from the bookstore before he passed last year. 'It's been over a decade, Mary Louise. No one is going to come looking for your parents' taxes from the eighties.' Now, I'm no hoarder, mind you. But there are some parts of history that are worth holding on to."

She crossed over to Owen and held the envelope out to him. "Seeing as this letter was addressed to your grandfather—and he's no longer with us—I suppose it belongs to you."

Chapter Thirty-Eight

Violet, 1973

It had been almost thirteen years since Violet left Burdock Creek—and her sister—behind forever. Thirteen years since she lost the love of her life. Since the plans she'd so carefully set in motion fell apart, leaving her heartbroken and alone.

In that time, the lines at the corners of her eyes and along her forehead had settled in. The fullness of her cheeks had hollowed out. She'd grown her hair long and shaggy not so much in the style of Jane Fonda as a reminder of the way Tillie always wore hers full and wild and free. She'd started to go gray at her hairline, and she imagined Tillie would've said it made her look distinguished. Regina would've told her to dye it. Once, the thought would've made her laugh. Now, it was a reminder of how her sister had tried so desperately to control her.

Violet sat in the small living room of her Greenwich Village apartment, listening to an old Billie Holiday album and settling into her melancholy and grief with a freshly poured drink. She'd never found love again, not like the kind she had with Tillie. She'd tried, once or twice, managing a couple of good years with an older divorcee who had an apartment on the Upper East Side, but the weight of Violet's heartache was always too much for anyone she might start a life with. Even her magic had weakened, as if the flame in her heart had burned to an ember. Yes, the candles did their work, but in quieter ways. Where once Violet could bring in enough money for half the year with a single green taper burned, now one spell would pay her rent with only a little left over to buy a bottle of gin.

So she lent herself to helping other people who society thought didn't belong. She registered Black voters. She marched for an end to the war in Vietnam. She joined the Women's Strike for Equality and dipped candles for the Women's International Terrorist Conspiracy from Hell.

While these things brought her a sense of purpose, they were never enough to fill the hole of what she'd left behind. Selling spells had been a quiet existence—it could've been a happy one, had things turned out differently—now she offered her power freely to those in need, the double boiler on her small gas stove always warm and ready. But it would take more than a few weak candles to change a country hell-bent on maintaining a status quo built on oppression.

Still, she did what she could.

But for the past few days, none of her spells seemed to work correctly. Every candle dipped came out warped or twisted, the wax all wrong. It wouldn't cling to the wick, or if it did, the wick would get lost, and the candle couldn't be lit. With each failure, it felt like a light was going out inside of her, like she herself was the flickering flame and one gentle breeze was all it would take to snuff her out. She'd chalked it up to the approaching anniversary of Tillie's death and her own unhealed heart.

The lights softened overhead, a reminder that though Tillie was gone, Violet wasn't alone. Her magic had brought these seven hundred square feet to life, and while it was no Honeysuckle House, the apartment loved her, and that, at least, was something.

She took another sip of her drink, when the phone started to ring. She considered letting it go, ignoring whoever might need her. With how her candles had been coming out, it would probably be for the best. But the work she did was all she had. So, she set her rocks glass on the table and pushed up from her chair.

She picked up the handset and wrapped the cord around her finger.

"Violet Caldwell," she said.

There was a brief pause, a sigh. Then, a familiar voice. "It's me."

Cold crept along Violet's spine. She leaned against the wall for support, and it softened into her.

"How did you get this number?" Violet asked.

"Magic," her sister replied.

"Don't call here again." Violet set a finger on the switch and prepared to press it down, but she stopped short at what her sister said next.

"I have a daughter."

Violet's hand fell to her side as she stood shocked by this confession and her sister's hypocrisy. "So you can have a lover, but I can't?"

"There is no lover," Regina said. "There's only my child, and I'm afraid I'm going to lose her."

"If you treat her the way you treated me, that will be your own doing." Violet tried not to imagine her niece. She couldn't let herself guess at her age and wonder if she had Regina's dark hair and worry after how a child would turn out, raised by her sister's hand.

"That's not what I mean," Regina said. "Our family is cursed."

"If you mean the way you tried to tear me and Tillie apart—"

But her sister cut her short.

"No," Regina said. "Actually cursed. I realized it after you left. The whole town did. It was thirteen years to the day after our parents' deaths."

Violet narrowed her eyes. "That's not proof of a curse." But something about the word felt right. Tillie's death hadn't made sense. The police had told her bathtub drownings were rare, but they happened. A person who's too tired or had too much to drink slips below the surface of the water and doesn't come back up. But Honeysuckle House should've saved her. It should've woken her up or drained the tub or done anything other than let the water fill her lungs. It was part of the reason Violet had left that same week.

Not only had she lost Tillie, but the house she trusted had failed her. Her own spells had failed her. All of her protection candles hadn't been enough. For thirteen years, Violet wondered if her sister had found a way around them. If she'd taken Tillie's life with magic. But she had no proof, and she feared that, had she accused Regina, her sister would've made Tillie's family suffer even more.

But if there really was a curse, then Regina hadn't hurt Tillie after all. Yes, she'd tried to break them apart, and Violet didn't know if she could ever forgive her. But there might be a chance for at least some sort of peace between them.

"It takes someone we love," Regina said. "Mother and father were the first. Then your . . ." Regina trailed off.

"The love of my life?" Violet supplied.

No one spoke for a few seconds.

"Her name is Linda," Regina said. "My daughter. She has Mom's eyes and your way with the bees."

"If we're cursed, I don't know how you expect me to help," Violet said.

"I thought maybe the two of us together could break it. My magic has felt off kilter for almost a week. My candles are all wrong, and some of them won't even light."

Violet pressed a hand over her heart, where she'd felt herself fraying. She'd thought it was grief that had wormed its way into her spellwork, but if it was happening to Regina, too, there might be something else at play.

"If it was only me at risk, I wouldn't bother you," Regina said. "But it isn't. It could take Linda from me. Or me from her. Or you before you get the chance to know her."

"If it takes someone a Caldwell witch loves, I don't know how that puts me at risk," Violet said.

A sharp intake of breath came through the receiver. Violet tapped her fingernails against the wall.

"You may have left, but I still love you." Regina's voice came out slow and measured. After what she had said about the curse, it felt more like a threat than an olive branch.

"You drove me away," Violet said.

"I didn't . . . I couldn't . . ." Regina stopped. After a few seconds, she said, "You were all I had."

Violet didn't speak.

"Please," Regina said. "I can't do this without you."

Violet gently set the receiver back on the switch, cutting off the line. Then, she rested her forehead against the doorframe and started to cry.

* * *

A few hours later, Violet had given up on her Negronis and started drinking her gin straight from the bottle. She'd turned up her music, trying to drown out the memory of her sister's voice and her growing guilt. Part of her wished Regina had told her about her niece sooner. She didn't think she'd have gone back to Burdock Creek, but she could've sent gifts and postcards and things to make sure the girl didn't turn out like her mother.

If this supposed curse claimed Regina, then Violet would be the only person left to care for her. She couldn't leave her niece to fend for herself.

"It's not my responsibility," Violet said aloud as she held up the gin, prepared to take another drink. She'd started with less than a quarter of it gone, now there was less than a quarter of it left. As she brought the lip to her mouth, a whistle came from the kitchen. She lowered the bottle and narrowed her eyes.

"Are you trying to tell me I'm drinking too much?"

Her apartment had gotten in the habit of suggesting Violet switch to tea on her most melancholy nights. Normally, she ignored it. When she was deep in her grief, the last thing she wanted was a clear head.

But this time, things were different.

Her niece might not be Violet's responsibility, but she knew she'd never forgive herself if she didn't at least try to protect the girl. All these years, Violet had blamed her sister, but if what Regina said was true, then Violet had no one to blame but herself. She'd loved too deeply, and it cost Tillie her life.

As angry as she was with Regina, Violet still loved her sister. Even if a part of her wished for Regina to feel the kind of loss Violet had experienced—some sort of penance for making those last few days with Tillie a fight instead of a memory Violet could cherish—she didn't want her sister to die.

With a heavy sigh, Violet abandoned the bottle and pushed herself to her feet. The kettle whined louder.

"I'm coming."

By the time she got to the kitchen, the stove had turned off, and a fresh cup of chamomile tea sat waiting for her on her small kitchen table, right on top of her calendar. When she picked it up, there was a ring mark over the thirteenth. If Violet left by noon, after she'd slept off the gin, she might be able to make it before midnight. It wouldn't give them much time, but enough to attempt a spell.

"I don't want to go back there," Violet whispered, closing her eyes.

Tillie would've told her to trust her intuition, but Violet couldn't hear it through the gin and heartache. When she opened her eyes, she found the tarot cards Tillie had hand-painted sitting on the table.

She set the mug beside the calendar and started to shuffle.

"What will happen if I go?"

After she cut the deck, she pulled the top card. The old tree that used to stand in front of Honeysuckle House stared up at her, and Violet's heart stuttered. Across the top, one word: death.

This was where her parents' car had crashed, the first losses Violet had ever felt. Tillie had painted the card in their memory. The tree, fallen. Honeysuckle vines wrapped around its trunk.

Violet tapped a finger against the card. It could be a literal interpretation, but the death card so rarely was. Most often, it was a symbol for something ending in order to usher in a new beginning. And if her family truly was cursed, then this could portend the end of that curse. Death was only part of the way through the fool's journey, which meant there was more to come.

She drew another card.

Honeysuckle House stared up at her. This time, two women stood on the front steps, arm in arm. They each held a cup. People looked out from the windows, eight in all, each of them with a glass of their own.

The ten of cups. A card of family. A card of home. And a promise for the future.

Violet took a deep breath. The second card was all she needed. She stood and picked up the phone then dialed her sister's number. On the third ring, Regina picked up.

"Violet?"

The hope in her sister's voice almost broke her.

"I'll try to be there before midnight."

She didn't give Regina a chance to reply before hanging up. Though the ten of cups promised a future for the Caldwells, Violet couldn't ignore the warning of the first card she'd pulled. She might not be coming back from this trip, and if that was the case, Tillie's family deserved to know what Violet feared had happened the night she died.

A part of her wanted to believe her family was cursed, that Tillie's death couldn't have been prevented. Another part of her was terrified of her sister. But she couldn't leave a child in Regina's hands.

She pulled out her stationery, addressed an envelope to Tillie's brother at their old shop, and then, she started to write.

Chapter Thirty-Nine

Florence, Now

Florence and Owen took the letter back to Ink & Pages. They found the back room much the same as they'd left it earlier that day. A fresh pot of tea was waiting for them, so they sat down and pored through the pages together. They didn't just include Violet's last night alive. They detailed the days leading up to Tillie's death. Violet's arguments with Regina, the candles she and Tillie dipped. Florence found more family history in that one letter than she'd been told her whole life.

When she'd finished reading, Florence looked up from the pages, wishing she could reach through time and take her great aunt's hand. In Violet's words she'd found a different story of her family than any her mother had told her. Violet was the type of ancestor Florence wished she could've known. She imagined sitting at Violet's feet as a child, watching her dip wicks in the workshop, helping her pull the comb from the hives and prepare the wax to be melted. In that moment, her heart broke for what the curse had taken from them both.

Violet would have only been five years older than Florence was now when she penned the letter. She feared her love had cost Tillie her life. If she'd known what the curse would take from her, would she have kept her distance from Tillie the same way Florence had locked her own heart away?

"She lost so much." Florence's voice caught in her throat, and she set the pages on the coffee table.

"So have you," Owen said.

"Both of us," Florence replied.

"It's hard to think what my life would've looked like if Tillie had survived. If my family hadn't left Burdock Creek," Owen said, his eyes searching hers. "Maybe we'd have become friends."

"I think I would've liked that," she whispered.

Owen set his cup down and leaned forward to fill Florence's mug then handed it to her gently. She fought back tears at this small gesture of comfort. So few people had offered her moments like these over the past thirteen years. She didn't quite know how to respond.

"Thank you." A tear slipped down her cheek. Owen raised a hand to her face as if he was about to brush it away, but he let it drop and reached for his tea instead. They looked at each other for a few more moments, the air around them growing warm. Florence found herself leaning toward him, but when the lights in the room dimmed, she pulled back, quickly, splashing tea over the side of the cup.

They both started to laugh, and Florence shook her head. "Sorry," she said as she wiped her hands on her sleeves, then put her mind back on the pages in her lap. Her aunt's grief wouldn't help her break this curse, but maybe something else in the letter would.

"Violet thought Regina might've killed Tillie," she said. Of anything her aunt had written, that stood out to her the most.

"That surprised me, too," Owen said. "The report showed Tillie drowned in a bathtub. Could magic do that?"

It had been over a decade since Florence had worked the flame, but she knew her family's power could be used for bad as well as good. Her mother's spells were evidence enough. But to take a life? That would require more than a simple candle.

"It could," Florence said. It was the sort of magic that would have consequences—maybe even the kind that could bring about a curse. "But what about the deaths thirteen years before? And then Regina's own death thirteen years later?" Florence asked. "Even with Regina trying to tear Violet and Tillie apart, it doesn't add up."

Something else in Violet's retelling of the days leading to Tillie's death had struck Florence. She set her tea down and flipped through the pages. Then, she started to read. "The night Tillie moved in, Regina accused her of trying to take the house from her the same way her family took the shop from our parents."

Owen sat up a little straighter. "That's sounds like what we found in the police reports."

"If we hadn't gone through those, I would've thought Violet was just trying to make sense of her sister's hatred for Tillie, but maybe there's something to it."

The rest of the paragraph read:

> But the Greys paid us for the shop, and I still worked in it. At the time, I thought Regina was lost in her own grief with the anniversary of our parents' deaths looming. Now, I realize she was trying to turn me against Tillie, to keep me from having love because she was afraid of being alone.

"If Regina thought my great-grandfather killed her parents, that would give her motive," Owen said. "But she and Violet were together when Tillie drowned."

Florence pursed her lips in thought. The pieces were there, but she couldn't quite see how they fit together. "Tillie died in the bathtub—in a house where, without the curse, she should've been safe."

The Caldwell curse always took its victims at Honeysuckle House, and each death looked like an accident. Florence herself had almost been one of those victims when the honeysuckle had attacked her. But only one thing controlled the vines in her childhood home—Honeysuckle House itself.

That was when it hit her. What if they had it all wrong? What if her great-grandparents weren't the first victims of the curse at all?

She looked up at Owen. "What if the house drowned Tillie?"

The house had tried to kill Florence. It had knocked her grandmother down the stairs and crushed her mother with a chandelier and pushed her dad out the window. But it hadn't killed her great-grandparents.

She paused, a hand over her mouth as the words from the report came back to her: *Thirteen years to the day after the deaths of Helen and Christopher Caldwell.*

"Violet wasn't the only one who was there when Regina accused your family." Florence leaned back against the couch and pressed her hands to either side of her face. "Honeysuckle House would've heard her, too."

Owen turned to look at her. "You think the house killed her in retaliation?"

Even hearing the words took the wind out of her. She didn't want to believe it. It was one thing to know the house was somehow wrapped up in the curse, but for it to be the cause? For it to be a murderer? The house had attacked her once, but before that, it had been her protector, her friend, one of the only people who looked out for Florence after her father was gone.

"Helen brought the house to life," she said. "The grief of her death could've pushed it over the edge. It lost someone it loved, and so it took someone the Greys loved."

"But why does it keep happening?" Owen asked. "Violet and Regina and Linda were all Caldwells. Wouldn't the house want to keep them safe?"

"Using magic to hurt has consequences," Florence said. "I saw it with my mom throughout my whole childhood. Every time she lit a candle to control me, it twisted her. She was even worse the next time."

"The house *is* magic," Owen said with meaning.

"Maybe it killed once on the thirteenth anniversary of Helen and Christopher's deaths," Florence said, her voice a mixture of fear and loss. "And now it's doomed to kill again. Every thirteen years."

Chapter Forty

Evie, Now

Evie stood in the kitchen of Honeysuckle House as Angela made grilled cheese and Clara sat at the table playing with Florence's kitten. Though yesterday's events worried Evie, the house had been declared safe, and aside from its antics in the workshop that afternoon, it had almost felt normal. She didn't know exactly what would happen if she moved forward with her mother's binding spell tomorrow, so she wanted to give Clara—and herself—this last chance to sit with the house as she'd always known it.

"I wish Aunt Flo was here right now having dinner with us," Clara said as Angela shuffled a sandwich onto one of the many vintage plates Evie had thrifted over the years and handed it to her.

Now that Evie had cooled off a bit, part of her regretted pushing Florence away. Another part of her felt justified. All their lives Florence acted like she knew what was best for the both of them. She never paused to wonder if Evie might be just as capable as she was. After all, Evie had raised Clara, and it was Clara whose spell had led them to her mother's altar. Not that Florence knew about any of that.

"We all make our own choices," Evie said bitterly.

Angela wrapped an arm around Evie's waist and leaned her head against her side. "At least she tried."

"I'd rather she'd stayed at the shop if she was just going to come here to tell me I was wrong," Evie said.

Angela pulled back and arched her eyebrows. "You don't mean that."

"Fine," Evie admitted. "It was nice to have her here again." Even if she wished things had gone differently.

"Did you tell her about what you found?" Angela asked as she started on another sandwich.

Evie shook her head. "We started fighting before I had the chance."

"Maybe if you call her and tell her Angela is cooking, she'll come back!" Clara said over a mouthful of soup-dipped sandwich. "If it was me, I'd come. Angela makes the best grilled cheese."

"Better than mine?" Evie asked.

"Yes," Clara said. "Much better."

Evie and Angela both laughed.

"It helps that Honeysuckle House never lets it burn," Angela said.

Evie leaned against the counter beside Angela, watching her. It wasn't the first time Angela had cooked for her, but after what they'd shared the night before, the moment felt brand new. Angela looked up from the frying pan, her twists framing her face, and when she caught Evie watching, she smiled and set down the spatula. Then she grabbed Evie by the belt loops of her jeans and pulled her in for a quick kiss. Evie wanted to linger there, but Angela released her hold on her and went back to the sandwich.

"Are you two kissing now?" Clara asked.

The question filled Evie with a sort of contented warmth not even her magic had brought her. For a brief moment she forgot about the curse, and it was only her and Angela and Clara in the place Evie loved most.

Angela handed over Evie's sandwich and tilted her head to the side, a smile playing at her lips as she let Evie take the lead on how to answer Clara's question.

"We are," Evie said, keeping it simple.

Clara sighed dreamily. "Kissing's nice."

"It is," Angela agreed.

"We certainly like it," Evie said, that warmth in her chest spreading.

"Maybe one day I'll have a best friend who I want to kiss!" Clara said brightly as she tilted her head, clearly deep in thought. "But for now I have Honeysuckle House. And Ink, even though technically he's Aunt Flo's best friend."

"Maybe he can have two best friends," Evie suggested.

Beside Clara, Ink reached for her sandwich, claws sinking into the bread. She gently removed his paw before tearing off a piece and offering it to him.

"Ink likes the sandwich, too!" Clara said as he nibbled on it.

Evie took a bite of her own. "I wish the house would make my grilled cheese taste this good."

"I don't see why we can't stay here tonight," Clara said. "If it's safe enough for dinner, why isn't it safe enough to sleep here? I miss my bed."

As much as Evie wanted that, the house *had* caught fire the day before. She'd been careful not to leave any unattended flames burning today, but that didn't mean she was ready to trust the house with her daughter's safety. "With dinner, I can keep an eye on everyone," she said. "If we're sleeping, it's harder to do that."

"We could all stay in the same bed," Clara suggested. "Like a sleepover!"

Evie glanced at Angela, and they both laughed softly.

"As fun as a sleepover sounds, your mom is right," Angela said.

Clara took another bite and made a thoughtful noise. "Has the house ever done this before?"

Evie shook her head. "Not that I can remember."

"Then how do you know it's the curse making it like this?" Clara asked.

"I suppose I don't," Evie said as she sat down across from her daughter. "Not for sure." The only time the house had ever been unsafe was on a curse day—the attack on her sister, her dad falling out the window. Catching fire before the thirteenth didn't line up with the curse as she knew it. But something about it felt familiar, like the way Evie's own magic had become erratic, as if, this time, the magic that brought the house to life was affected by the curse, too.

Angela flipped the last sandwich, the oil popping as it met the hot surface of the pan. She gave it a pat with the spatula, then turned to face Evie, but the sound had drawn Evie's focus. The flames traveled up around the side of the pan, bigger than they'd been a moment ago. She tilted her head as one of the other burners came on. Then another.

Her eyes went wide, but before she could say anything, flames shot straight up from the burners, engulfing the pan. The sandwich caught fire. The pot of soup, too, started to boil. Red liquid bubbled up and spilled over the edges, dripping down the front of the oven onto the floor.

Angela stood, staring at the flames. Evie jumped up from the table and pulled her out of their path. The lights flickered on and off. Pots and pans fell from their places on the racks overhead.

Evie ran for the fire extinguisher. She struggled with the release pin as she pointed it at the stove, the flames growing higher and higher, until, finally, it came loose. She squeezed the handle. White dust covered the burners, the oven, the counter, putting out the flames. Evie grabbed a nearby hand towel and reached into the smoke. She turned the knobs, cutting off the gas.

When she turned around, she found Angela standing behind her, holding onto Clara who clutched Ink against her chest. Evie took them both by the hand and pulled them out of the kitchen, down the front stairs, and into the yard.

Once they were safe outside, Evie lifted Angela's hands, checking over her palms. "Are you hurt?"

Angela shook her head, but the color had drained from her face.

"I thought it would be safe," Evie said. "I was so certain the other fire was from Clara's spell."

"My spell." The regret in Clara's voice almost broke something inside of Evie as Clara clutched Ink tighter and looked back toward the front door.

Evie knelt down beside her. "This wasn't your magic, honeybee. This was something else. The house it's . . ." She shook her head, not quite knowing what to say. "It started before your candle."

"I should've talked you out of dinner here," Angela said, her body shaking.

"This isn't your fault, either," Evie said. "I'm the one who pushed us to come back. I was so sure after the fire didn't cause any serious damage . . ." She looked up at the turret window where just yesterday she'd watched the flames from this very spot.

Beside her, Clara slipped her hand into Angela's and leaned her head against her side. Ink hopped out of her arms and wound his way around Angela's legs.

"Don't worry," Clara said. "Mommy won't let anything happen to us."

Evie ruffled Clara's hair, but her eyes were on Angela.

"I want to believe that's true," Angela said. But she wasn't looking at Clara, either.

"It will be," Evie said. "It has to be."

* * *

That night while Clara slept with Ink curled against her chest, Evie slipped from the bedroom. She paused at Angela's door, considered opening it to see if she was still awake, to apologize again for putting her in danger. Instead, she padded down the hallway to where she'd left the journals stacked on the coffee table.

The night before she'd found almost the same spell her mother had cast in her grandmother's journal. As she reached for the diary to see what her grandmother had written about it, her eyes landed on a different one. It was from 1973, thirteen years after her grandmother's, and she started to wonder.

Had her family cast that spell every time? If so, why hadn't it worked?

She reached for the later book, flipping through the pages as she searched for anything that might resemble a list. There! A spell, just like her mother's—brown candle and all. She reached for the next journal in the stack, Regina's from 1986, the year Florence was born. It too, had the spell. Though this page had Florence's name scrawled across the top.

Evie traced her fingertip over her grandmother's writing, trying to account for the change in the spell. Had she tried to use Florence as the anchor before she was even born?

Evie plucked her mother's 1999 journal from the stack, turning page after page until she found the spell there, too. This time, Evie's name was added to the list. Her mother, it seemed, had tried to evolve the spell, too, instead using Evie as her anchor. Then thirteen years ago, she must have anchored the spell to Evie and Florence both. But even with two Caldwells, it hadn't been enough to bind the magic.

Now, though, things were different. Evie had all the spells the Caldwells before her had cast to stop the curse. More than that, Evie had Clara, which meant there were three Caldwell witches to ground the spell's magic.

She hoped it would be enough.

Part X

The Two of Cups, Reversed

A soulmate card. Points to a deep emotional bond between two people.

When reversed, it indicates a lack of trust.

Chapter Forty-One

Regina, 1986

Regina Caldwell had never been one for domesticity. Dipping candles, harvesting honey, and managing her bees, yes. But these were things witches did; these were acts of magic. She supposed there *were* witches who enjoyed setting a table or infusing intention into sweeping their entryway. With Honeysuckle House, there was no need for a broom.

All that to say, she never expected to take up crocheting.

Yet here she was at fifty-two years old, sitting on the lounge chair in her living room, alternating between rows of single and half-double stitches. No matter how many times she counted her chains, her work always came out slightly misshapen. After her fifth attempt, she gave in to the imperfections. Her granddaughter wouldn't notice them until she was much older anyway, and by then they'd feel charming rather than lazy.

Her daughter lay across their couch, one hand on her over-large belly and her feet on her husband's legs. After Regina mentioned wanting another little witch in her family, Linda had dipped and lit a couple of pink candles, and despite the town's avoidance of the Caldwells and their curse, Robert had only had eyes for Linda. They'd married a couple of months later, Linda already pregnant with a child that was due any day now.

Robert had settled into their lives like he'd always been there. While Regina had no particular love for the man, she did enjoy his passion for cooking, something neither she nor Linda had ever picked up. Besides, he'd provided Regina with a grandchild, and that was more than enough of a reason to tolerate having a man in her home for a short while.

"Are you not worried about the curse at all?" Linda asked as she sipped a cup of raspberry tea. "After it took Violet . . ."

"Aunt Violet," Regina corrected her. Though her daughter may never have had the chance to get to know Regina's sister, it felt important to remember her in this way. After all, Regina had never loved anyone quite so much as she'd loved her sister.

Linda rolled her eyes, then winced. "Ouch."

"Sorry," Robert said. "Too much pressure?"

But Linda shook her head. "Not you," she said. "Florence. Seems she's just as worried about all of us as I am."

"I'm sure your mother's magic will take care of us," Robert said.

"I can't believe you're taking her side," Linda said with a sigh she had no right to. Her eyes met Regina's. They both knew about the candles Linda had dipped and burned to keep Robert's worries at bay. To her mother she said, "Your magic didn't work last time."

"I've had another thirteen years to work things out," Regina said. "This time, we'll be safe."

Her daughter tapped her fingertips against her belly, her lips pressed thin. "Last time you let me help you."

"Last time, your magic wasn't affected by it," Regina said.

The past week had been like 1973 all over again. As soon as October arrived, Regina's candles started looking like the blanket in her lap—rough and haphazard—the work of a novice. When Linda had come to her after trying to dip a candle for the baby's health, Regina discovered her daughter's magic hadn't fared any better than her own. And with each day that brought them closer to the thirteenth, things only got worse. They'd stopped dipping candles altogether a few days ago after Linda's shirt had caught fire while she was trying to light a stubborn wick.

"I still think we should work the spell together," Linda said. "Two witches are better than one."

"You need rest," Regina told her.

What she didn't say was she'd already prepared the candles she needed, well before the changes to her magic took hold. Now, it was only a matter of time before the curse day arrived. Then, she could light them, and all would be as it should.

Chapter Forty-Two

Honeysuckle House, 1986

Though Regina may have tried to ease Linda's fears about the curse, the house knew Linda was worried about what the day's magic might bring. Just as worried as Honeysuckle House itself. It had lost so many of the people it loved. It didn't know if it could handle any more deaths. When the sun rose, it pulled Linda's quilt from her sleeping form. She tried to tug it back up, but the house wouldn't let her. Linda rose from bed with a hand on her lower back and threw a robe over her nightgown, then slid her feet into a pair of slippers.

The house watched as she made her way downstairs, carefully cradling each of her footsteps to prevent even a single creaking floorboard. When she reached the kitchen, a steaming cup of raspberry tea waited for her on the counter beside still-warm toast.

"Thank you," she said.

The house was glad to offer her this comfort.

"Mom wants to deal with the curse herself, but I'm not so sure," Linda said, hands wrapped around her mug. "She has only me to lose. I have Robert." She set the tea down and held a hand over her belly and, with a certain reverence in her voice, said, "I have Florence."

The house opened the window above the sink, sending a gust of cold October air into the room, trying to draw Linda's attention to the yard.

"A little chilly, don't you think?" Linda started to close the window, but the house wouldn't let her. Not until she saw her mother outside making her way toward the apiary. Because if Regina was at the apiary, it meant she wasn't in the attic with the spell she'd been preparing all week.

The house made the lights in the kitchen glow a little brighter.

"You wanted me to see her?" Linda asked.

The kitchen bulbs blinked off then on. Behind Linda, the house dropped a frame from the wall, drawing her attention back to the doorway. When she turned, the house turned off all the lights save one in the hallway.

Linda set her cup down and walked toward it; as she did, the house made the next bulb glow and the next, leading Linda all the way up to the third floor. She paused at her mother's bedroom, gripping the doorframe as she took several steadying breaths. If the house could've, it would've carried her the rest of the way.

"Just hold on a little longer," she said as she rubbed her belly before she made the final climb into her mother's attic room.

Part XI
Death

The end of something old to make way for the beginning of something new.

Chapter Forty-Three

Clara, Now

The day after the house lost control of the gas stove, Clara held Angela's hand as they crossed the street from the coffee shop to Ink & Pages. Angela's mom had put extra whipped cream on Clara's hot chocolate. All down Main Street flags hung from the lampposts. Though Clara was still learning to read, she had no problem piecing together the words "Burdock Creek Fall Festival," which curved over and under an illustration of Honeysuckle House. She hugged Ink tightly to her chest as she tried not to cry reading them.

She'd kept the kitten overnight. Angela had called Florence and told her about the second fire while her mom sat at Angela's kitchen counter with a cup of tea and the look she only ever got when Aunty Flo "was being particularly difficult."

Clara had shouted, loud enough, she hoped, that Florence could hear, "Do you want us to bring Ink back to the shop? I don't want you to be lonely!"

With a smile, Angela handed Clara the phone.

"Aunty Flo!" Clara said.

"Are you and Ink okay?" Florence asked.

"It was scary, but I know Mom will protect us."

There was a pause on the other end of the line. "It sounds scary. I think maybe you should hold on to Ink for tonight, so he feels safe."

Ink hopped onto the counter beside her and butted his head against her hand.

"I can do that," Clara said.

"Then tomorrow you can bring him by the shop," her aunt said.

"I gave him goat cheese for dinner," Clara told her.

Her aunt had laughed and thanked Clara for taking care of her kitten. Now, Clara held him tight against her chest with one arm as she and Angela neared the bookshop.

"I wish Mom was coming with us," Clara said. "She's going to miss out on the hot chocolate."

Angela held a drink carrier in her free hand—pumpkin spice lattes for her and Aunt Flo and Owen, and the cocoa for Clara. When they reached the bookshop door, Angela said, "Your mom has to have some difficult conversations today."

Clara nodded sadly. That had been the other part of what they'd talked about last night. Her mom was canceling the festival and the honey harvest and the candle dipping. Three of Clara's favorite things. Clara had been sad enough she started to cry, even though she very much didn't want to cry because she wanted to be brave for her mom. But, to Clara's surprise, her mom hadn't seemed terribly sad at all.

"If her candles work, maybe she won't have to cancel the festival," Clara said hopefully.

Angela paused with one hand on the door, and she looked down at Clara. Something flashed in her eyes, reminding Clara of the fear she'd seen there just the night before.

"What do you mean, her candles?" Angela asked.

"The ones she made yesterday," Clara said. "Before we came over and had grilled cheese and the kitchen caught on fire."

Angela blinked a few times.

"I saw them in the workshop," Clara explained. "Well, Ink led me to them. They were a little lumpy, nothing like Mom's usual candles. But one of them was black, and the other was brown, like in Grandma's spell. They weren't dry yet, so Mom must've made them yesterday. Do you think if she burns them today it will fix the house, and we can still have the festival?"

Angela stared at her without responding for so long Clara said, "Angela?"

The door opened, and Florence stood on the other side.

"You brought coffee," Florence said. "And my favorite niece."

"I'm your only niece," Clara said.

"You're my favorite only niece." When she reached for the coffee, Angela still hadn't spoken.

"Angela?" Florence asked, concern in her voice.

"I think we need to go to Honeysuckle House," Angela paused. "Your sister . . ."

Clara's heart stuttered. "You think she's doing the spell by herself. And we're not there to keep her safe."

Clara wasn't particularly familiar with fear. The dark had never scared her and the bees had never stung her and her mom had always, always been there. These past few days had been the first time she'd really felt it grip her. But it wasn't until that moment that something cold settled into her chest, and with it came the realization that her mother might be in danger and the house wouldn't be able to protect her.

Chapter Forty-Four

Evie, Now

Evie stood on her mother's side of the attic room, the wall still gaping with the damage from the fire. After Florence had left, Evie had taken a few good swings at it to get her anger out, but she hadn't had a chance to finish. Not with dinner and then the second fire.

Flames were at the heart of the Caldwells' magic. Yes, the wax and the dipping of the candles all played into it, but it was the burning that sealed their spells and brought them into being. The house's inability to control fire within its walls seemed important somehow. Had Evie more time, she'd sit with that fact. Were she and Florence on speaking terms, she'd talk it over with her. But tomorrow was the thirteenth, and time was the last thing Evie had.

She wouldn't lose anyone to this curse and to her own mistake in thinking her benevolence was enough to break it. She'd had thirteen years to pick it apart and undo it, and she'd wasted them.

She wouldn't waste this last day.

Yes, she told Angela she was canceling the festival. But she hoped after her work was done, there would be no need. Whatever dark magic lurked inside the house would be bound, and any danger to those she loved would be gone forever.

She'd prepared everything from the spell she'd found in her mother's journal. The candles hadn't turned out as perfect as the ones she'd found in this room, but she trusted her own magic more than she trusted her mother's. She sat in the antique chair and read over the list of components one more time.

Black candle
Brown candle
Tourmaline, obsidian, and quartz
An anchor
Objects belonging to spell subjects
String
Something offered
Temperance card
Magician card

She placed the crystals in a triangle, quartz at the top to lend its power and amplification, tourmaline and obsidian in each bottom corner to ground and protect.

The floorboards creaked beneath her. Evie bent down and rested a hand against them.

"I know you're scared," she said. "So am I. But I promise this will help."

There was a low groan from the pipes in the walls.

Evie set one of Clara's pebbles in the center of the spell circle. Then she placed the necklace her mother had taken from Florence beside it. She unclasped her own necklace and set the tourmaline pendant with them. Three witches to anchor the magic. Finally, she added the doorknob to represent the house, the subject of the spell, or so she thought.

She took a long piece of cotton twine—the same she used for dipping her candles—and tied the objects together. She set both of her misshapen candles in the circle and the tarot cards along with them.

She didn't know what she could offer to make the binding take hold, what would be powerful enough to undo whatever darkness had her home in its grip. She loved Honeysuckle House deeply, thought of it as her own family. Whatever offering she made had to have an equal weight. Her mind drifted to Angela, to the love growing between them. It wasn't something she wanted to give up. She wanted to explore it, to uncover every facet of it for the rest of her life, but if letting go of her love for Angela meant keeping her safe—if it meant keeping all of them safe—that was worth it.

And so, she struck a match.

Chapter Forty-Five

Florence, Now

"Evie came up with a spell to end the curse?" Florence asked. Then, a little breathless, said, "Evie came up with a spell to end the curse."

Pride mingled with jealousy and disbelief. Florence knew her sister had always had the more powerful magic between the two of them, even if she'd lost some of that spark after their father's death. If anyone could find a way to stop the curse, of course it was Evie. But something in Florence wanted to feel the power flowing from her heart into the wicks and wax once more, to be the one to set her family free.

At the very least, she wanted Evie to include her.

"No," Angela said, as she shook her head. "I . . ." The coffees were coming very close to spilling over the edge. Owen squeezed around Florence and took them from Angela. She gave him a strained smile then said, "It's not her spell."

Florence blinked slowly. Her gaze shifted to her niece. Clara had summoned a cat with a single candle.

"You did this?" There was wonder in Florence's voice.

But Clara stood there, biting her lip, tears welling in her eyes. She shook her head.

"It's your mother's," Angela said. "Evie found it in the attic the day it burned."

Florence braced herself with one hand against the doorframe.

"Evie said it was a binding spell for the house," Angela said. "She thought your mother had found a way to stop the curse."

Florence stared at her for a few moments. Evie had come to the same conclusion Florence had: It was the house that was cursed, not the Caldwells. Then, the rest of what Angela said sank in.

"She's going to try to cast one of my mother's spells?"

Linda Caldwell was the one person they couldn't trust. The person who had ensured their father's death.

"Tell her what you saw," Angela said to Clara.

"There were candles in the workshop," Clara said. "But we can't let her burn them alone. What if something goes wrong? What if there's another fire?"

Florence pushed herself off the door and stood tall. She rested a hand on Clara's head and said, "We won't let anything happen to her."

Florence knew her sister was reckless. She knew Evie never once listened to Florence's warnings after their mother was out of their life and her need for Florence's protection had left along with her. But this went beyond recklessness.

"Why didn't you tell me sooner?" Florence asked Angela.

"Evie was afraid you'd try to talk her out of it."

"That's exactly what I would've done," Florence said. "I can't believe *you* didn't."

"What if she's right?" Angela asked. "What if it works?"

"What if it kills her?" Owen said.

"We can argue about this later," Florence said. "Right now, we need to make sure Evie is safe, and we need to stop her from casting that spell."

The four of them piled into Angela's Jeep. Florence sat up front. Owen and Clara in the back. Florence passed the drinks around as Angela turned off Main Street to avoid the tourists who had come early for the festivities—the hayride and the pumpkin patch and the craft fair ran the day before and after the events at Honeysuckle House.

"At least Evie canceled the festival," Angela said, her hands tight on the wheel and her latte untouched in the cupholder. "Not that any of these people seem to have heard."

Florence almost spit out her coffee. "When? How did you convince her?"

"It wasn't me," Angela said. "It was the second fire."

Clara, who sat taking a giant sip of hot cocoa, swallowed loud enough for them all to hear, then said, "If she's casting the spell, then when is she going to tell everyone she canceled the festival?"

Silence fell over the car.

"She was supposed to be meeting with the businesses who are running the events they moved downtown." Angela's words were a whisper.

"She lied," Florence said.

But Angela shook her head. "She wouldn't. Not after . . . She wouldn't lie to me. Not about this."

"Knowing Evie's logic, it wasn't a lie," Florence said. "If the spell doesn't work, she'd cancel the festival. But if it does, there's no reason to turn people away yet."

As Angela neared the curve leading to Honeysuckle House, Florence felt the familiar well of panic rising up inside her. She gripped her thighs tight, her knuckles going white. She almost jumped when a hand came down on her shoulder. She pulled the visor down and met Owen's eyes in the mirror.

She reached up and gripped his hand with her own, still amazed at how he'd slipped into the cracks in her heart in such a short time. She didn't know where things would go between them after the curse—if they both made it that far—but she found herself wanting to find out.

"You okay?" Angela asked with a sidelong glance.

"I think so." It wasn't getting any easier for Florence to face her trauma when it was triggered in such a deep way, but she found it more tolerable now that she wasn't alone.

Angela rolled to a stop. She had her door open the moment she pulled her keys from the ignition and was halfway to the porch before Florence even had a chance to catch her breath and still her racing heart. Florence unbuckled her seat belt to find Owen on the other side of the door, opening it for her.

"Angela!" Florence called. "Wait!"

But Angela didn't slow. "She could be hurt."

The door to Honeysuckle House opened wide like a mouth.

"Keep an eye on Clara," Florence said to Owen. Then she took off after Angela.

The lights flickered in warning as Florence burst through the door and started up the steps, each footfall reminding her of the night before her father died. Fear ricocheted in her chest. Memory and trauma bled into the here and now. It was enough to stop Florence in her tracks, to have her bent double with panic. Instead, she let it carry her up and up. Past the floor where her childhood room had been. Past the pain and the heartache and the loss.

When she reached her parents' old bedroom, a deeper sort of terror reared up inside her. She gripped her scarred forearm and could almost feel her mother's nails digging in. As she stood, staring through the open door at the spiral staircase, Angela's feet disappeared above her. Florence found she couldn't follow. All of her panic, all of her fear coalesced right here in this moment. She'd made it through yesterday, but that had been on her terms. She'd been facing her fears with support and purpose. Yes, her panic had been simmering beneath the surface, but now it had her in its grip.

Owen came up behind her, Clara at his side. She slipped past Florence.

"Clara!" Florence managed, her voice breaking. "You need to go back outside, where it's safe."

"Mom needs me."

Then she, too, was running up the steps.

Owen rested a hand on Florence's upper back. His soft touch sent tears falling down her face. The feeling of them shocked her enough to break her out of her frozen stance, and she started up the spiral staircase.

When Florence reached the top, Clara was slipping through the damaged wall. Florence ran after her to find her sister standing in front of her mother's altar. She took in the spell circle, the candles, the tarot cards. In front of Evie sat a pile of spent matches. The window had opened wide, and an unnatural gust blew through the opening. Evie held a lighter in her hand.

"Evie!" Florence said. "Don't do this. You don't know what that spell will do."

"I know enough," Evie said without looking up. She pulled the trigger on the lighter and brought flame to wick.

As the fire took hold, there was a loud crack, like a tree branch breaking. A few feet away, Angela looked up as one of the attic beams started to fall. Owen pushed past Florence and dove for Angela, knocking her out of the way. The wood only just missed crushing him beneath its weight, but not before it hit his shoulder and sent him sprawling. His head hit the attic floor with a thud, and his eyelids fluttered shut.

Chapter Forty-Six

Regina, 1960

Nothing had gone how Regina planned. First, her sister's magic had overpowered her own. Then, Tillie's brother hadn't been as easy to manipulate as she'd hoped. She rushed home after their conversation and pulled out her tarot deck. She needed a spell, but if it was going to work, she needed guidance.

The house, as always, greeted her, turning on lights as she hurried up the stairs to her room. When she made it to the attic, she started for the bookshelf. As beautiful as Tillie's painted cards were, after the three of swords Regina had pulled, she didn't want a repeat. Instead, she turned to her everyday deck.

When she reached for the cards, the shelf tilted, pushing the box toward her.

"Thank you," she said.

The lights flickered in what felt like a question.

"It's Tillie," Regina said. "She wants to take Violet away from us."

The bulbs dimmed in response.

"Don't worry," Regina said. "I won't let her."

She whirled around and hurried to her altar, where she shuffled the deck then fanned it out in front of her. As soon as the familiar heat warmed her palm, she flipped the card to reveal the seven of swords.

She held it up in front of her.

It was the same one she'd pulled the other night, when she'd wanted clarification about the three of swords. The floorboards shuffled under Regina's feet. The house was always curious about her tarot readings.

"I thought it was a card of deception when I pulled it the other day . . ."

But it was more than that. In the original Rider-Waite-Smith artwork, the card depicted a man stealing five of the seven swords. And that gave Regina an idea. She wanted her magic to be stronger than her sister's. Perhaps with the right spell, she could borrow from Violet's power.

She tapped her fingertips against her altar. Using magic to take something not rightfully hers had consequences, but if it meant keeping her sister and keeping the life she loved, those consequences would be worth it. She pulled out her journal, hurried down to the workshop, and began preparing a spell.

In her haste, she didn't see one of the tarot cards had slipped from the table, as if the house had decided to do a reading of its own. The card landed face up on the rug. The five of cups. A symbol of loss and grief and regret.

She'd find it later, but by then, it would be too late.

Chapter Forty-Seven

Violet, 1960

The closest Violet had ever come to having words with her sister was that day in the workshop when Violet announced Tillie was moving in. It had come from a place of fear—that Regina wouldn't accept her, that she wouldn't understand. Now, that fear was gone. Anger had taken up its spot, and with every thought and every breath, it grew.

She pulled the Pontiac in front of Honeysuckle House and killed the engine.

Tillie reached for her hand. "Are you sure about this?"

Violet nodded; she'd never been so sure of anything in her life. She stepped out of the car and looked up at the house. "Where is she?"

The front door opened wide in response.

"Do you want me to go with you?" Tillie asked.

Violet shook her head. "I need to do this on my own."

Tillie leaned her head against Violet's shoulder and took her hand. "You shouldn't have to."

"But I do," Violet said. "And when I'm done, I'm all yours."

Tillie stood up on her toes and pressed her lips to Violet's cheek.

Violet turned her head, catching Tillie's mouth with her own. Tillie made a surprised sound but returned the kiss.

"For good luck," Violet said.

Together, they started up the stairs. When they stepped inside, Tillie squeezed Violet's hand before they parted ways. As Tillie started for their room, Violet asked the house, "Where is Regina?"

The chandelier winked on, and the front staircase creaked. Up the stairs, the hallway lights led her to Regina's room, where the door swung open silently. Violet found her sister in the attic loft, sitting in her armchair and scribbling away in her journal. Violet stood there for a few moments watching her. Violet had given up so much of her life to become the parent Regina needed. All she had ever wanted was her sister's happiness, and it broke her heart to realize Regina didn't want the same for her.

"Regina," Violet said.

Her sister looked up, dazed. She closed the book and set it to the side.

"I didn't hear you come in." Regina's voice sounded like an accusation, and the way she glanced at the wall confirmed it. Whatever she'd been doing up here, the house had wanted Violet to see it. She glanced at Regina's altar. Nothing seemed out of the ordinary—a pile of crystals, her new deck of tarot cards, a stack of candles in the corner with a single black taper on top.

"Joshua told me what you did," Violet said.

Regina's nostrils flared, but her voice came out calm and flat. "I told him I was worried about your safety."

Violet crossed her arms. "That's not the way he tells it."

"And you trust him over me?"

"You threatened his sister," Violet said. "You threatened me."

"I would never do anything to hurt you," Regina said.

"That's just it." Violet's voice cracked. "You already have. I love Tillie. I want to spend the rest of my life with her, and you want to tear us apart."

Already Regina was shaking her head. "I don't want to lose you."

"You wouldn't have," Violet said. "But if you keep going like this, you will."

"You're the one who cast spells to stop my magic!"

Regina's words landed like a blow. Violet had dipped and lit those candles out of an abundance of caution. She'd wanted them to be unnecessary, a defense born of paranoia.

"You *were* casting spells on me." Betrayal and disappointment filled Violet's voice.

Regina's eyes widened. "I. . ."

"My magic is stronger than yours," Violet said. "And if you think going around town and telling our secret will get you what you want, then you've underestimated just how far I'll go to keep Tillie safe."

"It's not fair," Regina said. "You brought her into our lives without thinking how it would impact me. You're all I have, Violet, and she's taking you away from me."

"No, Regina." Violet's words came out sad but firm. "You're pushing me away."

"Mother and Father are gone." Regina's voice was low and thick with emotion. "You said we'd always have each other."

Violet's heart twisted. She almost crossed the space between them and wrapped her sister in her arms, as if she could keep all this pain from getting in. Had Regina's grief driven her to this? If Violet had waited until after the anniversary of their parents' death, would things be different? But, no. Regina was an adult, just as much as Violet was. She'd been trying to keep love out of Violet's life for years.

"I don't want to turn you out of this house," Violet said. "But if you don't give this up, I will."

Then, she turned on her heel and started down the stairs.

Chapter Forty-Eight

Florence, Now

For thirteen years, Florence had been meticulous about protecting her heart. She didn't let anyone in because she couldn't bear the thought that caring for someone would put them in danger. Owen had changed that.

Now, he lay unconscious, crumpled on the floor, the beam beside him. She should've known better. She should've never opened herself up to the possibility of loss. Or worse, opened someone else up to the possibility of death.

But it didn't make sense. The curse didn't come until the thirteenth. Owen should've been safe until tomorrow. They all should have. But there he was, the sunlight shining through a hole in the ceiling and casting shadows over his face.

Though Florence wanted to run to him, she had to stop her sister. Evie stood dumbfounded, staring at Angela who, only moments before, had been right where the bulk of the beam lay. Already more wood in the roof was starting to creak.

"Angela," Evie whispered, horrified, as Angela dropped to her knees beside Owen. Clara ran to Angela and wrapped her arms around her.

"Are you okay?" Clara asked.

Angela pulled her in close and pressed a kiss to her forehead. "We need to worry about him, not me." But Florence could hear the fear in Angela's voice, a tremor that cut through her usual confidence.

Florence closed the space between herself and her sister. She grabbed the candles and blew them out. Then, she threw them to the ground, the spell unfinished. Evie flinched as the floorboards shook, rolling the tapers even further away from the two of them.

"How *could* you?" Florence's voice was quiet and low and so much like her mother's.

Evie flung a hand toward the fallen beam. "I was trying to prevent this! It would've worked if you hadn't interrupted me."

Florence shook her head. She wanted to let her anger overtake her. To scream and sweep her arm across the altar and scatter the remnants of Evie's spell. To make her sister feel the weight of what she'd done. But she wouldn't be her mother, not even now.

She ran toward Owen and Angela.

"He's breathing," Angela said. She had one hand on Owen's chest.

Florence's own chest gave as she watched it rise and fall. She brushed Owen's hair back from his forehead, revealing a trickle of blood from where his head had hit the floor. "This is all my fault. I shouldn't have let him in."

But Angela shook her head. "That beam was meant for me."

Owen's eyelids fluttered open. He looked up at them, eyes unfocused, and said, "I wouldn't be so sure about that."

"Owen," Florence breathed, and she almost kissed him. Instead, she pressed the back of her hand to his forehead, then his cheek. "Are you all right?"

He started to sit up then tipped back. Florence caught him before he could fall over, one arm around his back, the other pressed up against his chest.

"Alive," he said. "Dizzy. Head hurts."

"It could be a concussion," Evie said.

He closed one eye and squinted at her through the other. "This is my fault. I shouldn't have come inside."

The beam had fallen the moment Evie cast the spell. Maybe it wasn't the curse that had caused it, Florence thought, but whatever magic Evie had found in her mother's journal.

"If this is anyone's fault, it's Evie's," Florence said at the same time Evie asked, "How could it be your fault?"

"The house heard us yesterday," Owen said. "It knows who I am."

The realization hit Florence square in the chest, knocking the wind out of her. No, her feelings for Owen hadn't put him in danger. But by bringing him here, by mentioning his aunt, she'd risked his life all the same.

"It tried to kill you just like it killed Tillie," she breathed.

The lights snapped off. Florence glanced at the hole in the ceiling, eyes tracking for more loose beams. The creaking had stopped the moment she blew out the candles, but she still needed to get Owen out of there. If the house had taken revenge once, it could very well do it again.

"Tillie?" Evie asked.

"Grey," Florence said. "She was Owen's great-aunt."

"She's why I came to Burdock Creek," he said. "I was looking for my family history."

"But it wasn't the curse that killed her," Florence said. "It was the house. Because *her* parents killed Helen and Christopher."

"I'm not following any of this," Evie said, confusion clear on her face.

Yesterday it had been a theory, but now, in light of what had just happened to Owen, it was a theory Florence was willing to bet on.

"We looked at the police reports from the deaths. We found a letter from Aunt Violet. There's no other explanation. The house killed Tillie," Florence said. "And now, it's forced to kill every thirteen years. That's the curse Evie—it's on the house. Not us."

"No," Evie said with disbelief. "It wouldn't. You have it wrong."

There was a rattling from the pipes in the walls, and Florence tightened her grip on Owen.

"Then how do you explain it dropping that beam on him?" Florence asked.

Evie looked up at the ceiling. "Did you do this?"

The lights slowly came back on, then winked out. Evie crossed her arms. "See?"

"We can't trust the house," Florence said.

"Honeysuckle House protected us from Mom, or did you forget that?" Evie asked. "It loves us, Florence."

"If it wasn't the house and it wasn't the curse, it must have been the spell you tried!" Florence said.

This time, the lights came on and stayed that way.

Fear and shame flashed across Evie's face, and if Florence wasn't so angry, she might've held her tongue. But she was long past that. "If you trust the house, then you can't ignore it now. The spell did this. *You* did this."

"I was trying to save the house—to save all of us!" Evie yelled.

"We need to go," Angela said. "The house isn't safe, and we're all sitting here waiting for the next thing to go wrong. That's why I told Florence about the spell."

"*You* told her?" Evie asked.

"Clara saw your candles, and I was afraid something was going to happen to you," Angela said. "I didn't want you to be hurt here all alone."

"I came here alone so *you* wouldn't get hurt," Evie said.

"A lot of good that did," Florence said.

"Really, Florence? Can you not? Even if the house *did* kill Tillie—which I absolutely do not believe—we still have a curse to contend with," Evie said, her voice sharp. "A curse that, despite our theories, we're no closer to breaking."

"You always said if you knew how the curse started you could undo it," Angela said. "What about the journals?"

"Journals?" Florence asked.

But before Evie could answer the lights started to flicker, and the walls began to shake.

Chapter Forty-Nine

Evie, Now

"We need to go. Now!" Evie grabbed her mother's journal then scooped Clara up from the ground.

Florence and Angela scrambled up from the floor. They helped Owen get to his feet. He swayed a little but stayed upright.

"Hold on tight." Evie tried to keep the fear from her voice, but the words came out shaky. Clara wrapped her legs around Evie's waist and gripped her around the neck. The spiral staircase creaked under every step. Lights blinked on and off as Evie hurried through the house with Clara in her arms.

The walls groaned as if the house might fall down around them at any moment.

When they reached the front room, they burst onto the porch and into the yard. The wind whipped up, and the lights flickered erratically against the storm-darkened sky, as if the house was looking down at them.

The window to Evie's attic room slammed so hard the glass shattered in the pane and rained down on the side yard. Evie stared up at it, waiting for the others to appear in the doorway. Florence was the last one through, and as soon as she reached the porch, the door closed with a bang. Honeysuckle vines covered it, barring their reentry.

"Is the house mad at us?" Clara asked. The fear in her voice made Evie's heart ache.

"I'm not sure, honeybee," Evie said. But it certainly seemed that way. At least it wasn't trying to hurt them anymore.

Angela came up behind her and rested a hand on Evie's back. Evie relaxed into her touch, and if she hadn't been holding onto Clara, she would've collapsed into Angela's arms.

"I know you were trying to help," Angela said, her voice soft, "but you shouldn't have done this alone."

"I didn't want you to get hurt," Evie said.

"And you thought I'd stand by waiting for the house to hurt you instead?" The pain in Angela's voice only undid Evie further.

"I wasn't thinking about my own safety," Evie said.

"Maybe you should've been," Angela said.

"She's right," Florence said. "You didn't have to do this alone."

Evie glared at her sister and tried not to cry. "I almost brought you into it yesterday, but all you wanted to do was fight."

"If I remember correctly, you're the one who picked a fight with me," Florence said as she helped Owen walk to a nearby tree that could better support his weight.

"If you'd come the day the house burned, we'd never be in this mess," Evie said. "You would've seen everything in the attic whether I wanted you to or not."

Clara scrambled out of Evie's arms and landed on her feet. She planted her hands on her hips and said, "Mom! We need to work together. *All* of us."

"Clara's right," Florence said with a heavy sigh, almost as if the fight had gone out of her. "What was that you were saying about journals?" she asked Angela.

"Something I'm guessing the house didn't want us to hear." Owen cast a wary look at Honeysuckle House.

"Clara's magic didn't just burn a hole through the wall," Evie said. "We found a pile of diaries in front of the bookcase. Mom's spell was in almost all of them in some form or another. I didn't have a chance to read much beyond that. I was too focused on the spell."

"With all of us, we might be able to get through them fast enough to see if there's something else in there that could help," Florence said.

"All of us?" Evie shot Owen a glare. "He took a job here under false pretenses!"

"I didn't," Owen said. "Not on purpose. I came looking for answers about my family. I was going to ask you about the curse, but after I heard you talking about it, I didn't think that was such a good idea. I didn't want you to fire me."

"I wouldn't have," Evie said. Then, she paused, and with a sigh said, "I might have." She'd been so caught up in trying to get everyone to believe her efforts to break the curse had worked, that anything having to do with it could've set her off. "I still don't understand why you think the house killed Tillie Grey."

"The police reports—" Florence started.

"Called the house a murderer?" Evie asked.

"Well, no, but—" Florence tried again.

"You're just as in the dark as I am," Evie interrupted again.

"If you would let me talk," Florence said, then paused, eyebrows arched.

"Sorry," Evie said. "It's just . . . this is Honeysuckle House we're talking about."

"The house was there for every death," Florence said. "It could've told us how the curse started a long time ago, but it never did."

"For all we know, Mom was the one who locked those journals away." Evie was still unable to view the house as a killer, even though she knew it had hidden at least one of the diaries from Evie.

"Not the journals," Florence said. "Ink & Pages showed us a memory of Regina and Violet at the shop, back when it was still Grey's Gifts. I lit a candle, and it came to life in the smoke. If it could do that, then why couldn't Honeysuckle House do the same?"

The house communicated with them in all sorts of ways, but it had never used smoke, at least not as far as Evie knew.

"I wasn't sure why the memory was important, so I did a tarot reading that pointed us to the house. The curse, the deaths, all of it goes back to Honeysuckle House," Florence continued. "If we want to fix it, we have to start there."

"How? By burning it to the ground?" Evie's voice came out sharp and pointed, but her sister didn't even flinch.

"If that's what it takes," Florence said.

Behind them, Honeysuckle House shuddered.

"No!" Clara said. "We can't hurt the house."

Evie rested a hand on her daughter's head and said, "Clara's right. Even if the house *did* cause the curse, we're not going to undo it by tearing it down. We have to find a way to bind the magic making it kill—like mom was trying to do."

"If that's even what the spell was for," Florence said.

"You can look at it yourself," Evie replied. "Maybe you'll see something I didn't."

"If you had showed it to me—" Florence started, but Evie held up a hand.

"We've both made mistakes," Evie said. "There's no point punishing each other for them. I need to call tomorrow's guests and let them know the bed and breakfast is closed."

"And actually talk to the festival council?" Angela asked, her tone both gentle and admonishing.

Evie winced. "I was planning to talk to them if the spell didn't work."

"Well," Florence said, arms crossed. "It didn't work."

"I am very aware of that, *Florence*." Evie said her sister's name with a certain sharpness. "I'm not going to let anyone get hurt here. I never was."

"You were going to hold the festival," Florence countered.

"And now the house has caught fire twice and a beam fell and almost crushed my girlfriend," Evie said the words without thinking, but as soon as they left her mouth, they felt right. More right than anything had felt in a long time.

"Wait," Florence said. "You and Angela . . . ?"

Angela stiffened beside Evie, and a new sort of doubt crept up on her.

"I didn't mean to say anything." Evie said the words fast, wishing she could take them back, that she hadn't put a name on what had started between them before it ever had a chance to grow. "I don't even know if that's what you want."

Angela gripped Evie's hand. The warmth of her touch spread from Evie's palm, up her arm, and settled in her chest. "It's absolutely what I want."

"Even with the curse?" Evie asked.

Angela looked up at the house. "I think we're a little far in for that."

Evie wasn't about to let the curse take Angela from her. She wasn't going to let it take anyone ever again.

"Why don't we make those calls on the way to grab the rest of the journals," Angela said. "Then we can meet Owen and Florence back at the bookshop."

Chapter Fifty

Honeysuckle House, Now

Black-shuttered windows stared out over the lawn, and though the family had gone, the bulbs still flickered on and off, on and off. At first, the lights had been a warning, a way to get the witches out, but now, it couldn't seem to stop, as if all the magic that had brought the house to life couldn't be contained within its walls.

It had been coming out in bursts. Not the first fire—that had been a magic beyond the power pumping through the pipes like a beating heart. The beam, too, had been out of the house's control.

But the fire the night before? That should never have happened. The house had been so overjoyed for one final dinner with its family. After Florence had come—even if it did end with a fight between the sisters—Honeysuckle House knew it could finally rest, its work complete and the family free. It hadn't expected them to risk a dinner, and it should've warned them away. But it only had precious few moments left, and it wasn't prepared to waste them.

That had been its mistake.

It couldn't risk hurting the people it loved the most ever again.

Part XII

Temperance, Reversed

A symbol of balance.

When reversed, something is out of balance.

Chapter Fifty-One

Florence, Now

When Florence and Owen got back to the bookstore, Ink sat waiting for them by the front window. The sign on the entrance read *Finish your book tonight, and we'll be back tomorrow to help you find the next one!*

Florence turned the key in the lock. The lights flickered on as she pushed open the door. "Hello, Shop," she called. In response, there came a sound from somewhere deep inside the building, like a person flipping through a book.

Ink pounced onto her jeans and climbed his way up. Florence grabbed him before he reached her chunky sweater and cradled him in her arms. She brought her nose to his nose, his breath fogging up her glasses, and he let out a small, delighted meow. She rested him gently on her shoulder, but rather than settle there, he squatted back and leapt for Owen.

Owen caught the kitten with a laugh, set him on his own shoulder, and said, "It's nice to see you too."

"I think we should start with a tarot reading," Florence said. "The cards called me home. They foretold the house catching fire. Evie and I may have misinterpreted the reading thirteen years ago, but with all of us together, I think we'll have a better chance at getting it right this time around."

The register started to beep, and there beside it sat Florence's tarot deck.

With a whispered thanks, she grabbed it and whirled around, smacking right into Owen's chest. She pulled back quickly, almost falling over, when he steadied her with his hands on her forearms. The heat of them seeped through her sweater clear to her skin, and a flush made its way up her throat in response. She tilted her head back to look up at him, and for a moment neither of them moved.

"Sorry," he murmured.

Her eyes fell to his lips, and she swallowed.

"It's my fault," she said. "I didn't realize you were right there. I . . ." She almost rose up on her toes, almost pressed herself into him. If they were right about the house murdering Tillie, then maybe the house wouldn't kill someone Florence cared about. Maybe it was only doomed to kill someone *it* loved. But that wasn't a risk Florence could take. There was still a chance Owen was safe, that whatever this mess of emotions she felt toward him wasn't enough to count, wasn't enough to put him in danger if they couldn't break the curse tonight. But if she kissed him, she'd be done for.

She tore her eyes away from his mouth. Then she cleared her throat, and he dropped his hold on her.

"Tarot?" She held up the deck.

"Tarot," he said, his voice deeper than it had been a few moments before.

Before they could start toward the ever-changing back room—before they even had a chance to recover from their almost-kiss—the door opened behind them. Clara barreled through the entrance then stopped short in front of Owen.

Ink hopped from his shoulder into her arms.

"Hello, Ink," she said to the kitten.

Evie followed behind her with an armful of journals. "The festival is officially canceled. Let's get reading."

Angela stepped inside and locked the door behind them.

"We can use my room!" Clara said before she took off, darting between the shelves. Owen and Evie followed after her, but Florence lingered behind, falling in step with Angela.

"So," she said. "You and Evie."

Angela ducked her head and stared after Evie with so much love in her eyes that Florence had to look away. It wasn't something meant for her to see. "I know she's your sister."

"I'm surprised it didn't happen sooner," Florence said.

Angela shot her a glance. "Like you would've been okay with that."

"You've been in love with each other for years," Florence said. "I never wanted to admit it, but I knew. I'm sorry if I got in your way."

Angela took Florence's hand and gave it a squeeze. "It happened when it was meant to happen."

Florence bumped her shoulder against Angela's as they made their way to the back room. They found the door flung wide, the room transformed into a cozy study space. Squashy chairs big enough to sit cross-legged in surrounded a broad table. Once again, a steaming teapot and a collection of mismatched mugs rested in the middle. The overhead fairy lights had been replaced with lamps on small round tables, giving the room a homey, well-lit glow without any of the eyestrain of fluorescents. A fireplace with a cozy fire burned in the corner of the room. There was even a small cat bed, though Ink ignored it and jumped up onto one of the chairs.

Clara claimed the seat with Ink; Angela sat beside her. Evie took the chair next to Angela. Florence and Owen shared a look, and at his arched eyebrow and her answering nod, she took the chair next to her sister, surprised to find herself communicating with this man without a single word.

Florence opened her deck and started to shuffle.

"Tarot?" Evie asked. "Are you sure that's a good idea? The last time we did a reading together . . ."

"The last time we did a reading together, we were at odds," Florence said. "This time, we have the same goal."

She fanned out the cards on the table in front of them, heat starting in her chest. She held her hand over each one. Like last night, it took the magic a moment to make its way down to her hand. Finally, her palm warmed. She glanced up at Evie.

"You want *me* to flip it?" Evie asked, surprise in her voice.

When Florence nodded, Evie leaned forward and did just that.

The seven of swords stared up at them. The card depicted a woman with shoulder-length brown hair standing on the front porch at Honeysuckle House. She held a vine in one hand. In the other, a pair of gardening shears. She'd cut the vine so she had five of the thorns on the piece in her hand, leaving only two on the rest of the plant.

"Remind me what this one means?" Owen asked.

"Resourcefulness and strategy!" Clara said from where she sat with Ink in her lap.

"Very good," Evie said.

"Exactly what we're going to need if we're going to break this curse," Florence said. "But it can also point to deception."

"Like what my great-grandparents did," Owen said. To Evie and Angela, he explained, "We think they punctured the brake fluid reservoir on Helen and Christopher's car, causing the accident."

"To what end?" Angela asked.

"To steal the shop," Florence said.

"But how does this help us now?" Evie asked.

"Another card?" Angela suggested.

With a nod, Florence said, "How do we break the curse?" Then, she turned to her sister.

Evie leaned forward in her seat. She shook out her hand and held it over the fanned-out cards, moving it back and forth a few times until she paused on a single card; she flipped it over.

They were greeted by the sight of Honeysuckle House on fire.

"The tower," Owen said.

"We *do* have to destroy the house." Sadness threaded through Evie's voice, and she slumped back in her seat.

"No!" Clara shouted, jumping up from her chair. "I love the house. We can't hurt it. Mommy, you said the tower can be a meta . . . a meta . . ."

"A metaphor?" Angela offered.

Clara crossed her arms and nodded. Then, she started digging through her backpack.

"It wasn't the last time it was pulled," Florence said.

"But that fire also didn't burn the house down," Angela said.

Florence tapped her finger against her lip. "Let's say it *is* a metaphor. The tower is a card of destruction—of cutting ties with the past." She leaned forward in her chair, her arms on her knees as she tried to suss out how that related to the house. "I'd hoped things would be a little more clear. That we'd have a direct answer or at least something to tell us *how* to do what the cards said."

"We have the journals," Evie said.

But each book was filled with writing. There was no way they could get through every page, even with all of them reading.

Clara held up a small pink-and-blue candle. "I made a spell for us! Ink helped me." She set the taper in a candlestick holder next to the cards, then looked up at Florence.

"You brilliant girl," Florence said.

Clara beamed. Then, she frowned. "What about your rule?"

"I think it's time we changed it," Florence replied.

With a broad smile, Clara struck a match and lit the wick. The candle burned faster than any taper Florence had ever seen or lit herself. The blue and pink waxes pooled on the table. As the fire went out, the journals opened, the pages flipping of their own accord, until almost all of the journals sat face up, waiting to be read.

Clara reached for one of them and brought a finger to the page, her lips moving as her brow furrowed. She looked up with a frown.

"I can't read this. The words are all swirly." At the despair in Clara's voice, Florence almost jumped up to wrap her niece in a hug.

Evie took the diary from her. "It's in cursive, honeybee. You'll learn it soon."

"But I want to help, now!" Clara said.

"Your magic got us this far," Evie said.

"Why don't you keep Ink busy?" Florence suggested.

Clara nodded slowly. "I can do that." She scooped up the kitten and went to sit by the fireplace the shop had conjured.

Evie's eyes met Florence's, and the warmth Florence found there had her wishing they'd done all of this much, much sooner.

"This is Mom's spell." Evie opened the one journal Clara's spell hadn't. "I found it on her altar when the wall first burned down." She held it out toward Florence. "Maybe you'll see something I didn't."

At the sight of her mother's handwriting, Florence's heart rate kicked up. Her hands trembled, the notebook shaking.

"It's okay," Evie whispered, voice soft. "She's not really here."

Florence looked up at her sister. "I wish my body understood that."

"One step at a time," Evie said. "You made it to the house."

"Not without help."

Evie glanced past Florence to Owen and said, "Thank you."

Then, Evie leaned forward in her chair and picked up her mother's diary from 1986. "The house gave me this one thirteen years ago. It's the reason I thought I needed to use my magic for good. But it disappeared before I could read it all."

"The house hid it from you," Florence said. "It didn't want you to see it."

She expected Evie to start reading right away, but her sister set the notebook back on the table and took their mother's childhood journal instead. Florence almost reached for it, almost took it out of Evie's hands.

"Are you sure you want to read that one?" Angela asked before Florence could.

Evie glanced up from the front page and shook her head slowly. "For so long I've wanted to know who my mother was before I came into her life. I wanted to understand why she became the person she did. But I think I'm done making excuses for her."

Angela held out her hand. "I can read it."

The warmth in Angela's voice and the relief on Evie's face made Florence smile. There was a bittersweet sadness in it as she realized sparing her sister from heartache wasn't her job anymore.

Florence started to reach for her grandmother's journal from 1959 when Owen cleared his throat.

"Do you think I could read that one?" he asked. "I'd like to see Regina's side of things—compare it to Violet's letter."

With a nod, Florence handed it over. She glanced at her sister. "What do you think?"

Evie looked taken aback by Florence giving her the lead, and though it stung for Florence to realize she'd so rarely let Evie have the final say in anything, it felt right giving Evie this choice.

"Why don't you start with Great-aunt Violet's journal?" Evie suggested. "Since you use her tarot cards."

"Good idea," Florence said.

"I'll take grandma's other journal, from the year she died." As each of them settled in to read, Evie said, "We only have a few hours until midnight. If you find anything at all that you think could help, speak up."

Chapter Fifty-Two

Regina, 1960

Part of Regina wanted to chase after her sister. To grab her and pull her back up into the attic, to make her understand. Another part of her wanted to push Violet down the stairs and be done with it. She gripped the bottom of her chair to keep herself grounded as she watched her sister disappear. Only when she heard her bedroom door close did she open her journal and go over the list one more time.

She'd crossed out a few ingredients, added a few others, but ultimately, she was satisfied with the end result. This would give her the boost she needed for her spells to be more powerful than Violet's. She rose from her altar and walked to her bookshelf. She considered using the cards from the deck Tillie had given her, but she needed something far more precious to her if this spell was going to hold.

She reached for her very first deck, a gift from her mother when Regina was only five years old. She hadn't touched it since Helen died. Even now, Regina could remember the light in her mother's eyes, her excitement to be sharing that moment with Regina. They'd lit a blue candle for clarity, and Regina had pulled a card: the magician.

Helen had said drawing it as her first card was an auspicious start. Regina held the card now between her thumb and her forefinger. Her mother had been right. Nothing could stop her.

She flipped through the rest of the deck until she found the last piece she needed. The temperance card—a symbol of balance. Burning it would tip the scales in her favor, allowing her to strengthen her own power and weaken Violet's in the process.

The journals and books on the shelf shifted back and forth with curiosity. Regina rested a hand on one of them.

"Just a little magic," she said. "You might feel something when I light the candle, but it's nothing for you to worry about." The house would be the perfect anchor. It had more power than either sister, making it strong enough to ground her spell.

Beneath her feet, the rug curled up to touch the tip of her shoes. "I love you, too."

She sat back down in front of her table. She hoped her spell would be enough. Had she more time, she could've put together something more elegant. But there was no magic quite so powerful as pain.

The loss of her father.

The loss of her mother.

And now the loss of her sister.

That was what she'd poured into the wax in her workshop that afternoon. That was what had dripped out of her heart into her fingertips and along the length of twine. She'd felt every moment like she was living it again.

The crash of the car into the tree. The breaking of glass and bending of metal. The crack of the trunk as it crushed her parents beneath it. She'd been so young then, only thirteen. She almost couldn't believe she'd lived as much of her life without her parents as she'd lived with them. She wouldn't let the same thing happen with Violet.

"If it does, I'll never do magic again," she mumbled.

She set her circle, and she placed her candles. A Caldwell's power put magic into the world, it wasn't meant to take it. If Regina wanted this spell to work, she had to offer something in return. Something that would be worthy enough to trade for what she'd be drawing from her sister. The only thing Regina had that came close to that, was her love for Violet. But that wasn't something she was willing to give up.

Instead, she offered something that was never hers to begin with, something that would make all of this go away.

"I offer Violet's love."

As she spoke the words, the walls creaked and the floorboards shuffled and the lamps flickered. She ignored all of it. The house may have come to care for Tillie, but it would get over her leaving Violet in time.

Then, Regina struck a match.

Chapter Fifty-Three

Violet, 1960

Violet left the attic room with her shoulders squared and her head held high. There was a part of her that feared Regina's retribution, but she knew her magic was stronger.

Still, it wouldn't hurt to light one more protection candle.

She hurried back to her room, but as she neared it, she heard soft music spilling from beneath the door across the hall—the bathroom she now shared with Tillie—and she smiled. Regina could never take this from them.

She turned the knob and slipped inside. Steam hung heavy in the room. Tillie's portable record player sat on a stool in the corner, while Tillie lay in the clawfoot tub, her arms hanging over the edge. At the sight of Violet, Tillie tilted her head up. It felt like coming home.

"How'd it go?" Tillie asked.

"Regina won't try to come between us again," Violet said. "If she does, she'll no longer live in this house."

The pipes under the pedestal sink creaked, a soft, sad sound.

"I don't want to lose her either," Violet said to the house, "but she doesn't get to decide how I live my life."

The bulb above the sink glowed brighter in agreement.

"I'm proud of you," Tillie said. "I know that couldn't have been easy."

"I never thought I'd have to stand up to my little sister," Violet said.

"I hate the timing of all of this," Tillie said. "Your parents' accident was devastating. If you hadn't been with my family, if our parents hadn't fought, it never would've happened."

"None of that was your fault. It wasn't anyone's fault but my dad's. He had too much to drink before we left. He shouldn't have been driving."

Tillie held a hand over her mouth. "I didn't know that."

With a heavy sigh, Violet said, "No one does." She hadn't told the police about the whiskey she'd seen him drinking before her mother and sister came out to the car. "I didn't want to ruin his memory."

"The secret's safe with me," Tillie said sadly. "But I wish us being together didn't mean me coming between you and your sister."

"It doesn't," Violet said. "Not as far as I'm concerned. If she were in love with someone, I'd welcome them with open arms."

Tillie gestured to the tub. "Join me?"

Violet crossed the space between them, her eyes trailing over the outline of Tillie's form beneath the bubbles. All of her anger, all of her frustration, melted away. This was what mattered, this woman who'd filled a void in Violet's heart. She knelt down and pressed her lips to Tillie's shoulder, then her collarbone, then the side of her jaw. With one hand behind Tillie's head, she brought her mouth to Tillie's mouth. Tillie's lips parted, and Violet kissed her long and slow and deep.

When she pulled back, there were wet handprints on the back of her blouse.

"I'm going to go mix us a couple of Negronis," Violet said, a little breathless. They drank Manhattans when Regina was around, because it was her drink of choice. But Tillie preferred gin.

"Who needs a drink when someone kisses you like that?" Tillie asked, voice husky.

Violet leaned over once more, planting a small kiss on Tillie's cheek. She hurried into the hall. A splash came from the room behind her, and Violet smiled, letting herself relive the moment, reminding herself this was what life was about—love and joy and being seen.

As she reached the staircase, she ran right into Regina.

Her sister took a step back, bringing her close to Violet's height. They stood there for a few moments in silence. Regina opened her mouth to speak with something like hope in her eyes, but Violet held up a hand.

"I think you've said enough tonight."

Regina frowned, but before she could reply, the house started to moan, as if the pipes were about to burst. It was a desperate sort of sound, and though Violet wanted to reassure the house she would patch what Regina had broken between them, she couldn't make that promise.

"Vi . . ." Regina started to say, but Violet turned back the way she came. Tillie was right. They didn't need gin with a love like theirs.

As much as Violet wanted to run for the bathroom, to leave her sister behind and crawl into Tillie's arms, she held her head high and walked slowly. She wouldn't let Regina get the best of her. But as soon as she rounded the corner, she picked up her pace. When she rested her hand on the doorknob, she took a long deep breath.

"No Negronis," she said as she stepped inside. "I ran into—"

Violet stopped short.

Tillie lay in the tub, her arms hanging limp over the edge, almost like she'd fallen asleep.

"Tillie?"

There was no response.

"Tillie," Violet said again, this time louder.

When Tillie didn't move, Violet ran toward her, slipping on water that had spilled over the edge. She steadied herself with a hand on the wall. Then, she dropped to her knees. Tillie's eyes were open and unblinking, her lips blue. Violet grabbed her by the shoulders, trying to lift her out of the tub, but she was too heavy for Violet to move on her own.

"Regina!" Violet screamed her sister's name. "Help me!"

Within moments, Regina was there in the doorway. Violet held Tillie by the arms.

"What happened?" Regina asked, shock in her voice.

There was no time to explain. "Grab her legs."

Together they lifted Tillie from the tub. Water splashed over the edges, drenching them both. Once they had her on the ground, Violet dropped to her knees, squeezed Tillie's nose, and brought her mouth to Tillie's. She breathed and breathed and breathed, but no matter how many times she tried to force air into Tillie's lungs, Tillie never coughed up the water.

Violet rested a hand on Tillie's chest, right above her heart. It moved weakly beneath her palm.

Thump.

Thump.

Then, it stopped.

Violet thought her heart might have stopped with it. Fear clawed at her throat, and tears sprang up in her eyes.

"No," she whispered.

As the words left her mouth, the walls started to shake. The tap on the sink and the faucet in the tub turned on, like the house, too, was crying. She pressed her ear to Tillie's chest, listened for one more beat, but she was met with only the groaning of the pipes.

A sob tore from her throat.

Violet felt her heart breaking. She grew cold, right in the middle of her chest where once she had felt every warm and wonderful thing. It was as if the light inside of her dimmed, and she didn't know if it would ever burn brightly again.

Chapter Fifty-Four

Florence, Now

Florence glanced up from Violet's journal. She hadn't known much about her grandmother. But from what Violet had written, Regina Caldwell really was a monster. She may have been there with Violet in Tillie's final moments, but she'd done everything she could to tear them apart. It was because of Regina that the house thought Owen's family murdered Helen and Christopher.

"Your great-grandfather didn't kill them," Florence said.

"What do you mean?" Owen asked. "How do you know?"

"It's in here." She held the journal up. "Robert had been drinking. He drove into that tree all on his own. Violet never told anyone—not even Regina."

There was a pause as Owen took in her words. "Then the house killed Tillie for nothing," he said with a deep sort of sadness.

But Florence shook her head. "I don't know. From what Violet wrote, the house seemed as heartbroken as she was."

That got Evie's attention. She looked up from the journal she'd been reading. "You don't think the house did it?"

"I don't know what to think." Florence reached for the diary containing her mother's spell and looked it over.

She ran her fingertip over the list and bit her lip. "I don't think this spell is what you think it is."

"It's clearly a binding spell," Evie said. "The string, the black candle, the objects."

Florence shook her head and tapped the list with her fingertip. "The temperance card is throwing me. It's a card for balance. If she wanted to bind, she'd have been better off using the eight of swords or the devil or even the hanged man."

"It's the same card you pulled thirteen years ago," Evie said. "When we were looking for a way to end the curse. Just because we can't see how it works, doesn't mean that it won't."

"Did she write anything about it in what you read?" Florence asked Owen.

He flipped back a few pages. "No, but she *did* write about drawing the seven of swords."

"That's the card Mom pulled before you started reading!" Clara said from where she sat with Ink by the fire.

"We thought it pointed to Helen and Christopher's deaths." Owen shook his head slowly. "But if my great-grandfather didn't kill them for the shop, then it must mean something else."

"It can also represent stealing something!" Clara added.

"That's right, honeybee," Evie said.

Owen held up the journal he'd been reading. "Regina wanted to strengthen her own magic. She'd been casting spells on Violet—"

"—but Violet was more powerful," Florence finished. "Violet wrote about that, too." She glanced over her mother's spell one more time, then took the journal from Owen and flipped to her grandmother's spell.

Evie leaned over the edge of her chair to take a look. "I thought it was a binding spell because of the string and the candles—black to bind and brown for the house. But Grandma left out the brown candle. I couldn't figure out why, but after what you both read . . ." she paused as she pressed her lips together. "With the temperance card and the offering, what if it's a siphoning spell?"

Florence took a surprised breath. "You think she was trying to take Violet's magic."

"It would strengthen her power," Evie said.

But Regina wasn't the only Caldwell witch to cast that spell. Their mother had as well.

"Why would Mom need a siphoning spell? And what would she have offered to make it happen?" Florence looked up at her sister. "What did you offer?"

A flush crept up Evie's neck and settled into her cheeks. "I . . ." She paused, shook her head. "My love for Angela."

"Oh, Evie," Angela said, reaching for her hand.

"It was the only thing I had that felt big enough," Evie said. "And if it meant keeping you safe, keeping all of you safe . . ."

"When you lit the candle, the beam fell on her," Florence said. "The spell didn't try to take your feelings for her, it tried to take *her*."

Beside Florence, Owen stiffened. "Regina must have done the same thing," he said, voice low. "But she offered up Violet's love."

They sat in silence for a few moments as Owen's words sank in.

"Violet's fears were right," Florence said. "It *was* Regina who killed Tillie."

"And it wasn't the only time Regina used the spell," Evie said. "She was preparing it in the journal I read, too. She didn't list out the ingredients, but she mentioned dipping candles for the curse."

"I found something like that in your Mom's childhood diary," Angela chimed in. "Your grandmother was having trouble with her magic, so she had Linda dip two brown candles for her. One to call someone home, and one that was used in a spell later the same night."

There were only two diaries left to read, the pages splayed out by Clara's spell—Regina's from 1973 and their mother's from 1986. Florence glanced at her sister. "What do you think?"

Evie reached for the journal from the year Florence was born. "The house gave me this one. I want to see what I missed."

Florence took her grandmother's journal. Beside her, Owen leaned closer to see over her shoulder while Angela did the same with Evie. Together, all four of them began to read.

Chapter Fifty-Five

Violet, 1973

It was almost midnight by the time Violet made it to Burdock Creek. She turned down the driveway to find Honeysuckle House rising up in the dark, and with it came a deep sorrow in her chest.

She killed the engine and stepped out of the car. As she approached the house, the porch lights flickered on, and a honeysuckle vine made its way toward her.

"It's nice to see you, too," Violet said sadly as the vine loosely wound its way around her waist and up her torso. She plucked a blossom free, pulled off the end, and brought the base of the flower to her lips, drinking the nectar. When she finished, the vine released her, and she continued to the stairs. She stopped short as she found a child she didn't recognize sitting on the steps, and Violet's sadness grew even deeper.

"You must be Linda," Violet said. "Isn't it past your bedtime?"

"You know me?" Linda asked.

Violet crossed her arms and shook her head. Of course Regina had kept the truth of her from her child. "You don't know who I am, do you?"

"Should I?" The girl sounded scared.

"I'm your mother's sister," she said. "Violet."

Linda mouthed the word *sister,* surprise clear on her face. She came down a few steps until she was at eye level with Violet. She studied her for a few moments, head tilted to one side.

"I like your beauty mark," she finally said. "I wish I had one."

Violet pressed the tip of her finger to the freckle at the corner of her eye. It had appeared after Tillie died and had been another thing she was certain her sister would've insisted Violet cover up.

"Mine came later in life," Violet said. "Maybe yours will, too. How old are you?"

"Eleven," Linda said shyly.

Violet stood staring at her niece, this young girl who looked so much like Violet and almost nothing like Regina. Yes, she had the same eyes—hazel, like all the Caldwell women—but at eleven Linda was already well on her way to Violet's height. When she smiled, her right incisor came down over her lower lip, so much like Violet's. And even the way she held herself, confident but wary, as if she, too, had seen her fair share of tragedy felt all too familiar. She looked thin for her age, and she had the shadow of a bruise on her cheek, which had Violet worrying over how Regina had cared for her, or if she'd cared for her at all.

"Have you eaten?" Violet asked.

Linda shook her head.

"I need to talk to your mother, but as soon as I'm done, we'll take care of that."

"I'm fine. Mom's been busy." There was a touch of defensiveness in Linda's voice. "If you care so much, why didn't you come sooner?"

"I didn't know about you," Violet said. "Just like you didn't know about me."

"But my mom is your sister. Didn't you want to see her?"

"It's a long story, and one we don't have time for," Violet said. "Not right now—not if we want to keep you and your mother safe."

"You're here because of the curse." Then, with a gasp, Linda said, "The candles were for you."

Her aunt's eyes narrowed. "What do you mean?"

"My mother had me dip brown candles to call someone home. And here you are."

"Wait," Violet asked. "Your mother called me home? With magic?"

"She was having trouble doing it on her own, so she had me make them."

Violet pressed a hand to her chest to where she, too, had felt a shift over the past few days, an erratic flickering of power that felt like it might go out at any moment.

"Where is your mother now?" she asked.

"Upstairs," Linda said with a shrug, but Violet could see the fear in her eyes. "She said she was going to stop the curse, and I didn't need to worry."

Violet glanced up at the house. Inside the lights flickered. On and off. On and off. Then, they held that way. The only glow came from the window at the top of the turret where her sister had always cast her spells after their parents died.

"She said it was very important I didn't interrupt her." At first, Linda's voice was matter of fact, but it slowly shifted as fear crept in, and with it, sadness. "If I distract her, she might mess up the spell and the curse will kill her and leave me all alone."

"She told me she needed my help with the spell," Violet said.

"I don't know anything about that."

Realization dawned on Violet. "She wanted you to talk to me. She wanted you to keep me busy."

The night Tillie died sped through Violet's mind like a film. The fight with her sister, the black candle on her altar, the bathtub. Her confidence that nothing Regina did would be more powerful than Violet's magic.

Unless Regina had found a way to change that.

"No," Violet whispered. She stepped around her niece and started up the stairs at a run.

Chapter Fifty-Six

Regina, 1973

Regina stood in her attic room, her spell prepared, as she watched her sister's car—the car they were meant to share—pull up the drive. She'd done everything she could to keep Violet in her life, and still her sister had left. Yes, Regina's siphoning spell had gone wrong. She hadn't intended for Tillie to die, though it did solve the problem of Tillie being in her house.

The moment it happened, Regina had felt it deep inside her. With the sacrifice of Violet's love—of Tillie's life—the siphoning spell was complete. Her sister's power flowed through her. A hot, burning flame, brighter than any candle. And with all that light, came shadows. A darkness had found its way inside Regina, twisting her thoughts, her hopes, her fears.

It wasn't until the light that cast those shadows started to flicker almost thirteen years later that she'd realized her true mistake. In casting her siphoning spell, she'd been careless. She'd said she'd give up her magic if her spell didn't return Violet to her, if things didn't go back to the way they were before Tillie. Those words had tangled up with thirteen years of grief on the anniversary of her parents' death, and here she was, about to lose her magic forever if she didn't cast the spell once more. If she didn't make a sacrifice that would allow her to continue to siphon another witch's power.

Only, this time, all she had left to sacrifice was Violet, which meant she would have to siphon her daughter. She'd make sure Linda couldn't leave the same way Violet had, because in thirteen years, she'd have to find a way to do it again.

Regina had everything ready. The brown candle to trap Linda. The black candle to siphon her sister. The doorknob to anchor the spell to Honeysuckle House, her unwilling accomplice. Regina held a match poised to strike as she listened for the sound of footsteps on her spiral staircase.

There!

Violet stood at the top of the landing, and just behind her, Linda.

"Hello, Violet." Regina's voice was love and loss and anger all rolled into one.

"Regina," Violet said, her eyes sweeping over Regina's altar. "What are you . . . ?"

Something in Regina considered setting the match down and letting her magic die, but the darkness was louder than whatever love she still harbored for her sister. She struck the match and brought the tip first to the brown candle, then the black.

As the darker candle started to burn, there was a cracking of wood. The floorboard beneath Violet snapped in two. She stumbled.

"Mom!" Linda shouted. "It's not working! The curse is going to take her!"

Regina hated that her daughter had to see whatever would come next, but maybe it was better this way.

"You're right," Regina said, voice flat.

The window opened wide, and a breeze blew through the attic as if to put out the flame, but the candle only burned brighter.

Another board snapped. Then another, tipping Violet forward. As she fell, a jagged plank tilted up.

Regina almost looked away, but though Violet had abandoned her, Regina owed her sister this: a witness to her final moments.

The wood pierced Violet's sternum. At first the sound was thick and wet. Then there was a popping of bone after bone as it tore through her rib cage and came out the other side, through her back.

Violet's eyes shifted up to meet Regina's. She opened her mouth, but whatever she wanted to say was lost as blood spilled from her lips and her eyes rolled up in her head.

"We have to call someone!" Linda cried from behind Violet.

"They won't be able to help," Regina said. "They probably won't even come, not with how afraid they are of this place. We were too late, but don't worry, these candles will protect the two of us."

As the brown candle sputtered out, spent, Regina lifted two tarot cards from the table and held them over the last bit of fire from the black taper. The flames started up the paper toward her fingertips. Once they reached her hand, she dropped what remained of the cards into a small cast iron bowl. Then, the candle winked out.

Across the room, her daughter leaned forward, one hand clutching her heart as the heat in Regina's chest—that flickering flame that had threatened to go out—steadied, and her magic was safe once more.

Chapter Fifty-Seven

Honeysuckle House, 1986

The sight of Violet on the front steps thirteen years ago had sent a current through the house's wiring unlike anything it had felt before. Honeysuckle House had been heartbroken after she'd left. It had welcomed Tillie Grey with open doors and turned records and crisp sheets. It had watched as that welcoming created a rift between Violet and Regina the house didn't understand. When Tillie had slipped under the water, the house had felt her hands pressing against the sides of the tub, unable to surface as the water pushed her down. Though it had tried to pull the drain or tip the tub over, it had lost control of itself in that moment. It wasn't until Tillie stopped thrashing that it had any autonomy at all, and by then all it could do was rattle its pipes with grief.

It had done its best to be at Violet's side after that, to let her know she wasn't alone. But Violet had left anyway. For the next few years, it was only Regina and the house. Though they comforted each other, there were days when Regina went without speaking a word to the house, lost as she was in her own head. There were others where she yelled and raged and threw things at the walls, as if the spell she'd cast the day Tillie died had twisted her.

That's why the house had been overjoyed when Regina welcomed Linda into the world. She'd dipped and burned a red candle, left for the night, and a few months later, her belly had grown. Honeysuckle House had watched over her as she gave birth on the bed upstairs—no doctor, no midwife—just a determined witch and a host of candles in various colors to call in good health and good fortune. The house had done its best to keep the lights soft and low, but every moan out of Regina's mouth was echoed with a flash of incandescent worry. Only when Linda's first cry tore through the air did the house finally gain control of the bulbs, turning them all the way down so mom and babe could sleep peacefully.

It wasn't until well after Linda had come into the world that the house learned of the curse, when Regina explained to Linda why they stayed home, why so few people visited. It didn't fully understand how anyone could fall victim behind its walls, how Tillie had died under its watch. Shouldn't the house have been able to save them?

This time, though, the house understood. When Regina lit that black candle, the spell had taken over. It made the house drown Tillie. It pulled up the floorboard that pierced Violet's heart. Over the past few days, it had watched Regina prepare the spell once more.

This was why it had drawn Linda upstairs—so she could stop her.

"What is it you want me to see?"

Linda's eyes swept over the room, landing on her mother's altar. She approached the table slowly. There she found a list of spell components written out, and at the top of the paper, her unborn daughter's name.

"Mom's protection spell," Linda said.

The pipes groaned, as if to say, look closer.

As she took in her mother's handwriting, Linda's eyes narrowed. The string, the blanket her mother had made for Florence, an old doorknob, and one of Linda's tubes of lipstick. Beside them, the tarot cards and candles.

Linda blinked rapidly as she put the pieces together.

"This isn't a spell meant to protect us from the curse." Horror tinged her voice. "Mother plans to cast a spell on me. On *Florence*."

The house tipped Regina's tarot deck from the shelf, ensuring a single card landed face up. The seven of swords.

Linda examined the illustration, then looked up at the shelf. "She's stealing something?"

The lights glowed brighter, and Linda gasped.

"This is a siphoning spell," she said as she turned back to the altar. "The temperance card. The magician. She's upending the balance of magic among the spell's subjects."

She pressed a hand to the side of her face, where her witch's mark was. It had appeared the night her aunt died; the house remembered it well. Regina had claimed it happened to some Caldwells. The last time the house had seen it had been the day Tillie died.

"It's no witch's mark at all," Linda whispered, more to herself than the house. "It's the mark of a witch who's been siphoned."

She picked up the list of ingredients. "An offering," she murmured. "Last time she gave up Violet, didn't she?"

The pipes moaned their sadness.

"And this time . . ." Linda trailed off. Then, she braced herself with a hand against her mother's altar. "She plans to sacrifice my husband."

Her voice was a mixture of sadness and rage, and the house wanted to cradle her and hold her close, but there wasn't time. Already, Regina was making her way back, and Linda was too lost in her thoughts to see her. Honeysuckle House opened the window and slammed it shut so hard the glass rattled in the frame. Linda jumped at the sudden noise. She looked up and out at her mother.

Regina saw her, too. She stopped, but only for a moment. Then, she broke into a run.

Linda turned back to her mother's altar.

Below them, Regina ran toward the attic, the house creaking every board in warning. Linda crossed the room and stood at the top of the spiral staircase. She gripped the banister with both hands. The house warmed the wood beneath her touch. It was on her side.

The door opened in the room below, and Regina bounded in.

"Hello, Mother," Linda said.

Regina's head shot up. She started for the stairs, a little breathless.

When her foot landed on that first step, Linda said, "I wouldn't if I were you."

Regina paused. "I don't know what you think you found up there, but my spell is the only thing that can break the curse."

"You think I couldn't piece together the purpose of your spell?" Linda held a hand over her belly. "Florence is my daughter. *Mine*."

"And I'm trying to keep her safe," Regina said. "That spell is our only chance. We don't know who cursed us, so there's no undoing it. We have to make our power stronger than the magic that caused this."

Linda narrowed her eyes. "You mean your magic? The same magic that killed Aunt Violet and took Tillie Grey? Did you kill your parents, too?"

Red flooded Regina's cheeks. "How dare you." Her voice came out low and dark.

"Tell me I'm wrong," Linda said.

The house, too, wished she was wrong, but it knew better.

"You think you've put it all together." Regina took another step. "That I've been killing to grow my own power." Another. "And what? If you push me down these stairs, it'll all be over?"

"I'm warning you," Linda said.

"If one of us doesn't cast that spell, come midnight our magic will be gone forever," Regina said. "Taking my sister's life was the last thing I wanted. She's why I did this in the first place. When I realized I was losing my magic thirteen years ago, I couldn't stand by and let it happen. I didn't know how to survive in this world without my spells. And by then, I had you to care for. I had to make a choice. I had to siphon your power."

"I won't let you do this," Linda said, as Regina reached the top of the steps. She grabbed Linda's arms and pushed her back, but the house steadied her.

"You don't have a choice."

Regina threw her weight against Linda, forcing her back. The house helped Linda regain her footing to keep her mother from pushing past her. As the two of them struggled there at the top of the steps, Linda gripped her belly and cried out, bracing herself with one hand against the wall.

The lights flashed their worry. The baby was coming.

Regina slid around Linda and ran for the candles. Linda tried to follow after her, but another contraction wracked her. Regina's hand hung poised over the black candle. The house shuffled the floorboards, but it wasn't enough.

Regina struck the match.

"No!" Linda shouted. The house shifted the floor beneath her, propelling Linda forward, and she collided with her mother. The match slipped from Regina's fingers and landed on the rug. The house quickly rolled up the corner to put out the flame.

Linda grabbed her mother by her thin frame, turning so her back was toward the room. She forced Regina away from the spell circle and her candles toward the staircase until the back of Regina's foot hung off the step.

Regina grabbed Linda, trying not to fall.

"You won't take Robert from me." The quiet rage in Linda's voice gave the house pause. "And you won't take my magic, either."

With that, she grabbed her mother's hands where she clung to Linda's arms, and she pried them free. Regina's eyes widened with fear. Then, Linda pushed her, hard. So hard Regina hit the back banister and fell over the edge, landing on the ground below with a heavy crack.

The pipes rattled in response. The house knew this was the only way. Regina would simply continue to cast the spell every thirteen years, taking the people the house loved most, until she, too died. Still, the house couldn't bear to watch her fall.

Linda turned back toward the altar, when something wet spilled down her legs and pooled on the floor. Linda stumbled, but the house moved one wall inward, just enough to catch her.

"Thank you," she said. The lights glowed brighter. Linda closed the gap between herself and her mother's altar as she let out a groan. She looked over the journal one last time before she picked up a match.

At first the house didn't understand. It showed Linda the truth, the cost of the spell. It flickered the lights, trying to warn her.

"It's okay," she said. "I'm going to keep this family together."

The house shook the floorboards and the walls, but still, Linda struck the match. It flung the window open, blowing out the flame.

"I have to do this." Desperation laced her voice. She turned away from the window and lit another, cupping her hand around the tip as she brought the candle to meet it. At first, the wick wouldn't light, and if homes could breathe, Honeysuckle House would've sighed with relief. But then, the candle burned.

"I offer my mother."

Linda used the candle to light the brown taper beside it. As she stared into the flames, there came a dragging sound from the steps. The house had been so focused on Linda, it had turned its attention away from Regina, not realizing she still lived. Now, the older woman pulled herself up the stairs. Blood stained the back of her head, and her leg was bent at an angle, but still she climbed.

The house tried to stop her. It tried to stop Linda. But the moment Linda lit the black candle, the house had lost control of itself.

Linda grabbed the tarot cards and put the edge of each into the flame. They caught fire instantly. She held them for a few moments before she dropped them into a cast iron bowl and watched them burn. As they did, fire engulfed the black candle. It burned fast and strong, and then, it went out.

Three of the steps fell from the spiral staircase, right where Regina was standing. Though the house tried to catch her, it was powerless to do so. The moment she hit the ground, the house regained itself. But it was too late. Her neck was broken.

The spell was complete.

Chapter Fifty-Eight

Evie, Now

After they'd shared their findings, they sat in silence for a few moments. Finally, they had the truth. Evie pressed her fingers to her witch's mark. When she was a child, she'd wished to have one just like Florence, but it wasn't until after her father died that it appeared.

"She siphoned our magic." Evie tried to imagine the amount of power her mother must've had once she'd claimed Evie's in addition to her sister's. It was no wonder they'd never been a match for her.

Evie bit her lip to try to stop herself from crying. Her mother had feared for her family, and she'd made a choice. Seeing her mother's pain and her fears right there on the page had shifted something inside of Evie. She would do anything to protect her daughter. She recognized that same resolve in Linda. She knew, were she the one trying to stop Clara's magic from being siphoned or protecting Angela from being offered as a sacrifice, she would've pushed her mother over that railing, too.

But that's where things would've ended. Evie would rather lose her magic than force this on Clara.

"This is what Mom was doing thirteen years ago." Florence held a hand to her throat as she said the words. "It's why the honeysuckle attacked me. I'd been her offering."

"But it didn't work," Angela said.

"Your mom died," Owen said. "Not you."

"Then how do we still have our magic?" Evie asked. "Why is all of this happening?"

Beside her, Florence clapped a hand over her mouth. "The house," she whispered. "The chandelier."

"It stopped her," Evie said.

"It *saved* me," Florence replied.

"But not in time." Evie had seen the remnants of the completed spell on her mother's altar.

Florence nodded slowly. "The spell took Mom's death as the offering."

"And the house has been siphoning our magic ever since," Evie said.

"Is that why it's been so scary?" Clara asked.

"I think so, honeybee," Evie said.

From what they'd read in those journals, completing the spell hadn't only put their magic at risk, it changed the witch who cast it,. twisting them. Tillie's death had been unintentional. Yes, Regina had offered Violet's love. But she hadn't meant to kill her—like what Evie had almost done to Angela. But Violet's death had been calculated. The very person Regina wanted the most, she'd murdered. Linda, too, had gone from protecting Florence and their dad only to take Robert's life thirteen years later. Though the house hadn't tried to hurt them, it had changed in other ways. The paint chipped; the cobwebs ever present. But the past week had been different, almost like the house couldn't control itself.

"It's about to lose its magic," Evie said. "And mine and Aunt Florence's along with it." The two of them would live, but it would be a magic-less existence. The same one her grandmother and her mother had been unable to contend with.

"That's why it gave you Mom's journal thirteen years ago," Florence said sadly. "It knew our magic would end, and it wanted you to use it to the fullest."

Evie gasped and held a hand over her mouth. "And our tarot reading," she said. "The hierophant was never about the house at all."

Her sister had thought it meant the house couldn't be trusted as a guide. Evie had thought it meant *Florence* couldn't be trusted as a guide. But more than a helping hand, the hierophant was a card about the passing along of tradition, and it seemed the only tradition their family had was one of abuse and control. The card had been a call to put an end to the siphoning spell.

"Temperance reversed pointed to our magic being out of balance *because* of the spell," Evie realized.

"And the hermit never meant that we needed to give up our magic or to stop hoarding it," Florence said. "It was telling us the house planned to give up *its* magic by not repeating the spell."

Clara shook her head, hard. "But magic is what makes the house alive!"

"It is," Evie said, the weight of it almost too much.

"You mean . . ." Clara paused, her voice thick. "The house is going to die?"

Chapter Fifty-Nine

Florence, Now

Florence had given up on Honeysuckle House long ago. She never believed the house had hurt her on purpose, but it had still hurt her. Even so, there had always been a part of her that hoped by not using her magic, she'd put an end to the curse. That one day she'd feel safe enough to go home. The house would open its doors wide and welcome her in with the sort of warm embrace she'd never had from her mother. She'd lost so much time with Honeysuckle House, so many years gone because she'd thought she could stop a curse that ended up being nothing more than a twisted need to control. Her grandmother and her mother had been so desperate to hold on to their magic, so unwilling to imagine a world without it, that they'd killed to keep it. Generational trauma was its own sort of curse.

Their tarot reading from a few hours ago came back to her. The woman cutting the vine in the seven of swords represented how the curse began, and the tower—the destruction of Honeysuckle House—was how it would end.

"What do we do now?" Evie asked. "We can't let the house die and take our magic with it."

But that was exactly what they had to do.

"You can't complete the siphoning spell," Owen said.

"Obviously I know that," Evie said, exasperated.

"It isn't easy," Florence agreed. "I know how much your magic means to you."

What Florence didn't say was how much she'd missed casting spells of her own, how the thought of never being able to dip a candle again opened something wide inside of her. Yes, she'd given up her magic. But that had been her choice. Now it was being taken from her. Even in death, her mother still found a way to control her.

"Don't you get it?" Evie asked. "Losing our magic doesn't just mean Honeysuckle House dies and my candles don't work. You'll lose the bookstore, too."

The walls around them creaked with a sound so low and sad it felt as if they were crying. Florence brought a hand to her mouth.

"No," she whispered. But the shop had been born of the magic inside Florence. Without it, the shelves and books and lights would go back to what they'd once been.

"Isn't there anything else you can do?" Angela asked.

"It's too late," Evie said. "It's almost midnight."

They all glanced up at the clock above the door. It hadn't been there when they'd walked into the room, but once the bookstore understood what was happening, the clock had suddenly appeared. With the small hand past the eleven, they had less than five minutes to go. Less than five minutes until Florence's magical bookshop turned back into an ordinary storefront.

Florence gripped her sister's hand as they watched the minutes tick by. Soon, the fire in her heart would die. The house as they knew it would be gone, the bookstore right along with it.

"We have to go home," Clara said, pulling Ink close to her chest. "We have to say goodbye."

But Evie shook her head. "We'll never make it, and with the house's magic as unsteady as ours, we don't know if it's safe."

Both hands aligned on the twelve, and Florence closed her eyes, afraid of what she'd find when she opened them. She took a deep breath, gave Evie's hand a squeeze, then forced herself to face the loss of her store.

She blinked her eyes open to find the room exactly as it had been moments before. The warmth in her chest still pulsed alongside her beating heart, erratic, but there. Even the witch's mark on Evie's cheek was as dark as it had been the day it appeared.

"Shop?" Florence asked.

The lights glowed brighter.

Florence shook her head slowly. She turned to her sister.

"I don't understand," Evie said. "I can still feel my magic."

Owen reached in front of Florence and picked up one of the journals. "Linda completed her spell on the morning of the thirteenth."

Beside Florence, Evie gasped. "Dad died in the morning, too."

"And Mom in the afternoon," Florence said.

"The spell isn't finished at the start of the thirteenth, but at the end," Angela said.

"We still have time." The hope in Evie's voice was contagious.

"To do what?" Florence asked. "How can we fix this?"

Evie tapped a finger against her nose—a gesture they shared. For the first time in years, Florence loved seeing herself in her sister. "With temperance reversed, the cards showed us the curse was actually a siphoning spell. Maybe . . ." She reached for Florence's deck but glanced up at her sister before taking it. When Florence nodded, Evie started to shuffle.

She fanned out the cards and held her hand over them. "Come on." She shook out her hand and tried again. Then, she flipped a card, revealing an illustration of a honeysuckle vine with a single, unnatural, thorn in its center. The ace of swords.

Evie glanced up, meeting Florence's gaze. They spoke the words at the same time.

"A cord-cutting spell."

"The tower," Angela said, a little breathless. "It was about more than the house dying."

Evie nodded slowly at first, then more quickly. "The tower is an undoing. A breaking of foundations."

"If we can sever ourselves from the house before the siphoning spell ends, then we won't lose our magic," Florence said.

"It wouldn't save Honeysuckle House." Evie had tears in her eyes. "But it would save your shop."

"And it's what the house wants." The words were thick in Florence's mouth. "It's what it wanted all along. It wasn't Mom's magic keeping you from the attic room. Honeysuckle House didn't want us to find the spell because it was prepared to be the final victim."

"It was afraid I would siphon Clara and keep the cycle going," Evie breathed. "I almost did."

Florence grabbed her sister's hand and squeezed it hard. "But you didn't. That's what matters."

Evie leaned her head against Florence's shoulder. "Thank you for stopping me."

"Thank you for wanting to save my shop, even if we can't do the same for the house."

Evie looked up into Florence's eyes. "You'll do the spell with me?"

Florence didn't hesitate to nod. "I only ever gave up our magic because I thought it would protect us. But it was never our power that endangered us."

A pause. Then, Evie said, "It was Mom."

Florence threw her arms around her sister and pulled her close, and for the first time in a long time, Florence felt like she was home.

Chapter Sixty

Clara, Now

Clara held Ink tightly. She pressed her face into his fur and she cried and she cried. It wasn't fair that Honeysuckle House had to die so her mom could keep her magic and her aunt could keep her magic (which she didn't even use) and Ink & Pages could live.

It wasn't the house's fault everything had gone so wrong. The house had saved her aunt. It had saved her mom.

Maybe Clara could save the house.

As the others sat preparing their cord-cutting spell, going over possible candle colors and crystals and herbs and tarot cards and every sort of magic they had at their fingertips to sever the link the siphoning spell had forged, Clara skirted the edge of the room, chewing at her lip all the while.

"Maybe add some basil for protection," Evie suggested. "And the death card?"

"Definitely not the death card," Owen said, horrified.

"It's metaphorical," Evie said, something Clara had heard her mom say more than once, and if she wasn't so focused on saving the house, she would've repeated the words Evie had said when she first taught Clara about the card: *Death is a transition, the end of something old to make way for the beginning of something new.*

The only problem was, Clara wasn't ready for something new.

"I'm with Owen on this," Florence said. "We thought the tower was metaphorical, and then the house burned. Besides, we've never done a cord-cutting spell. We can't afford for anything to go wrong. Regina did her spell last minute without thinking through the consequences, and look where that got her."

If Clara had her way, they wouldn't have to worry about the cord cutting at all. She gripped Ink close and whispered in his ear, "Go make a mess of things."

The kitten looked up at her and blinked his little moon eyes. When she set him down, he ran straight for Florence, jumped up on the table, and sat beside her cup of tea. His tail twitched. He looked at Clara. When she nodded, he butted his head against the mug, nudging it toward the edge of the table. One. Two. Three times. It hit the ground with a crash of broken porcelain.

Florence and Evie jumped up from their seats as Ink leapt from the center of the room, forcing them to turn their backs on Clara.

"Ink!" Florence said with worry in her voice as she checked the kitten to make sure he wasn't hurt, and it made Clara feel even worse for what she was about to do. Her aunt held him up. She inspected his paws, scratched between his ears, and said, "No harm done."

As they set to cleaning up the spill, Clara darted in. She plucked the journal with her grandmother's spell from the table, then slipped out of the room. Ink followed close behind.

Clara couldn't walk all the way back to Honeysuckle House. Well, she could. She knew the way. But the longer it took her to get home, the more she risked being found out. That, and she was very tired from a very long night and it was much too dark for her to walk out there all alone. Not that Clara was afraid of the dark. But she wasn't exactly *not* afraid of the dark, either.

Instead, she headed for the back door of the bookshop. When she reached it, she said, "I'd like to go outside without the alarm going off, please."

The door opened silently, and Clara stepped into the night. Sometime after they'd arrived at Ink & Pages, the sky had opened up again. Clara stayed as close to the wall as she could to stay dry under the overhang. She shrugged off her backpack and hid the diary safely inside. Then, she pulled out a brown candle and a box of matches. She had several such candles nestled deep inside her backpack and had used one after her mom tucked her into bed the night before to get the candle she'd dipped from the workshop.

They were one of the first spells she taught herself. Evie wasn't strict about much, but when it came to Clara being home before dark, she was a stickler. Clara had found a way to make sure she never had to worry her mom.

A streak of lightning flashed across the sky, and thunder rumbled so loud Ink pressed himself closer to Clara's legs. She slid the box open, pulled out a match, then struck it against the side. She brought the red glow to the candle's wick and said, "Take me home. And be fast about it." She paused. "And may my loved ones be safe, my magic be good, and my work be a blessing."

Like the taper she'd burned that brought Ink into her life, this one melted fast with the urgency of her intention. She let it fall from her hand before the wax could hit her skin, and as it did, a door appeared in the side of the shop.

Beside her, Ink looked up and gave a soft meow. Clara's heart twinged and she started to cry all over again. But she smiled through her tears, because that's what brave girls did, and Clara had to be brave for Ink.

"Don't worry," she said. "I'll make sure it doesn't hurt."

Then, she opened the door and stepped into her bedroom at Honeysuckle House.

Chapter Sixty-One

Evie, Now

Once the spilled tea was cleaned up, they got back to work on their plan for the cord-cutting spell. Evie tapped a pen against her mouth as she jotted down notes—Florence's ideas and her own, combined with input from Angela and Owen. The two of them might not be Caldwell witches, but their knowledge of tarot and crystals helped things along.

"I'm thinking selenite," Angela said.

"Oh, that's good," Florence replied.

"What about the ace of swords?" Owen asked. "You could burn it the same way Regina used the magician and temperance cards."

"It represents the start of a new journey," Florence said. "One focused on truth instead of the deception of the seven."

Despite everything that had brought them to that moment, Evie found a soft sort of joy had come alight in her heart. For the first time in years, she and her sister were working on a spell together—Angela and Owen right along with them. This was the sort of future she'd imagined for herself when she was younger, before her mother died and everything went so wrong between her and Florence. She let that warmth fill her, let it block out the reality of what the spell meant. Honeysuckle House had been in her life longer even than her sister. It was the family she held onto when Florence turned her back on the

Caldwell magic. If Evie let herself dwell on the thought of losing it, she'd never have the strength to finish the spell.

"Can someone hand me Mom's list?" Evie asked. "I want to make sure we don't use any of the crystals she did."

Owen rifled through the journals. After a few moments, he looked up. "It's not here."

"Do you have it, Florence?" Evie grew impatient as the impending loss set in.

"I put it on the table before I started reading Aunt Violet's journal," Florence said.

Angela looked around the room. "Clara's not here, either."

Evie's head shot up. Clara had been sitting in the chair on the opposite side of the table only ten minutes ago, before the kitten made a mess of things.

"Ink's missing, too," Florence said. "Maybe they got bored and went to play in the shop."

But Evie's eyes met Angela's, and she saw the same fear there that she felt in her own heart. Honeysuckle House wasn't only Evie's family, it was Clara's, too. It had played the part of older sister and grandmother and friend, and though Evie knew the cord cutting had to be done, Clara might not see things the same way.

"You don't think . . ." Angela trailed off.

"Oh no," Evie said. Then again, "Oh no." She jumped up from her spot on the couch. "We have to stop her."

Florence, too, stood. She gripped Evie by the shoulders. "I'm sure she's fine. We'll ask the shop where to find her, then get back to work."

"You don't understand," Evie said. "Clara's been so worried about the house. She took Mom's spell. She's going to try to save it."

Her sister stiffened. Her grip on Evie tightened. "And Ink . . ."

"She plans to use him as the offering," Angela whispered.

Evie ran for the door and threw it open. "Clara!" she called.

But there was no answer.

The main lights flickered on, and Florence came to stand beside Evie in the doorway. "Show us where she is," Florence said.

Nothing in the room changed.

"She's gone." Evie imagined her seven-year-old daughter walking along Burdock Creek's main thoroughfare after midnight during a storm.

"She can't have gotten far," Florence said. "We should be able to catch her."

"She's already there," Angela said, voice low with despair.

Evie whirled around. Her eyes searched Angela's. "What do you mean?"

"The other day, when I took Clara to pack her bag after the fire, she filled her backpack with crystals and candles," Angela said. "She had a bag full of brown tapers."

Evie and Florence shared a look.

"She told me she uses them when she's out playing too late," Angela said. "I thought she was being clever. But I think she meant it literally."

Clara meant everything she said literally.

A mixture of pride and terror shot through Evie. Her daughter's magic was unlike anything Evie had ever seen. Her own magic—before her mother had bound her—had been strong like Clara's, but she'd been afraid of it. Except for the hummingbird she'd summoned for her sister, Evie had rarely done any spells on her own until much later in life.

That her daughter had dipped a candle that could take her back to Honeysuckle House? From anywhere? If Evie weren't reeling from what she knew her daughter intended to do, she'd be beaming. But if they didn't hurry, Clara would complete the spell, siphoning not only Evie and Florence's magic, but the house's, too. All that power would twist her. It would change her like it had Evie's mother and her grandmother. And in thirteen years, unless Clara cast the spell again, her magic would be gone. Forever.

Chapter Sixty-Two

Clara, Now

Clara stood peering through the hole her spell had burned into the attic, larger now thanks to her mother's sledgehammer, but no less her fault. Even though her spell had hurt her home, without it, she wouldn't be able to save Honeysuckle House. At the thought, she found herself feeling sad all over again and then mad—madder than she'd ever felt before. It wasn't right what her grandmother and her great-grandmother had done, what she now had to do.

She cradled Ink in one arm and pressed a hand to the wallpaper.

"I'm sorry I hurt you," she said.

The pipes groaned and the floorboards creaked and something in the walls rattled.

"I'm not afraid of you," she said. "I know you love me."

The room looked exactly as they'd left it. The beam still covered the far side. Rain poured through the hole in the roof. If Clara let the house die like her mom and her aunt planned to, they'd have to patch it themselves or call someone to come out and do it. A stranger would have to stomp around on the roof with no thought for what the house might feel, and it wouldn't matter because the house wouldn't be able to feel, and that realization only made Clara more determined to make things right.

She pulled the stolen diary from her bag.

"Light, please," she said.

The house obliged, still not aware of why she'd come. She wouldn't tell it. If Clara had learned anything from what the others had said about the journals, it was that sometimes you had to keep secrets from the people you loved.

Clara looked over the words her grandmother had scribbled on the paper. She was still learning to read, but these ones she knew. Most everything was still here. She wouldn't use the brown candle—she wasn't trying to make anyone stay where they didn't want to be—but she needed the black one. Her mom had put her own intention into it to offer up her love for Angela, but if Clara made her offering first, maybe that wouldn't matter. After all, the house had been able to stop her grandma's candle.

But she didn't want to *kill* Ink. She just wanted to make him disappear. She still had the other taper she'd made from the day she'd summoned him. If she could use it to bring him into the world, then she could use it to take him out of the world, too.

Ink leapt up onto the altar, then sat right in the middle of the broken spell circle. His tail twitched.

"You are a very good boy," Clara said through tears.

Her mom had taken one of the crystals with her—the obsidian. That was just as well because Clara's obsidian had been a part of what she'd used to call Ink to her aunt. She fished the small, crystalline cat out of her pocket. She grabbed the tourmaline and quartz then set them up in a triangle in the middle of the floor—along with her figurine—leaving plenty of space for the real kitten.

The lights flickered on and off.

"Don't worry," Clara said. "I love you as much as I love Mom and Aunt Flo and Angela and . . ." her voice got caught in her throat. Clara was unused to crying so much, and she found she didn't like it.

"And Ink," she managed. The kitten looked up at her. She scratched him between the ears. It was only fair he get as many pets as she could give him before she had to say goodbye.

With tears streaming down her face, she took the items her mother had tied together with string—Clara's rock and her mom's pendant, the doorknob and her aunt's necklace. After setting them in the center of the circle, she took the black candle and the tarot cards and added them to the mix. Finally, she turned back to Ink who sat all alone on top of the table. She picked him up and buried her face in his fur.

"It's not fair," she said.

Ink meowed in response. Then, he began to purr, and Clara cried even harder.

The window opened and closed.

"I have to do this," she said. "I'm not ready to let you go."

She took Ink and set him in the middle of her spell circle. He looked up at her through his big yellow eyes, then he turned around a few times before lying down and resting his little head on his little paws.

Clara bit her lip.

"Big girls don't cry," she said to herself. It wasn't something her mother had ever said to her. In fact, Evie told her all of her emotions were beautiful and important and needed to be given space. But she'd heard a teacher at school say it to one of her classmates, and it had seemed to work then. She thought it might work now.

It didn't.

With shaking hands, she pulled the extra blue-and-pink candle from her bag. She picked up a knife from the table to cut off the top. The blade slipped the first time, nicking her finger. Though blood welled from her skin, she made the cut, then she flipped the candle over, and made two more on the bottom so she could light the wick. She set it in the circle beside Ink. He rubbed his head against her hand, and Clara bent down to press a kiss on the top of his head.

She struck a match, and the house began to shake.

Chapter Sixty-Three

Evie, Now

"We're never going to make it," Evie said as she dug her keys from her pocket and took off at a run for the door. Nothing mattered to Evie as much as her daughter—nothing—but she'd been so worried about the fate of her own magic she forgot to keep an eye on Clara. Now, Clara was about to do something she'd never be able to undo, and it was Evie's fault.

"Evie!" Florence called. "Wait!"

But she didn't stop. She didn't even look back.

"Evie!" This time it was Angela, and she was right behind Evie. She grabbed Evie's hand, slowing her movement.

"We don't have time."

"Look," Angela said. Evie paused at the wonder in her voice.

She turned to find Angela pointing back the way they'd come. There, beside the door to the room the shop had created for them, was another door. Florence and Owen stood in front of it, and when Florence turned the knob, it opened into the hallway outside Evie's bedroom.

Evie's breath caught in her throat. Though she knew her sister had not cast a spell to bring the door into being, she also knew this *was* her sister's magic. Ink & Pages was the home her sister had created after she'd left Honeysuckle House behind. It knew her, it loved her, and because Florence loved Clara, because she loved Evie, it had given them a chance.

Evie ran for her sister, for the door, for her daughter.

She stepped through it and into Honeysuckle House. The floorboards shook beneath her feet. She stumbled, but Florence caught her as she, too, crossed into the hallway. Once Evie regained her footing, she pushed through her bedroom door and took the spiral stairs up to the attic. She landed on the threshold to find the lights flickering on and off on the other side of the broken wall.

Lightning crackled across the sky.

"Clara!" Evie shouted as she ran through to the other side to find her daughter with a match burning in her hand.

Chapter Sixty-Four

Clara, Now

"Mommy?" Clara asked, taking her eyes off the match. The flame traveled down the stick and brushed up against Clara's fingers. She yelped and shook it out. Then, she cried harder.

"I can't do it."

She felt the failure of the moment in her chest and her throat and her stomach. She wanted so much to save the house and to save her family's magic. She was so close to doing just that, but she loved the kitten too much to give him up.

"I can't hurt Ink."

As the words left her mouth, the house stopped its shaking. The lights steadied, electricity humming softly in the air. Thunder rumbled outside as the rain continued its assault.

One minute Clara's mom stood at the top of the spiral staircase, in front of Florence and Angela and Owen, the next she was right there beside Clara. She scooped her up off the floor and crushed her against her chest, somehow both gentle and firm and Clara wished she'd never let her go.

"Oh, honeybee."

"Mommy," Clara mumbled into Evie's chest.

Evie ran her hand over Clara's hair and pressed her mouth to the top of Clara's head. Her tears dripped onto Clara's scalp, and

Clara sobbed when she realized she was the one who had made her mother cry.

"I wanted to save the house," Clara said. "It's not fair we have to let it go. It was trying to keep you safe. It didn't mean to siphon your magic, and now there's no one left to protect it but me."

"You're right," Florence said from behind Clara's mom. "It's not fair."

Clara looked up at her aunt. She brushed the back of her hand over her eyes and hiccupped through her tears. "Then why can't we fix it?"

"We can't always fix the things other people break. All we can do is find a way to live with the pieces that are left behind." Her aunt, too, had tears in her eyes, and that only made Clara cry more.

"I wish we could," Evie said. "But the only way to put an end to all of this is to let the house go. To let it have what it's wanted all along."

"To die?" Clara pulled back from her mom, wriggling free of her hold. "No one wants that!"

"No, honeybee." Evie held her arms out to her. "To make it so we can live the lives we were always meant to have, without the women who came before us getting to choose what that looks like."

As her mother said the words, the lights in the room glowed brighter.

"See?" Evie asked.

"But this was what my spell was for," Clara said. "To bring us all back together. We can't let the house go, now."

"Your spell worked," her aunt said. "It brought me home. It opened this room so we could release the house without your mom and me losing our magic."

The light winked off then back on, almost like a question.

Florence knelt and rested a hand on the floor. "Thank you for protecting us. For saving me. I'm sorry I didn't understand."

Clara looked from her aunt to her mom. Evie dropped her arms to her side, then she knelt, too. "Without Clara's spell, we'd never have known the truth," she said to the house. "We'd never have had the chance to say goodbye."

The walls groaned and Clara groaned right along with them as she sat on the floor between her mom and her aunt. She leaned her head against her mom's shoulder, and Evie wrapped an arm around her.

"I love you, House," Clara said through her tears. The hardwood softened beneath her, and she sank into it like she might into one of her mom's hugs.

Part XIII
The Ten of Cups

A card of family, of home, and a promise for the future.

Chapter Sixty-Five

Florence, Now

As her niece said goodbye to Honeysuckle House and her sister cradled the girl in her arms, Florence watched them, a sadness boiling deep inside her, threatening to spill over. Though she couldn't stop her tears from falling, she wouldn't let herself break. She wouldn't make this moment about her.

This was their loss. Their home, something Florence had left behind long ago. She had no right to this sorrow. She'd turned her back on her family and on Honeysuckle House. She would do what she had to do to help make things right, but she wouldn't intrude on their heartache.

The house had other plans.

The floorboards underneath her lifted up, and Florence fell into Evie and Clara.

"Sorry," Florence said to her sister.

But before she could back away, Evie threw an arm around her and pulled her in close. Clara, too, burrowed against Florence's side. Even Ink, who hadn't moved from where he'd been lying in the middle of Clara's spell circle, jumped up and joined them.

"I never would've been able to do any of this without you," Evie said.

"I'm sorry I didn't try to help sooner," Florence replied.

But Evie shook her head. "You were hurting, just like I was. We dealt with what Mom did to us in our own ways. I can't rush your healing."

Florence's tears fell harder. "And I can't rush yours."

"Thank you for not letting me turn out like Mom," Evie said through tears of her own.

But Florence shook her head. "You were never going to be like her."

"The candle—"

"No." Florence cut her sister short. "You wanted to protect us. To keep us safe. Mom wanted to hold on to her magic, even at the cost of losing Dad. She could've put an end to this. She didn't have to light that candle."

Evie sighed, disappointment in her voice. "I still should've told you about the spell."

"We're not looking back anymore," Florence said, resolved. "It's time to move forward."

She waved Owen and Angela over, and they came to join them on the floor, Angela taking up the spot on the other side of Evie and Clara, and Owen settling in next to Florence. He draped his arm over Florence's shoulder, and she rested her head against his chest.

The rain slowed, and the clouds parted. Moonlight fell through the hole in the ceiling, bathing them in its soft light. They sat that way, crying and hugging and feeling the house all around them until dawn raised its head on the horizon, turning the sky the soft blue that heralded morning.

"We need to get started on the spell," Evie said.

The floorboards started to shake.

"Not that spell." Florence pressed a hand to the floor. "We're going to do a cord cutting, severing our bond so when the siphoning spell ends, it's only your magic that will fade."

The shaking stopped, but the lights in the room dimmed.

"You've done so well." Evie's voice was heavy with tears. "You kept us safe. You hid Mom's spell from us so there would be no more siphoning. We'll take it from here."

"Why don't Owen and I go get some breakfast while the two of you work?" Angela asked.

"No cooking in this kitchen," Evie said.

"I was thinking muffins from my parents' coffee shop," Angela said.

"And pumpkin spice lattes," Owen said. "For Florence's birthday."

All eyes turned on Florence.

"I can't believe I forgot," Evie said, a hand over her mouth.

With everything going on, Florence had forgotten, too. "You're not the only one."

"I can't believe *you're* the one who remembered," Evie said to Owen. To Florence she said, "I think you might want to keep him."

"I think I just might." Florence looked up into Owen's eyes. "Make my drink a double."

"You've got it," he said. Then, he pressed his lips to her cheek, feather light. The feel of his kiss unwound what remained of her fear. For so long she'd put up a wall between herself and the world around her, afraid someone would get hurt simply because she'd come to care for them. But she didn't need to fear love. Not then, not now, not ever again.

As Owen started to pull away, Florence turned her head, catching his mouth with hers. His lips parted in surprise, then answered in equal measure. It was a soft kiss, a moment of acknowledgment of this new and beautiful thing that had started to burn between them, and a promise of a fire that would grow even brighter in the days to come.

Florence was the first to pull away, her cheeks flushed and her heart full. Owen's eyes lingered on hers, his lips tilted up in a smile that, finally, Florence let herself return.

"If you're looking for a full-time job, I could always use a little more help around here," Evie said.

"But first, breakfast," Angela said. She glanced around them. "Do you think you'll be safe up here?"

Clara crossed her arms. "We're not leaving the house. This is our last chance to say goodbye."

Evie tucked Clara's hair behind her ears and said, "We'll have to if we want to dip a candle."

Clara threw up her arms. "We don't have time to make a new candle!"

"We'll set the wax with water," Evie said. "It'll have to do."

Clara shook her head. "This is too important."

It had been a long time since Florence had dipped a candle of her own, but even she knew their spells worked best when they had a full twenty-four hours to set, letting the witch's magic and intentions infuse the wax. It left less room for error.

Florence glanced at her niece's spell circle—the crystals, the twine, the candle Clara had cut—and an idea started to take shape.

"Is that the taper you dipped?" she asked her sister.

"I think so," Evie said.

"It is," Clara confirmed.

Florence gently lifted Ink out of her lap and set him on the ground before she crawled over to what remained of Clara's unfinished spell. She picked up the candle and held it between her hands.

She stood and crossed over to the table that had once belonged to their mother, and before her, their grandmother. She picked up the knife Clara had used earlier that night. Then she held it up and turned to face her sister.

"I think we can use this," she said.

Evie nodded slowly, and she, too stood. "You're right. If we cut it in half . . ."

"One side for the house, one side for us," Florence said.

Clara glanced between them. "Don't we need to put our magic in it?"

"You and your mom already did that," Florence said. Even now, she could feel the wax brimming with her sister's intentions—her niece's, too. Clara may not have dipped it, but she'd planned to use it to save the house, and it seemed some of that magic had made its way into the taper.

"By cutting the candle in half, we'll reverse those intentions," Evie said. "Like what you tried to do with the candle for Ink."

"But don't we need something more?" Clara asked. "Like the crystals and the tarot cards?"

Florence shook her head. "We have all the magic we need right here."

* * *

They spent the rest of the day saying their goodbyes to Honeysuckle House. Though the house was no longer trying to stop them from casting their spells, its own magic was still unstable, so they didn't go anywhere alone. They ate their muffins and drank their coffee in the warmth of the parlor.

When Florence suggested they put on some music, the turntable started spinning on its own. At first, the needle missed the vinyl, but Florence gently set it on the record. Billie Holiday's voice reverberated from the speakers, and could the Caldwells see ghosts, they might've found Violet and Tillie there in the room with them, dancing, chest to chest and cheek to cheek.

It wasn't until they'd walked into each room—until Florence pressed her hand against every door Honeysuckle House had used to keep her safe and Evie trailed her fingers across every wall that held her memories and Clara hugged every column that had watched her grow—that they finally made their way back up to the attic. The moon had risen high in the sky, and the clock ticked down the minutes toward midnight.

The damaged wall had fallen away. All the burned and broken plaster had disappeared, and the rainwater had dried up. The attic was whole once more. Painted honeysuckle vines trailed along the wall, the only sign the room had ever been locked away, the house's final act of magic and love.

Florence grasped her sister's hand, her heart both heavy and full. Evie glanced up at her and nodded. Rather than use the old table that had once belonged to their mother, they gathered around Evie's altar.

Together, they lifted the knife and severed the candle that would've siphoned their magic. One side for Honeysuckle House, the other for Florence and Evie. Then, Evie tied the two candles together with string and handed a match to Florence.

"You've been siphoned all your life," she said. "You should be the one to cut the cord."

"Are you sure?" Florence asked.

Her sister nodded, eyes shining with tears.

But when Florence struck the match and brought it to the candle, the wick wouldn't light. She tried again. Again, the flame wouldn't catch. A small sound escaped her sister's lips, and she lit her own match only to be met by the same fate as Florence's.

"Our magic is tied up in the house," Evie said, realization in her voice.

"We can't free it ourselves," Florence finished her thought.

They looked to Clara, who stood between them.

Chapter Sixty-Six

Honeysuckle House, Now

Honeysuckle House let out a low groan. The pipes rattled in the walls, and it lowered the lights. It had spent one last day with the people it loved most, but that wasn't enough. Nothing would be. The house wanted years. It wanted decades. It wanted to watch Clara grow up, to see Evie and Florence grow old, to welcome a new generation of Caldwells when the time came.

But all it had was this final moment.

"I can't do it," Clara said, shaking her head. "It can't be me."

The house stirred the nearby curtain, brushing up against Clara's cheek. As she cried harder, condensation formed on the windows. Water dripped from the faucets, and the house wept alongside her.

"This is all wrong," she wailed.

"It is." Evie rested a hand on the wall.

"It should never have come to this." Florence gripped the curtain gently, giving it a squeeze. The house squeezed back, and Florence's voice broke on her next words. "This weight should never have been put on any of us, but least of all you, Clara."

Evie crouched down in front of Clara, meeting her gaze. "But only you can set us free."

She held out a match toward her. Clara took it and held it up in front of her, staring at the little white tip. As her tears fell, splashing on the hardwood floor, the house wished more than anything that it could wipe them dry. Instead, it sent a honeysuckle vine through the open window, one final goodbye.

The vine wound its way up the legs of the dresser, and its flowers bloomed.

Clara bit her lip. Then, with a heavy sigh and a lot more tears, she struck the match.

Chapter Sixty-Seven

Florence, Now

Clara brought the flame to the candle that represented Florence and Evie, then to the candle for the house, and Florence felt something deep inside her begin to shift. At first, the tapers burned slowly. The fire worked its way down, embers sparking along the wicks. When the fire finally met the twine that tied the two candles together, there was a burst of heat. The flame erupted, engulfing string and wax.

The black candle melted, the wax pooled, and the fire sputtered out. Smoke rose from the spent wick in tendrils.

The honeysuckle vine withered.

The fluttering curtains stilled.

The lights resumed a normal, yellow glow.

As the fire went out on the table, it roared in Florence's heart. The ember of her magic that lay deep inside—the warmth of her power she'd tried her best to push aside and ignore these past thirteen years—caught flame. Possibility and hope whirled together. Florence staggered at the strength of it, bracing herself against the dresser.

When she looked up, she found her sister doubled over, too.

"It's just like before Dad died," Evie said breathlessly.

But Florence had never felt this. She'd never known the full strength of her power—siphoned first by her mother, then by the house. With this much potential, it was no wonder her bookstore had come to life. Tears pricked her eyes. She leaned her head back and let them fall.

The fire of their cord-cutting spell had burned away the last hold her mother had on her. And though Florence knew it might take a lifetime to heal from the other wounds her mother had inflicted, for the first time, Florence thought she might be able to do just that.

* * *

They met the others downstairs. Owen stood over the stove whisking a pot of hot chocolate. Angela had procured pumpkin pie from the festival that had carried on in downtown Burdock Creek without them. Ink lapped up oat milk from a saucer. All of them ate and drank their fill, and though the room was full of life and love and hope, the house was quiet in a way that made Florence's heart ache.

"Are you staying the night?" Clara asked as she looked up from her now-empty mug.

"If that's okay with your mom." Florence wasn't quite ready to be alone.

"You know there's always a place for you here," Evie said. "Your old room . . . ?"

But Florence shook her head. There were too many hard memories behind those walls.

"You can stay in my room!" Clara said.

Florence's eyes strayed toward Owen.

"I think your aunt might want her own room tonight," Evie said. "Why don't you take the Honeysuckle Suite. It's on the second floor above the kitchen—the one with the bay windows."

"That sounds perfect," Florence said.

Evie stood from the table and reached for Clara. "Come on, honeybee. I'll tuck you in."

"Where's Angela going to stay?" Clara asked.

Evie and Angela shared a smile.

"In Mommy's room," Evie said.

Clara looked from her mom to Angela then back to her mom before she nodded. "A best friend for kissing *and* sleepovers."

"I know someone who'd love to have a sleepover with you," Florence said as she lifted Ink from her lap and handed him to her niece.

Clara held him close, and he rubbed his head against her chest. "Come on," she said to him, "I never got to show you my room."

Once the kitchen was empty, Florence turned to Owen. She took a step toward him, and when he opened his arms, she relaxed into his hold. They stood there for several long moments, the smell of chocolate and nutmeg and cinnamon all around them, and though Florence had lost someone dear to her, she didn't have to bear that loss alone. Owen pressed a kiss to the top of her forehead. She pulled back and looked up into his eyes. There, she found an open sort of kindness that she was finally coming to realize wasn't only something she wanted in her life, but something she deserved.

"I know you have your own room here," she said, the words slow and careful. "And I know it's still early between us, but it might be nice to not have to sleep alone."

His lips curved up into the same grin that had first gotten her in trouble with him when he'd taken her sister's job offer and walked into her shop.

"Are you asking me to bed, Florence Caldwell?"

She rolled her eyes but flushed. "Not like that. Not tonight anyway, and certainly not in my sister's house."

He tucked a strand of hair behind her ear. Then, he pressed his lips to her cheekbone, just below her eye, where her witch's mark had once been, and said, "Don't worry. You don't have to be alone tonight."

Chapter Sixty-Eight

Evie, Now

The morning of the fourteenth came in a burst of color, the sunrise the most beautiful Evie had ever seen. Where in years past the house would've opened a window wide and called her to the glass with a soft breeze, this time it was Angela who gently shook Evie awake.

"We need to get going if you still want to make the honey harvest happen," Angela whispered from where she lay behind Evie.

Evie rolled over to face her and wrapped her arms around her. Their foreheads pressed together, then their lips. Angela was safe, and so was Evie. But that didn't mean Evie was ready to let her go.

When they finally broke apart, it was only because Evie's door opened with a bang and a "Mom! Time to get up!"

They spent the morning calling the festival committee. Each conversation brought with it a sigh of relief—and disbelief—that for the first time in seventy-eight years, no one had been harmed at Honeysuckle House.

The curse was finally broken. The cycle their grandmother started had come to an end.

Most of the tourists had already left, but that didn't stop the town from celebrating. Their neighbors filled the lawn outside the bed and breakfast. While Owen worked the honey extractor in the front room with Florence at his side, Evie helped her neighbors make their own candles in the workshop.

At sunset, they lit a large fire out behind the house and gathered around making s'mores dipped in honey and sipping cider and telling their neighbors the full story of what had happened behind the walls of their house.

By the time everyone left, Evie's heart was one part full and one part aching at the loss of one of her closest friends, a member of her family. They covered what remained of the fire with sand, and started to turn in.

Florence stood arm in arm with Owen, Ink on her shoulder.

"Do you want to stay here again tonight?" Evie asked, not quite ready to see Florence leave.

"I think we're going to go back to my apartment," Florence said.

"Before you go," Evie paused. "You never came out to dip a candle. I thought, maybe . . ."

Slowly, a smile spread across her sister's face. "You thought right. I'd love to make a candle with you." She turned to Owen, rose up on her toes, and pressed her lips to his. "You okay to stay up a little while longer?"

"I think I can manage," Owen said, taking the kitten from her.

Clara took his hand and said, "Let's go thank the bees for all their hard work."

"That's a wonderful idea," he said.

Once they were gone, Evie hooked her arm in Florence's and led her down to the workshop. She opened the door and waited for the light to come on. After a few seconds, she remembered it wouldn't—not anymore—and turned it on herself.

Together, they started up the boiler. As the wax melted, Evie turned to Florence. "What color?"

Florence looked over the shelf of dyes. After a few moments, she selected blue.

"For healing," she said. "And forgiveness."

"For Mom?" Evie asked.

But Florence shook her head. "For ourselves."

Evie pressed her shoulder to her sister's. Then, she cut a long piece of string. Together, they tied a weight to each end, like they'd done as children. They gripped the twine from the center and held it over the wax.

"May we always find peace and healing," Florence said.

"And the power to forgive ourselves and each other," Evie finished.

As the magic stirred in her heart, she saw it move in her sister's. Golden light spilled from Florence's fingertips and mingled with the light from Evie's. When they lifted the wicks from the wax, the curtains fluttered. A light flickered. And the boards beneath their feet creaked softly.

The Honeysuckle House they knew was gone—its memories, its history, its love for the witches who called it home. But a witch's house is a living, breathing thing, and it was only a matter of time before the building it had left behind would take on a life of its own.

Author's Note

I have wanted to write a sister book for as long as I can remember, but I could never find the right sisters or the right setting or the right story. Then, the Caldwells came to me. Florence with her need to protect. Evie with her desire to be seen. Violet with her eagerness to love. Regina with her fear of being alone. They are, each of them, themselves. But, of course, there's a little bit of me in all of them.

More than the sisters, Honeysuckle House is about what makes a family. It is about what makes a home. As someone with complex PTSD, I have a complicated relationship with the idea of "going home." My childhood was split between two homes—one that was safe and one that, if walls could talk, would tell stories I'd rather not relive.

As an author, writing has always been an act of healing for me, a way to alchemize my own pain into something new and beautiful, something where—I hope—readers can find belonging. Where they can find a safe place to examine the broken parts of themselves and take a step toward their own healing or where they might see someone they know and love and come away with deeper empathy and compassion. We don't always end up having the relationships with our families that we wish we had, but stories give us a place where we can imagine what those relationships might have looked like if things were different.

While this is a story of generational trauma, it's also a story of hope. It's an exploration of how that trauma ends. Of the choices we can make to heal and find a new path forward. If that is something you're seeking, I hope you've found at least a small part of it in these pages and that, some day, you find healing—wherever you may need it.

Acknowledgements

Writing a novel is a solitary craft, but putting a book into the world is something that's rarely done alone. So many people helped me bring this novel from the first glimmer of an idea to the pages you hold in your hands now.

Jessica Faust, thank you for falling in love with my writing and for bringing me into this next stage of my career. Melissa Rechter—who knew after you listened to me talk about *In the Shadow Garden* on the She Wore Black podcast, that you'd end up editing my next witchy book? Thank you for helping me fine-tune the story and giving it a place to call home. And thank you Agatha Andrews for serving as a sort of matchmaker.

To the whole team at Alcove, thank you for all you've done for *Witches of Honeysuckle House:* Dulce Botello, Mikaela Bender, Alexis Singleton, Megan Matti, Stephanie Manova, Rebecca Nelson, Julia Abbott, Thaisheemarie Fantauzzi Pérez, Doug White, and Matthew Martz. Lucy Rose, thank you for the stunning cover. To Layne Mandros, E.W. Martin, Ellen Whitfield, and the team at Books Forward, thank you for getting this book into the hands of readers.

Speaking of which, I'm so grateful for my readers. So many of you followed me from *In the Shadow Garden* and have hyped my books ever since. If you're just now finding me, I am so glad you're here. Specifically, I wanted to give a shout-out to the Emilys (@booksandbedtime and @emilyisoverbooked) for constantly talking about my books on social media. Thank you also to Britt (@brittyoreads), Kat (@itskatsteele), Erin (@erinsbookspot), Laura (@manosfrias.reads), Lindsey (@lindsey.thelibrarian), Brianne (@books_withbri), Jess (@readbelievelove), Kim (@thepeachmartini), Val (@valreadsbooks), and so many more. I've also been so fortunate to connect with booksellers online who continue to talk about my backlist with as much excitement as this new book: Claire (@wildsistersbookco) and Holli (@blackbirdreader & @blackbird.tea.peddler), thank you.

Thank you to Leah Hultenschmidt for your encouragement on the very first inklings of this idea and to Jacqueline Badessa (@purposelyunperfect), Lola Sharp, and Ally Malinenko for reading long before the book was finished.

Sara Biren and Tracey Neithercott are my bees who have been here from the very beginning and have read so many of my books over the years. Alison Ames, you kept me sane through so much of this process. Rebekah Faubion, I continue to be so grateful for our friendship, for your sharp critique, for the spells and tarot and astrologizing. Amber McBride, this book would not exist if you did not sprint with me through almost every page of it—thank you for your friendship and your brilliance at every turn.

Dad, thank you for believing me and encouraging me even when I was only drawing little aliens and mailing them to you with their stories. DFYP.

Nick Parker, this book is my heart, and you saw that from the very first page. Thank you for loving the Caldwells—for loving Clara, especially. This book came to life during one of the most intense healing periods I've gone through, and I wouldn't have made it to the other side without you. You are my best friend and the love of my life and one of my most trusted voices when it comes to my work. I am so glad to have found you so early in life and to have spent so much of it with you. I love you.